I Never Forget a Duke

The Night Fire Club
Book 1

Kate McMurray

ARE YOU SIGNED UP FOR DRAGONBLADE'S BLOG?

You'll get the latest news and information on exclusive giveaways, exclusive excerpts, coming releases, sales, free books, cover reveals and more.

Check out our complete list of authors, too!

No spam, no junk. That's a promise!

Sign Up Here

www.dragonbladepublishing.com

Dearest Reader;

Thank you for your support of a small press. At Dragonblade Publishing, we strive to bring you the highest quality Historical Romance from some of the best authors in the business. Without your support, there is no 'us', so we sincerely hope you adore these stories and find some new favorite authors along the way.

Happy Reading!

CEO, Dragonblade Publishing

Chapter One

HUGH BAXTER, THE twelfth Duke of Swynford, descended the stairs to the crowded Rutherford ballroom, intending only to perform the minimum social niceties before finding whichever room George Rutherford had set up for cards. He loved living in London, but he loathed these balls at the height of the Season. He attended for his mother's sake; the dowager duchess insisted it was important to the family legacy that he put in appearances at the major social events. Swynford was one of the oldest dukedoms in England, after all, and although the current duke descended from first duke, created by Charles II shortly after the Restoration, the Baxter family had been peers of the realm since the Hundred Years War and were related to the king via a cousin who had married into the royal family a few generations back. So his name came with some obligations.

Helena Baxter, Hugh's mother, was not about to let him forget these obligations.

If some trifle with her health had not kept her at home this evening, the dowager duchess likely would have been telling him which eligible debutantes he should dance with tonight in the hopes that one of them proved to be a suitable mother to the thirteenth Duke of Swynford.

Hugh loved beautiful women but did not love dancing and would have been content to let the title die with him on days his mother had not lectured him on the importance of the family legacy. On those days, he wanted to give his mother what she most wanted in the world, which was a grandchild. But he couldn't help but think that, though Helena Baxter was a spitfire, what she wanted for Hugh was a placid broodmare. He'd compromised with himself that he'd enjoy life to its fullest until forty, at which time he'd choose some willing young miss and make his mother happy. Aside from the current bout of sniffles, Helena was in the peak of health, so she'd surely be able to wait that long.

Thus he hoped to dodge the simpering young women and their calculating mamas while he made sure he was seen before he relieved his male social peers of a few coins in the card room.

As soon as his foot hit the floor, however, they descended on him.

"Your Grace, I don't believe I've yet introduced you to my daughter..."

"Your Grace, it is an honor to see you again. Do you know..."

"My daughter has a spot on her dance card reserved just for you..."

Hugh pressed his lips together and looked for an exit.

He chose three debutantes at random and took them around the dance floor before seeking out a friendly face and landing on Larkin Woodville.

Lark stood near the refreshments, seeming to be engaged in some sort of internal argument about how gauche he might appear if he drank more of Mrs. Rutherford's lemonade.

"Please tell me," Hugh said as he sidled up to Lark, "that George has a card table set up in a room full of whisky and cigars."

"Ah, the curse of being England's most eligible bachelor. It must be difficult to have so many lovely women willing to walk over their own mamas to win your affections."

"Far be it for me to complain about women clamoring over me, although the only difference between me and every other fool here is my name."

Lark seemed to make a decision and poured himself a ladleful of lemonade. "So if my name were Baxter, I'd be the beau of the ball?"

Hugh stopped himself from saying the first thing that popped into his head, which was that the only thing saving Lark from Hugh's fate was some ailment or accident overtaking Lark's father, the Marquess of Beaufort. But Hugh knew that was cruel and borne of his own sadness when he thought of his father's passing, so he pushed that aside. Instead, he said, "I believe if you let it be known that you would very much like to reform your profligate ways and settle down with a gently bred wife, there'd be a stampede of women yearning to be your future marchioness."

Lark frowned. "Dear god. All right, you've made your point. Let us adjourn to the card room."

Several hours later, Hugh told his driver to go ahead home, that he needed the walk to clear his head after indulging in a bit too much of George Rutherford's fine whisky.

Lark was pretty deep in his cups too, but his parents insisted he ride home in their carriage. Hugh bid him good night and began to walk the short distance to his home on Upper Brook Street. He considered cutting across Grosvenor Square but saw that the gate was shut. But that was all right; it was a crisp, cool night, and Hugh already felt all the better for being outside instead of in the crush of the Rutherfords' ballroom. He walked around the garden, lost in thought, contemplating what he would do the next day. He liked these quiet moments at night and often walked after dark, although his friends warned him against the practice, since one never knew who might be about in the shadows. Hugh wasn't particularly worried now, though; the only men he might run into in Mayfair were other drunk aristocrats.

Still, as he made the turn onto Upper Brook Street, he thought someone called his name, but dismissed it. No one else was around. He was nearly to his door when he heard a shuffle behind him. As he turned to see what it was, something hit the back of his head.

Then the world went dark.

ADELE PAULSON COULD not possibly endure the stuffy air in the Sweeney house for another moment. The old countess did not like open windows and was convinced the London air was responsible for her current poor health. Adele thought that was likely true, although she thought the next reasonable question was why the countess persisted in staying in London when her country house had much better air.

Adele walked out the front door with Wilton, the butler, on her heels.

"I just need a moment, Wilton," Adele insisted.

"Yes, Lady Adele, but the neighborhood is not safe for a young lady at this time of night."

"I do not intend to go far. I want some fresh air is all."

Wilton retreated but took up a post at the front door with his arms crossed, clearly determined not to let Adele out of his sight.

The countess's house was modest, a bit of a distance from fashionable Mayfair. The house did have a little backyard garden, but the last time Adele had walked there after dark, the gardener accused her of stomping on the flowerbeds. This was an unfair charge, and Adele was pretty sure Cook's dog had been responsible for ruining the flowerbeds, but she'd had no proof. Thus she avoided the garden at night.

Ever since reading a translation of the stories of the Brothers Grimm, she'd been fancying herself as a bit of a Cinderella, responsible for much of the household work and often the scapegoat for anything wrong in the house. Although in Adele's case, there was no handsome prince, she wasn't related to the family that persecuted her, and she was being paid for these indignities. Still, if Adele sought fresh air out front instead of in the tiny backyard garden, no one could accuse her of having nefarious plans for the backyard flora.

The countess had been trying Adele's patience lately. She'd grown forgetful, which seemed to anger her, and she took out the bulk of that anger on Adele. Adele tried not to take that personally and understood the countess's anger was borne of her frustration over her failing health, but Adele was tired of insisting that she was only trying to help.

She sighed and leaned against a lamppost. Not for the first time, she thought about how this was not the life she imagined for herself. Five years ago, she'd been engaged to Geoffrey MacDowell, Lord Paisley, heir to titles and property in England and Scotland. She'd loved him deeply and had her whole future planned. They would split their time between London, his country manor in Kent, and the grand estate in Scotland; they'd have three or four children; and Adele would have time to pursue things like gardening or painting, perhaps, and they'd be happy.

Geoffrey had never told her he'd been sick. And the Lord took him two weeks before their wedding.

Adele's devastation at the loss had kept her away from London for a season, and by the time she returned at the ripe old age of twenty-two, it seemed she was already on the shelf. No eligible man would send a second glance her way, not when there were so many new, young debutantes on the scene.

So what good was an earl's daughter so long on the shelf? Her father had been a close friend to the late Earl of Sweeney—the present earl was only a few years older than Adele and preferred the country to London—so here Adele was, the Dowager Countess of Sweeney's paid companion.

She closed her eyes and took a deep breath, then pushed off the lamppost, reluctantly taking a step back toward the house. She heard a noise and turned around, watching as a large carriage rumbled up the street. A door opened and someone inside tossed something at the sidewalk a few feet from where Adele stood. Then the carriage sped away before Adele could finish yelling about the man discarding his rubbish in the street. She glanced at the bundle and was content to leave it… until it moved.

Adele exchanged a glance with Wilton, who walked with her to the bundle. A long sheet of muslin or some other fabric was wrapped around what Adele assumed at first must have been a dog. But if that were the case, it was a huge dog. And then the bundle moaned.

Wilton stepped forward and lifted the edge of the fabric. There was a man. Adele did not recognize him and assumed he was not one of her neighbors. He was too well-dressed for the neighborhood, at any rate. He looked like he'd just come from a ball. He was tall and young, Adele thought, though his clothes were rumpled and there was a trickle of blood on his forehead.

"Do you know him?" Wilton asked.

"No, but I assume he is nobility of some sort, given his dress."

When the man moaned again, Adele said, "Sir? Who are you? What is your name?"

Then his whole body went slack.

Wilton touched his neck. "He's alive, but I believe he's passed out."

"We must get him inside."

"Are you sure?"

"We can't leave him on the street. We'll put him in the green bedroom, and I will tend to him."

"That is quite improper, my lady. Cook and I can see to his wounds. Young master John was quite the young hellion and was forever getting into scraps, so we have some experience with patching up cuts and bruises. Perhaps he will recover his senses by the morning and you and the countess can escort him home."

"Do you think he may need further medical attention?"

"Doctor Willis is scheduled to come to the house to attend to the countess on the morrow. We'll have him look after our young man. In the meantime, I will need your assistance, at least to get him to the threshold of the house. Can you carry his feet?"

Together, Wilton and Adele managed to get the man to the door. Wilton asked Adele to go in and fetch one of the footmen. Ten minutes later, the man was fast asleep in the green bedroom, the only bedroom in the small house not presently spoken for. Adele stood at the door and watched him for a long moment, and now that he was in a room with better lighting, she thought him vaguely familiar, but perhaps that was just the trappings of wealth. She'd traveled in the same circles as this man once, she knew that much, but she could not identify him.

Wilton returned with Cook, who nudged her out of the way. "Get some sleep, Lady Adele. He will still be here in the morning for you to fret over."

Adele nodded. She gave the mysterious man one last, long look and then went to her room.

Chapter Two

HE WOKE UP with the light shining through a window he didn't recognize.

He lay in bed for a long moment and took an assessment. His head pounded and the light hurt. His stomach felt tied in knots. He dimly understood that these were symptoms of the morning after a long night of drinking, but he did not believe he'd overindulged the night before. Had he? The fact that he could not remember where he'd been the night before was likely further evidence of too much drink.

He sighed and decided to roll over to sleep the rest of this off, but then there was a rap at the door.

The sound entered his head like a needle. He swallowed a groan. "Come," he said, but it came out hoarsely.

A woman entered the room. He did not know her, though something in the back of his mind said he would like to. She was quite pretty, albeit plain; her brown hair was swept off her face and tied into a twist at the base of her head. She wore a pale-blue dress that hugged her bosom in a way he found appealing. Her face was nicely drawn, with thin eyebrows and a slightly pointy nose and plump lips pressed into a line of concern.

"How do you feel, sir?" she asked.

"Like I was run over with a curricle. I apologize, but where am I?"

"Yes, of course. The apologies are mine. You were largely

unconscious when we escorted you in last night. You are in the residence of the Countess of Sweeney."

"Sweeney?" It seemed like a name he should know, but as he cast about his mind for a face to pair with the name, he could not do it.

"Yes. I will grant you, the countess is no longer quite a grand dame of the *ton*, more a wilting rose, although do not tell her I said that. And the house is, unfortunately unfashionably close to Regent's Park rather than Mayfair, but we can't all be dukes." The woman chuckled and shook her head. "Ignore me. My manners are ghastly."

"Are you… her daughter?"

"Oh, no. Apologies again, sir. I am Lady Adele Paulson. I am the countess's companion. Wilton and I, that is the butler and I, were getting some fresh air outside last night when you were tossed out of a carriage. You must have hit your head."

"I must have." He touched his hair, taking stock again. There was quite a lump on his crown.

"And you are, sir?"

He opened his mouth to tell her, but then realized he could not remember.

"Perhaps I should have begun with a simpler question. What is the last thing you remember?"

He closed his eyes, but his memory seemed a thing shrouded in gray clouds.

"I do not know," he said. "How can it be that I do not know?"

"I'm sure it will come to you in short order."

Her tone indicated she did not find this turn of events nearly as alarming as he did. He sat up in bed and realized he'd been stripped of all but his drawers.

"I do apologize also for absconding with your clothing last night, but I turned them over to the housekeeper for cleaning. In the meantime, I've found a few garments that once belonged to the current earl that I believe will fit you. As he's taken up residence at some pile in Yorkshire, I do not believe he will miss them. The current earl is the countess's son, so don't be concerned that these clothes are too terribly old fashioned." She walked out of the room and returned with a parcel wrapped in brown paper. She placed it atop a chest of drawers in the corner. She patted the parcel, so these were clearly the clothes.

It was like his thoughts were blocks he couldn't make fit together. "I am sorry, but I do not..." He gestured around him. "I cannot remember anything. Not where I was last night, not where I was three days ago, not even my name." Panic started to crowd into the edges of his mind.

The woman, Adele Paulson, stared at him for a long moment. It occurred to him that Adele was a lovely and somewhat unusual name, but he pushed the thought aside.

"You are serious," she said.

"I'm afraid so."

She frowned. "'Tis a good thing Doctor Willis is coming here this morning to attend to the countess. If you'd prefer to stay abed, I can have him visit you as well."

He lay back down slowly. "That seems like a good idea."

"What shall I call you?"

"Pardon?"

"You may not know your name, but I still feel like I may need to refer to you in some way."

"Let me think on it. Maybe I just need a few more minutes to recover my memory."

"I do hope so. All right. You must eat, so I will instruct Cook to send a tray up for you. Doctor Willis should be here within the hour, so I will send him to check on you after he sees to the countess. Does that seem agreeable?"

"Quite."

She nodded once. "All right. I will leave you. There's a bell pull to your right should you need anything."

She left the room, leaving him to sit and contemplate his situation. It was as if someone had erected a wall between himself and his memories. He glanced at the bell pull. It was a familiar object, in that he could recall seeing one before, although the handle was tarnished. Would one inside of his own home be thus? Was his home clean? Where was it? Miss Paulson had rambled about this neighborhood being unfashionable, had she not? But this was the home of a countess?

And how was it that he could recall social ranks but not his name or address?

He sighed and rubbed his forehead. He was somewhat relieved when a servant girl came in, left a tray of food on the bedside table, and left again with only a bow of her head. He was not certain he could endure speaking.

The offerings were modest: a few scones, a small bowl full of jam, a pat of butter, and a cup of tea. So he could identify food, but not himself.

He sighed, sat up straight, and tucked into his breakfast.

As she escorted Dr. Willis down the hall, Adele explained, "We discovered last night that he has a rather large lump at the back of his head." She touched her scalp near the top of her head to demonstrate. "He had a cut near his temple as well, although it was minor. The especially troubling thing is that he has no memory."

"An overindulgence of drink will sometimes wipe out recollections of the night before."

"No, you misunderstand. He has no memory of anything. He cannot recollect his name or where he lives or how he came to have a bump on his head."

Dr. Willis stopped walking and tilted his head. "I have heard of such things occurring but have never witnessed it myself. How curious."

Adele knocked on the door, and when a weary sounding, "Come!" came from inside, she pushed the door open. "Hello, sir.

May I present Doctor Willis."

The mystery man had put on one of John's shirts, which meant Adele could now look at him without being distracted by his bare shoulders. Who would have thought the bare shoulders of a man, the jut of his collarbone, the hint of hair on his chest, who knew any of that could be so… appealing. And on a fairly young man—Adele guessed he was older than thirty but younger than forty—who had a handsome face with a strong jawline and an aristocratic nose, those shoulders were something Adele would not soon forget. Seeing them had made her babble this morning, and she was mortified to speak with the man again, but he seemed intent on the doctor.

"My memories have deserted me," the man said.

"Yes, Lady Adele explained. I have not treated a case such as this myself, but I have read about them. You hit your head in some way, yes? May I examine?"

"Please do."

Adele looked on from the corner. Probably she should have left, but she found the mystery man mesmerizing. Who was this man? Was he a lord of some type? His clothes had indicated a certain amount of wealth. But how had he come to be in that carriage that had thrown him overboard?

"Did you fall?" asked Doctor Willis.

"I cannot recall."

"Another patient of mine achieved a bump like this when his brother hit him over the head with a flowerpot. That patient was nine years old, though, so I doubt very much you were having an argument about who owned the wooden horse, at least in a way that would have resulted in getting hit with a flowerpot." The doctor chuckled. "How do you feel physically otherwise?"

"All right. I woke up with quite a headache, but it has lessened somewhat. The rest of me seems to be intact. There's a bruise on my hip, but it will heel." He glanced at Adele in the corner, probably trying to signal to the doctor that he would not be displaying that bruise for the doctor with her watching. "It's not my body I am worried about, but my mind."

"Yes, quite. Well, in similar cases to this, the memory returned all at once within a few hours or days after the injury, or it returned in dribbles over a longer period of time, or it never recovered completely."

"Oh, god. Surely this state cannot continue on indefinitely." The man touched his head. "It's almost as though I can feel my memories are there, floating around in my brain, but I cannot get to them right now."

"Yes, and in all likelihood, your memory will return. I believe putting yourself somewhere familiar may help. Perhaps Lady Adele can help you discover who you are."

Adele smiled in a way she hoped was encouraging, although inside she felt nearly giddy at the prospect of an investigation.

How dull had her life become in the last few weeks of caring for the countess that this should excite her so much?

She shrugged it off and stepped forward. "I would be happy to help you, sir."

"Thank you," he said.

"And if you discover any other symptoms, if you have other injuries or feel nauseous," said the doctor, clearly preparing to leave, "Lady Adele knows how to reach me. Otherwise, try to be patient."

"I will see you out," said Adele.

"No need, I know the way." Dr. Willis tipped his hat and left the room.

The man narrowed his eyes at her. "He referred to you as Lady Adele. Are you nobility?"

"My father is the Earl of Canbury."

The man shook his head. "The name does not ring a bell, although that hardly signifies given my present mental state."

"You may not know him under better circumstances. Papa is not often in London these days. Says the air disagrees with him. He prefers the country."

"Then how is it his unmarried daughter is a caretaker for a

wilting rose of a countess?"

Adele couldn't keep the smile off her face. "I told you not to mention I said that."

"You said I should not tell the countess you said that, but I have not yet met this elusive woman."

"Yes, I'm afraid she is in poor health, hence the doctor's presence."

"Nothing too difficult, I hope."

"A fever. The doctor thinks she will be back to her old self in a day or two. She is also quite stubborn and would likely tell the devil he'll have to wait if she is not ready to go yet."

The man laughed. "She sounds like an interesting woman."

"We manage to find ways to entertain each other." Adele sighed. "You knew enough to know by the way the doctor addressed me that I must be nobility. Between that, your accent, and the quality of your clothing, I believe we can infer that you are a lord of some sort."

"Are you sure?"

"No. I was just hoping to narrow things down. Do you remember anything?"

"Nothing. My head feels as though it is stuffed with cotton instead of memories."

"Then how do we narrow it down? Because while I do not think you live in this neighborhood, my only evidence is that I have not seen you before. My father might be able to help, because he knows everyone, but since Parliament is not in session, he is not in town. I suppose we could check with Bow Street and see if anyone has reported that a man meeting your description has gone missing."

The man tilted his head. "Bow Street?"

"Law enforcement. A detective may be out looking for you as we speak."

"No, that does not seem right. My memories may return in short order."

"I do hope so. But perhaps if they don't, we can go out on the town tomorrow. Walk you through some fashionable spots, see if anything jogs your memory."

"That seems reasonable."

"In the meantime, you are welcome to stay here as long as you like. I already spoke with the countess, and she says it's all right. This house is not the fanciest, but we have a nice library and the little garden in back of the house is a nice place to sit. We have plenty of food if you're hungry. Regent's Park is not far if you want some fresh air, and—"

"Fresh air," he murmured.

"Would you like to go outside?"

"No, I have a recollection… I believe one of the last things I did before everything vanished from my mind was go for a walk for some fresh air." He rubbed his forehead and then dropped his hand and shrugged. "I can't recall more than that."

"Rest today. We'll walk in the park tomorrow, perhaps. Please ring the bell if you need anything."

"Will that summon a servant?" He asked.

"Yes. We have a small staff, but this is not a large house, so one of the maids or footmen will come quickly if you need them."

"How do I summon you?"

It occurred to Adele at first to take that as a jest, but he seemed sincere. "Pull the bell. A servant can fetch me. As I said, it is not a large house. I am always close by."

"Because you are caring for the countess. I do apologize if I get in the way of that. I did not mean to take you away from your duties."

She smiled. "You didn't. That is, things had gotten a little dull around here of late. The countess spends a great deal of her time either asleep or reading these days, so I have not had many people to speak to who aren't the household staff. Your intrusion was not unwelcome, sir."

"All right. Glad to be of service, then." He smiled and Adele felt it in her chest. He was quite breathtaking.

She swallowed. "I do need to attend to the countess now. She's always a little grouchy after the doctor visits. But ring if you need anything and I'll check back in with you in a little while."

"Yes, all right. Thank you, Lady Adele."

"'Tis my honor, sir."

She left, and as she walked down the hall to the countess's room, she tried not to feel anything about the way he'd asked if he could summon her. A girlish curiosity about whether he fancied her was ridiculous and beside the point. She was a spinster destined to spend her days taking care of the older women who had fallen out of favor with the *ton*, and he'd go back to whatever his actual life was as soon as he recovered his memories. So there was no use in dwelling on it, no matter how handsome he was.

Chapter Three

LARKIN WOODVILLE, EARL of Waring, heir to the Duke of Beaufort, loved gossip. He supposed he could feel fairly secure of his place in society, which allowed him to indulge in the sort of frivolity printed in the scandal sheets. He handed a few coins to a paperboy and started to unfold the paper as he walked to Hugh's house on Upper Brook Street. Most of today's tittering was about various people who were seen and heard at the Rutherford ball two nights before. Lark chuckled at the mention of his own name in connection to a young lady he'd danced with, but that was a nothing story; she was the sister of one of his schoolmates, not a prospective wife.

There was an interesting article about the Earl of Canbury being spotted in women's clothing again. That was an old story and Lark had long pondered the truth of it. Canbury was an especially loud voice in the House of Lords and was angling for a diplomatic position, so his political rivals were working hard to tear him down. Canbury was not especially well liked on a good day, and now that he'd been all been licking the Hessian boots of the Prince Regent in the hopes of gaining a government job, he had enemies coming out of the woodwork. Lark had always assumed the rumors that he liked to dress as a woman in public were just bad actors trying to embarrass him. Not to mention, the earl and his sister bore an uncanny resemblance to each other, so it might have just been a case of mistaken identity.

Not that Lark cared a whit about what people did with their idle time. If a man wanted to wear a dress in public, Lark took no issue with it. Women's clothing seemed so complicated, though, almost not worth the effort. And Lark himself had not exactly been a paragon of Christian virtue, so unless someone was doing something that harmed another person, he was content to let it be. Judge lest not ye be judged, right?

He certainly was not anxious to let it be known that he'd recently spent a few glorious nights in the bed of the Marquess of Beresford.

He arrived at Hugh's house, tucked the paper under his arm, and knocked on the door.

Hodges, the Swynford butler, opened the door with a concerned expression on his face.

"Is Swynford in to callers?" Lark asked.

"He is not in, my lord, but I believe Her Grace would like to speak with you."

This seemed like bad news. Lark stepped into the house. Hodges escorted him to the red sitting room, where the dowager duchess sat with a book in her lap.

"Good afternoon, Your Grace," Lark said.

"My goodness. Oh, Lord Waring, it is good to see you." She set the book aside and braced her arms on the chair as if standing would require substantial effort.

"Please don't get up on my account. What has happened? Is something wrong?"

She sighed and sank back into the chair. "It's Hugh. He... he did not come home after the Rutherford ball."

"He... what?" Hugh hadn't made it home? In more than a day? How could that be?

"The carriage returned without him. When did you last see him?"

Lark's knees felt a little wobbly, so he sat in the settee near the dowager. "We left the Rutherford ball together. But then Father insisted I ride in the family carriage because I'd... well, let us just say, Lord Rutherford has an excellent store of whisky. Hugh told me he intended to walk home to clear his head. Last I saw him, he was headed here on foot."

The dowager shook her head. "London is not safe at night. He thinks because he is a duke that no harm will come to him, but even in Mayfair, dangerous men lurk in the shadows."

Lark's heart pounded. It was very unlike Hugh to simply disappear; there were few men who understood their place in the world and their responsibilities better than Hugh Baxter. But more than that, Hugh had clearly intended to walk home, and he wasn't *that* drunk. Something must have happened to him en route.

"Have you told anyone?" Lark asked. "Alerted Bow Street?"

"No, not yet. Hodges and a few of the footmen did a thorough search of the area yesterday. So I know that he is not lying dead in a rose bush in Grosvenor Square. But where else could he have gone?"

"I'm afraid I don't know, but I will do everything in my capacity to find him."

The dowager gave Lark a watery smile. "I know you will. You and Hugh have always been like brothers."

Lark was about to get up when the dowager added, "Speaking of family, Collingswood is in town."

Lark had to work to keep his face from wrinkling with distaste. Lord Collingswood was Hugh's cousin. He was a small, petty man who, although he'd made a fortune from the family plantation in Jamaica, had the misfortune of not being born into the Baxter line destined to inherit the dukedom. Lark suspected this was why the dowager had been pestering Hugh about marriage lately; she wanted a grandson and heir to ensure Collingswood never got his hands on that title.

"Has he been to see you?" Lark asked.

"Yes, three days ago. He came by while Hugh was out meeting with his solicitor. He wanted to speak to Hugh directly and would not share the topic of his meeting with me, so we exchanged pleasantries and then he left. I was supposed to pass the message on to Hugh but did not get a chance before…"

Lark blew out a breath. "Collingswood should have stayed in Jamaica."

"Indeed, but I suspect he has business here in town."

The dowager reminded Lark quite a bit of his own mother, so he understood that she was implying that, in addition to trying to track down Hugh, Lark should try to learn why Collingswood was in town. He nodded. "It appears I have quite a bit of work to do."

"I recommend speaking with Hugh's solicitor. Matthew Hogarth. He has an office on Broad Street."

That seemed like a reasonable suggestion, so Lark nodded and stood up. "I will call on him as soon as practicable and report back when I learn anything."

"Much appreciated, my dear."

THE MEMORIES IN his brain might have gone missing, but the memories in his body were clearly still there. His body knew, for example, that when a man was on a walk with a beautiful woman, that man should offer her his arm.

Although "walk" was relative. They were slowly taking steps around the garden behind the house. It was a small garden, but it was well-tended, and he was content enough to take a few steps with Lady Adele at his side.

He still had a headache, though it had diminished to a dull ache instead of the incessant pounding of the day before. He still got dizzy if he moved too fast, so walking in the park seemed ill-advised. Still, it had felt good to get out of bed and put on clothing that morning. The earl's clothes were a little snug, but not obscenely so. He wanted to shave, but Adele had not yet been able to locate a razor, so that would have to wait for now. Still, his face itched, and he knew enough to understand that the easiest solution was to remove the stubble from his jaw. He wondered if he looked handsome and rakish with such beard growth, or if he just looked tired and haggard. Did Adele think him handsome? *Was* he handsome? What did he look like?

He stopped walking as he realized he could not recall the contours of his own face.

These moments of panic had been hitting him at regular intervals for the last day and a half, since he'd woken up in the countess's house. Things he didn't know kept occurring to him, or he'd feel confused or lost, and fear would begin creeping in. How could he not know what he looked like? How could his memories still be locked away? How would he ever find his family and his home again?

"Are you all right?" asked Adele.

He swallowed and tried to speak calmly. "I just realized I do not know what I look like."

Adele looked him up and down. "Well, my lord, you are quite tall. You have dark hair, which I imagine you've gleaned for yourself. Blue eyes."

He wanted to ask if she found him handsome, but that seemed quite forward. So he rephrased the question. "How old do you think I am?"

"Five and thirty, I think. Maybe a little younger or older."

"Perhaps when we go inside there is a mirror I could look at."

"Yes, there is one above the fireplace in the gold salon."

"Maybe seeing myself will jog something in my memory."

"Doctor Willis implied that seeing familiar things could help bring your memory back. I would like to be able to do more of that, but we are presented with the enduring mystery of where you came from and what might be familiar."

He nodded. He wished he could remember… anything. Feeling a little dizzy with the effort of just trying to recall his name, he sat on a stone bench in the garden. "Perhaps we should focus on my health first."

"I will admit, it is strange to see a man of your… stature feel so weak. But head injuries can be quite serious."

"Let us go back in when this dizzy spell passes."

"Please take all the time you need."

She sat beside him, so he took a moment to take her in. Her dress was off-white and unadorned. Her hair was pinned up away from her face, and the style was simple, but it gave him the opportunity to admire her. She had long eyelashes and high cheekbones. Her skin was like porcelain, and her lips looked…

But no. He should not admire her. Not like that. She was taking care of him and probably not very open to his advances.

"You really have never met me?"

"Not before a few nights ago. If we have met before, I don't remember you."

"But I feel like… that is, social rank matters, does it not?"

"In some circles it does."

"And if you are the daughter of an earl, I may rank beneath you."

"Perhaps. I honestly do not know. I don't believe it matters."

He nodded slowly. "Would it be inappropriate to tell you I find you very pretty?"

She laughed softly and bowed her head. "I don't know if it's appropriate, but I liked hearing it. And you are quite handsome, my lord."

That felt encouraging. He smiled at her, his dizziness forgotten. "You live here with just the countess and her staff, so I assume you are not married. How can that be?"

She shot him a startled look that he couldn't quite interpret.

"Oh," he said. "I apologize. Was that a rude question?"

"No. Well, yes, the question was a bit forward. I imagine had we met at a ball, you would have asked in a more delicate way."

"I was merely wondering, because you are pretty and compassionate, how it could be that you do not have a husband."

She sighed. "Well, if you must know, I was betrothed to a man whom I loved very much, but he died two weeks before the wedding."

That took him aback. "My deepest condolences. What happened? No, that is also too forward. I merely wish to inquire—"

"It is all right. He was sick. He never told me." Her voice sounded a little watery. She blinked a few times and shrugged it off. "Well, anyway. He became very ill about a month before the wedding, The doctor didn't know what was causing it, but suspected it was a weak heart. He'd been sickly as a child, but had never mentioned it to me. He may have thought he was healthy. But I wish he would have warned me. I could have prepared myself."

This was clearly something that still sat with her. He wanted to comfort her, but something told him touching her would be inappropriate. But then he did it anyway, touching her arm lightly. "You must miss him."

"I do sometimes. However, the point of this story is that I mourned him and stayed away from society for a while, and by the time I returned for a Season, there was a new crop of debutantes who were younger and prettier than me and no man of quality even looked in my direction. So now that I am on the shelf, I take care of gentlewomen in their dotage."

That seemed puzzling. Somewhere in the back of his mind, he understood that this was how things were done, but still he said, "So if you get to whatever advanced age you've arrived at... which is...?"

"Six and twenty."

"That is not even... that is, can it be true that women reach a certain age, and they are just... out of chances?"

"I am not out of chances. Life is just going in a different direction than I expected. I am setting aside funds so that I might purchase a home for myself. Then who knows? I may write or paint or garden. I imagine I will find things to fill my day."

"Do you not want a family?"

She looked wistfully toward a row of flowers in the garden. He took that to mean she did want a family. She let out a long sigh. "I love children. I always enjoy when the earl brings his family to visit the countess. But this is the hand I was dealt."

"It seems unfair."

"Maybe it is, but at this point, I believe I must make my own happiness."

"Are you happy here?"

She made that startled face again and clasped her hands together. "My, you ask a great many questions."

"I know… nothing. Well, that is not true. I know some things. I have this vague recollection of the rhythms of conversation. I suspect that if we were a couple courting that you'd also pepper me with questions so that we might get to know each other. But I cannot tell you much about myself. Or about conversational niceties like the weather."

"You seem to remember quite a bit. When I spoke with Doctor Willis about your condition, he said that some memory loss patients forget how to walk or how to speak. You seem to have merely lost your long-term memory, and it is quite possible it will return to you in due course once you have fully recovered from your head injury."

"Or I will be forever lost."

She patted his knee. "In that case, you will make new memories. Your life is not over."

"Yours is not either."

She frowned at that. "Perhaps not, but you are of an age when most men marry. Perhaps you will find a new occupation and you will marry and start a family."

He wanted to ask why it would have been impossible to start a family with her, but they'd barely just met, and he could tell the question would be unwelcome. Instead, he said, "You didn't answer my question."

"Which question?"

"Are you happy here?"

"Most days," she said. "Do you feel better, my lord? We could go look at that mirror now."

"Yes, all right."

He understood that she was putting him off, likely to avoid having to answer more questions, so he'd stop asking her things for now. But he sensed that she was actually deeply unhappy with her situation.

She helped him up, and as they walked slowly back inside, she said, "Some women would be happy to escape the trap of matrimony. It gives them the freedom to pursue their own interests and own property for themselves. What they possess is theirs, not their husband's."

"Yes, I am sure that is true." And it was likely that owning things for herself and pursuing her own interests were things Adele valued, but he still did not believe she relished in spending the rest of her life without a husband or children. Of course, he had no right to contemplate such things or to barge into her life in the way he had. He had no right to judge her choices or desires.

And yet this mix of yearning for something more than what she had and resigning herself to her fate intrigued him.

Wilton, the butler, greeted them at the door. "If I may," he said, "the countess suggested we purchase another suit of clothes for Mr. Smith."

"Mr. Smith?" Adele asked.

Wilton smiled. "Apologies. That is what I have taken to calling our guest when speaking with the countess."

Smith. He tried on the name but wasn't sure it fit. Still, it was a thing to call himself, an identity to cling to, and yet it was perfectly benign and anonymous. "Mr. Smith it is," he said.

"Very well. I took the liberty of measuring the clothing you arrived in and sending those measurements to a tailor I know on Savile Row."

"Is something wrong with the clothing I arrived in?" Smith—for he supposed that was his name now—asked.

"No, not at all. But they are evening clothes, as if you came from a ball or dinner party. We need something more appropriate for day."

"I hate to put you to that expense."

Wilton shook his head. "Not at all. The countess authorized it."

"Perhaps I should meet this countess."

Adele nodded. "Yes, I will take you to visit her when she is feeling a little better." She turned to Wilton. "Mr. Smith has requested to see a mirror, so I was going to take him to the gold salon."

Wilton opened his mouth, perhaps to ask a question, but then snapped his jaw shut. He nodded. "Very good, my lady."

Adele led him down a hallway to a room that seemed to be set up for people to sit and converse. It was indeed gold—gold curtains, gold in the wallpaper, gold thread in the upholstery on the chairs and sofas. There was a huge, gold-framed mirror over the fireplace. It seemed opulent at first glance, but on closer inspection, the room was well-worn. The curtains were slightly discolored in places, the wallpaper was peeling near the ceiling, the upholstery was threadbare, and the mirror's frame was tarnished near the bottom. Smith's mind whirred as he tried to process this with what he knew so far. A countess, but a poor one, perhaps, or one whose fortunes had greatly diminished in recent years. Why had she spent money on a suit of clothes for him? He put that away to revisit later.

For here was the moment of truth. Smith walked up to the mirror and gazed at himself.

The man looking back was familiar, but again, it was like a heavy gray curtain hung between his conscious mind and his recollections. He knew this man, but not well enough to say who he was or how he came to be in this house.

Then he had a flash: a man with graying hair saying, "You have your mother's eyes." He could picture a woman with dark hair and eyes very much like the ones looking back at him now. She was strict, he knew, and opinionated, but also loving. She was his mother. He knew that on an elemental level. Just as he knew the man with graying hair was his father. And they each put all their hopes in him.

"I have parents but no siblings," he said aloud. "I spent a lot of time with my mother when I was a boy, but not all of my time."

"You likely had a nanny and a governess."

A woman with stern eyebrows speaking to him in Latin popped into his mind. "Yes, I had a governess, until I was old enough to go away to school. The school I went to did not require a uniform, but the headmaster did not allow anything eccentric, and we were required to wear a neckcloth." He touched his neck. "Which I do not appear to be wearing now."

"That sounds like Eton," Adele said. "Which, incidentally, supports my hypothesis that you are a lord of some sort. Many of the best families in England send their boys to Eton."

"I had friends there. I can picture their faces but not recall their names."

Adele walked over to one side of the room and gestured toward a painting. "I do not know if you would have crossed paths with the Sweeneys, but this is a portrait of the countess with her late husband and her two sons. I believe the present earl is around your age, or maybe a little older, so perhaps you would not have crossed paths with him when you were children."

Smith looked at the painting. No one in it was familiar to him. "Is it a good likeness?"

"I believe so. That is, I did not know the Sweeneys well until I came to work for the countess a year ago, but I imagine that's what they all would have looked like twenty years ago."

"I do not think I knew them."

"Worth a try."

Smith nodded. He looked back at his reflection and studied it for a long moment. Those little flashes from his childhood had felt like the beginning of something, but now the gray curtain was back.

"I'm feeling quite tired," he said, rubbing his chin. He wished these whiskers were not there. He found the shadow on his face disagreeable.

Adele appeared at his side. "You should get some rest. Do you know the way back to your room?"

"If you could get me as far as the stairs, I know the rest of the way."

"Of course. Follow me."

Chapter Four

WILTON HAD MANAGED to find a razor, which he gave to Adele to bring to Mr. Smith.

"What if he does not know how to shave?" Adele asked. "Suppose he is a wealthy lord. It is likely his valet usually does this for him."

Wilton considered. "I shave my own face but I've never shaved someone else's. Do you know how?"

"I can't say I have ever shaved a man, either. This looks like quite a sharp blade."

"Yes. Here, I'll show you." Wilton demonstrated scraping the blade across his face.

"How do you not cut yourself?"

"Practice."

"You are not suggesting I shave Mr. Smith, are you? That seems wholly inappropriate."

Wilton looked chagrined, as though he had actually intended to suggest just that very thing. "You are right, I'm sorry. Bring him the razor, but if he does not remember what to do, ring for me and I will help."

Adele wondered why she had been appointed to bring this razor to Smith, but she supposed she had made herself his caregiver, as she was everyone's caregiver in this house. Wilton was a competent butler, but he was also shy with strangers sometimes. Something about Smith intimidated Wilton in a way it did not intimidate Adele. Perhaps it should have and Adele was foolishly naive, but she did not believe Smith would harm her.

She found Smith in the gold salon, reading a book.

"Have you read this?" he asked as she entered the room. He held up her copy of *Emma*.

"I have."

"Do you think the anonymous author is a woman?"

"I think she published it anonymously because she is a woman."

He nodded. "Something about her voice makes me recall how the women of my acquaintance speak, although I of course haven't the foggiest notion of whom those women might be." He sighed and set the book aside. "How are you, my lady?"

"Wilton has procured a razor for you." She held it out in both hands.

He picked it up and examined the blade. "I must say, I am elated at the prospect of looking more respectable, but I am not sure I know what to do. How do men remove their whiskers without cutting themselves?"

"It is curious that you remember how to walk and read but not how to shave. Wilton and I surmised that in your other life, you had a valet who did it for you."

He closed his eyes for a long moment. "Yes. That seems likely."

Adele wondered again if perhaps Smith was a very wealthy man. That was troubling, because as she grew more fond of him, it seemed increasingly likely that they were not even of the same social class. Not that she harbored any illusions that there might be a romantic connection between them; that was not Adele's fate and she knew it. But she could admit to passing fancies where this handsome man was concerned.

Smith walked to the door without explaining where he was going, and everything about him had the confidence of a man who was used to acting on his whims. Adele chased after him, all the way to his bedroom, where he stared at the washstand.

"Perhaps you could help me," he said, looking right at Adele.

"This is a bit outside of the scope of my normal duties. That is, I take care of an old woman. I've never shaved a man before. But Wilton said to summon him if needed." She crossed the room to grab the bell pull.

"I'd really prefer you did it."

"That is an extraordinarily terrible idea, sir. I have no experience with a razor. I might slice your head right off."

He laughed and looked back at the mirror. "All right, I'll start. I need a mirror, though. And do you have any… shaving soap?"

"Oh. Yes, I know where the earl keeps his when he stays here. I shall return swiftly."

She tried not to obsess over all the ways Smith could injure himself if he attempted to shave as she went to the earl's quarters. She took the old mirror the earl kept there; it had a crack at one corner and some tarnishing, but she figured it would do. She grabbed the shaving soap from its place there, too. On her way back down the hall, she passed the countess's bedroom. "Is that Miss Paulson?" she called out.

Adele sighed and stuck her head in the room. "Yes, my lady. Did you need something?"

The countess lounged in bed as she had for the last week, recovering from what Dr. Willis insisted was just a cold. Adele wondered sometimes if the countess was not being overly dramatic "Oh, not right now. I would like to ask you to add the bookshop to your rounds in town this week. I am nearly finished with my book." The countess patted the book on her night table.

"Yes, of course."

"Can you fetch me something to drink as well? I should like some tea."

"Yes, I'll take care of that."

"Thank you, my girl. That is all."

"If I may, do you intend to ever meet our house guest?"

"I will when am less tired and more presentable."

"Are you feeling all right?"

"Yes, I'm fine. A little sleepy. I think I shall take a nap now. Please close the door on your way out."

Adele questioned the wisdom of ordering tea if the countess was just going to sleep, although she wondered if perhaps claiming to want a nap was just the countess's way of dismissing Adele without seeming rude.

Some companionship. When Adele had taken this position, her father and the Earl of Sweeney had argued that they just wanted someone to sit with the countess, and Adele had imagined she'd spend the bulk of her time sitting with the countess as they read books or did needlepoint. That had been how it was the first few months, but as the countess's health failed, she seemed less interested in a companion and more interested in someone to wait on her.

She sighed and flagged down a maid. "Please convey to Cook that the countess would like some tea. I have to bring something to Mr. Smith."

"Yes, my lady," said the maid before reversing course to head to the kitchen.

Adele took a deep breath and headed for Smith's room. He sat in front of the water basin. A maid must have come by in her absence and put clean water in the basin.

"Apologies for taking so long. The countess needed my attention for a few minutes."

Smith gave her a long look and said, "No need to apologize. I am an unexpected guest taking you away from your duties."

Adele placed the soap on the edge of the washstand and took a step away, preparing to supervise while Smith shaved. He got right into it, probably some old muscle memory telling him what to do, and managed to lather up his face. He leaned forward and began to scrape the lather away from his face and into the basin.

Adele opted not to speak while he worked. This looked like something that required great concentration.

Well, that, and she was mesmerized.

She couldn't remember even seeing her father shave, although clearly he must have because he was always clean-shaven. She watched now as Smith ran the blade down his cheeks and chin, taking lather and his whiskers with it but somehow not cutting himself. Well, he did manage to nick himself near the base of his chin and a little bead of blood formed there. He grunted and touched a handkerchief to it, then finished the job. Every stroke looked steady and practiced. Adele wondered if learning to shave was part of some ritual all men went through, especially in these days when beards were not fashionable.

Her mind wandered to all kinds of places as she watched Smith work. She briefly entertained a fantasy in which they shared a bedroom and this was part of his morning ritual. What must it be like to share a room, share a life, with a man? She'd thought about it quite a lot when she'd been engaged to Geoffrey but never had the opportunity to even sleep under the same roof as him.

Smith finished the job and patted his face with a towel. He leaned forward and examined his reflection in the mirror. "That is much better. But I missed a few spots. This mirror is not the cleanest. Perhaps you could help me."

Adele sat at the foot of the bed and looked over Smith's face. He had done an admirable job, although he had missed a line of hair near his chin. He handed her a brush with lather. "Swipe some of this over the parts that still have hair. It will help protect my skin from the blade. Then just lightly scrap the side of the blade along my skin. Act as though your task were just to remove the lather, not to apply much pressure to my face."

"All right."

She swallowed and followed his instructions. Performing this task necessitated leaning very close to Smith, close enough to see the fine lines of his face, close enough to smell him. She did as he asked, adding lather and scraping it off.

She did nick him again on her last pass along his chin, although he claimed it did not hurt. She dabbed at his cuts with a wet handkerchief until the bleeding stopped. Then she met his gaze.

He smiled at her. His eyes were so kind and beautiful. The scent of the shaving soap swirled around them, and Adele found herself drawn to it. She leaned a little closer to smell the scent of the soap on Smith's skin. It was heady.

"I do thank you for your assistance," Smith said softly.

"You're welcome."

The thought passed through her head that he might like a bath next. Perhaps she could help him with that as well…

She laughed to herself and backed away. That was ridiculous. She had no business helping him with anything so intimate. She was not his wife. They barely knew each other.

Adele took the towel and the handkerchief, intending to put them in the bin for one of the maids to take to the laundry later. Her fingers brushed against his hand as she took everything from him. She hated to break the spell, but needs must.

SMITH WATCHED ADELE clean up, something she seemed to have done automatically. He wondered if she did this because it was her job to do so or if she were just the sort of woman who took care of everyone.

Being close to her was soothing in a way. She was so pretty and kind that he wanted to get closer to her.

As soon as he'd held the razor in his hand, he'd known what to do with it. He suspected he often let his valet do this, but enough memory was in his body to tell him he performed this task himself sometimes, too. But he'd left a little hair on his face because he found himself longing to have her take care of him.

This was now the third day of his convalescence, so to speak. He felt nearly cured, no pain in his head at all and very little dizziness, although his memory was still elusive. If he knew where his home was, now would be the time to go there. He knew a time would come, either because he recalled who he was or they found enough clues to determine his identity, that he'd have to go home. But he would have hated to leave Adele.

Selfishly, he liked having her fuss over him.

But he wanted to do something for her as well. There was not much he could do; he did not seem to have much in the way of domestic skills, nor did he have any money.

"Miss Paulson, is there perhaps something I can help you with as a return on this favor?"

She looked at him, her expressions surprised. "I cannot think of anything."

He stood and gave himself one last glance at the mirror. He looked quite agreeable, and he liked how smooth the skin on his face felt. He had dark hair and knew keeping the shadow off his face was likely a daily battle, so he figured he'd be repeating this every morning, although likely not with Adele present.

Then he had an idea.

"I am a bit parched. It is a lovely, sunny day," he said. "Perhaps we can ask the cook to put some luncheon together for us and then go eat it out in the garden."

She smiled. "That sounds lovely, my lord."

As they walked together to the kitchen, Smith thought that he was not the sort of man normally prone to trying to romance women over picnics. He did not think himself lacking experience with the fairer sex, nor did he think he'd been courting anyone recently, but he supposed he had no way of knowing. He hoped he did not have a young lady waiting for him somewhere. Or, worse, a wife. Could he have been married? Was he betraying that wife right now by his interest in Adele?

Lord, but it was frustrating not being able to remember anything.

Adele wore pale yellow today. Her light hair was pinned up in a simple twist at the top of her head, like a crown of hair. Smith found he liked the simplicity of her dress and style, that she was never fussy or, he supposed, impractical. She seemed to be part of the household staff and had a number of tasks she must complete each day, so perhaps the elaborate dress of an idle woman would not be a good fit for her.

He sensed a deep unhappiness in her, too. She was good at putting on the mask of a smile most of the time. He'd seen the mask slip when she'd returned to his room with the mirror and the soap however. He found something in him wanted to help her with whatever was bothering her. He wanted to take her sadness away.

Adele and Cook worked quickly to put a meal together, but Hugh insisted on carrying the hamper outside. Cook handed Adele a blanket, which she spread on a patch of grass as Smith carried the hamper to her. He sat beside her and began to unpack it.

It was a modest lunch. Fresh bread, a hunk of cheese, a few slices of beef. Smith did not like the part of himself that was focused on looking for signs of income. This led him to believe that his real self often spent time thinking about money, but whether it was because he had a lot of it or a little, he could not determine.

Was he cruel? Kind? Judgmental? Did he attend many balls? Did he work hard? He had no idea.

Adele primly folded her legs beneath her as she sat.

"I grew up in the country," she said. "I shall never quite get used to the cramped spaces of the city."

"I believe I like the city, but I cannot say for sure."

She laughed softly. "Part of me likes the pace of the city. Everything happens faster here. And I like that I am but a short carriage ride from being able to buy anything my heart desires, although I admit I am frugal and do not often indulge. But the city is also full of interesting characters. You don't see many street performers wearing purple cloaks singing bawdy songs for a few pence in the country."

"No, I suppose you wouldn't."

"There is a man like that who plays a large drum outside the bookshop I like."

"So you read a lot?"

Adele laughed. "There are books littered around the house like crumbs for mice. I'm surprised you didn't notice."

He smiled at her. "I did. I just wasn't sure whose books they were."

"The countess is largely confined to her room these days."

"Since she came down with the cold?"

Adele shook her head. "It started a few weeks before that. We used to spend a lot more time together, but lately all she wants to do is sleep and read her books. She is partial to novels that have some mystery to them."

"I think I must have liked reading before, but I cannot recall any of my preferences."

"I can only imagine what it must be like."

"In some ways, it is like discovering the world anew," he said, and he genuinely felt that way. He spent a lot of time wishing the gray haze would clear from his head, but he also liked exploring the world now. Getting to know Adele was the chief highlight, and as they discussed books she'd read recently, he admired how expressive she was, how intelligent. She had a dry wit, as well, something she only seemed to express when she let her guard down.

They made quick work of the meal Cook had prepared as they talked.

"Do you feel up for a walk in the park today?" she asked as they packed up.

He wanted to spend more time with her, but he conducted an honest assessment of his own strength. "I am not sure I could walk very far today. My strength is not quite all the way back yet. Tomorrow, perhaps."

"Very well." She sounded disappointed.

It took some effort, proving his point, but he managed to push himself up onto his feet again. "Please do not think I do not want to walk with you. It really is just that I'm tired. Trying to remember things seems to take a lot of energy."

"I shall look forward to a time when you are in better condition for walking."

"I may retire until dinner, in fact. Please do not feel I've abandoned you."

She smiled. She stuffed the blanket into the now empty hamper and picked it up and hooked her other hand around his elbow. "All I want for you is a speedy recovery. Let us not overtax you. I can keep myself busy until dinner."

"That is quite agreeable of you."

She chuckled. "I wonder at the women in your real life if you think I am so agreeable."

Chapter Five

LARK WALKED THROUGH the club and found Fletcher Basildon, Baron Fowler, and Owen Thomas, the Earl of Caernarfon, seated near a fireplace sipping whisky. To Lark—and to Hugh—these two gentlemen were Fletcher and Owen, schoolmates from Eton and thus lifelong friends.

"Cheers, mate," Owen said when he spotted Lark.

"Where is Swynford?" Fletcher asked. "We haven't seen him in days."

"That is actually why I've come to find you," said Lark, sitting in an empty chair. One of the club's attendants appeared with a snifter of whisky, which Lark took gratefully. "Hugh is missing."

Fletcher and Owen glanced at each other. "What do you mean he's missing?" asked Owen in his Welsh accent.

"He left the Rutherford ball three nights ago and hasn't been seen since." Lark quickly caught them up on what he knew so far and added, "Yesterday, I called on Hugh's solicitor, Matthew Hogarth, who was anxious to help, although he had no information about Hugh's whereabouts."

"Is Hugh tangled up in something right now?" asked Fletcher.

"Not really. Hugh recently came into possession of a new plot of land after some distant relative died, but I can't see how that would explain Hugh's whereabouts. If he'd gone out to see it, he would have told his mother he was leaving town, but she also has no idea where he is."

Owen frowned, finally catching on. "In other words, some menace may have befallen him. He could be in peril somewhere."

"Yes, that is what I'm saying," said Lark. He took a healthy sip of whisky. "I'd like to enlist your help."

"Of course," said Fletcher. "So he just… vanished?"

"It seems that way," said Lark. "Mr. Hogarth is making some discreet inquiries with hospitals for injured men and with Bow Street to see if any, er, unidentified bodies have turned up, but if Hugh were dead, I believe we would know that by now. Surely he'd be recognized."

"Do you suspect some other sort of foul play?" asked Fletcher. "Kidnapping?"

"I just don't know," said Lark. "I've been thinking on this problem for days and I honestly have no idea where he could have gone, if he went somewhere of his own volition."

Fletcher frowned and set his whisky aside. "What do we do?"

"If none of Mr. Hogarth's inquiries pan out, I was thinking we might let a newspaperman know. That was why I wanted to speak with you, specifically, Fletcher."

Fletcher nodded. One of his business ventures was a print shop in London, so he had connections to newspapers and could easily find someone to print something about Hugh's disappearance and let Lark have control over the message.

"Is Hugh courting some young lady he could have eloped with?" asked Owen.

Fletcher burst out laughing. "If that were the case, he was definitely abducted."

"Where do you think he went?" asked Owen, elbowing Fletcher.

Lark sipped his whisky. "Part of me hoped one of you might know. When I last saw him, he was on his way home. Something happened on his walk from Rutherford's to his house. That is a short distance, but the dowager duchess says he never came home after leaving for the ball."

Lark was momentarily distracted when Anthony, the Marquess of Beresford, walked over to greet them. Lark had made a decision that he would not alert anyone but those he trusted most that anything was amiss with Hugh, and he glanced at both Owen and Fletcher, who both nodded almost imperceptibly. Lark had a certain... fondness for Beresford, but didn't trust him entirely. Beresford was as bold and alluring as he was annoying sometimes and he gave off an air like he didn't care what anyone thought of him, something Lark found simultaneously attractive and terrifying.

Beresford said, "Your little quartet is missing a member."

"Swynford is under the weather," said Lark.

Beresford appeared to find this information of little interest and stood there posing, his hip cocked, as he examined his nails. "Pity. Nothing fatal, I hope."

"A few sniffles."

"I wish him the speediest of recoveries." He looked at Lark directly and made eye contact. "I wanted to share, Parliament is coming back in session. Prinny has some reason for calling them, likely for Parliament to appropriate more funds to his house decoration budget, but at any rate, my uncle is back in town from his sojourn to Bath."

Beresford's uncle was the current Lord Chancellor, a powerful position in the British government. The Lord Chancellor was of advanced years and had murmured about possibly retiring soon, meaning the position was likely going to be open at some point in the near future. This interested Lark only insofar as he was curious to see which lord made the bigger fool of himself jockeying for the job.

Lark's overtaxed brain tried to see if he could make some connection between Hugh vanishing and Parliament being in session. He could come up with no way to connect these two things. He rubbed his forehead and then realized that Beresford was busy gossiping about various MPs.

Trying to recover from having bowed out of the conversation so as not to alert Beresford to the fact that something was wrong,

Lark said, "This should keep the scandal sheets busy for a bit."

Beresford laughed. "Indeed."

"Is the rumor about Canbury true?" Owen asked.

"About his wearing women's clothing in public? No," said Beresford, "at least not as far as I know. However I heard he was seen leaving the molly house on Guildford Street. Some men are just not capable of discretion, I suppose."

Lark tried not to react. Beresford was hardly discreet himself—Lark would not have been surprised if he'd been the one to spot Canbury at a molly house—but perhaps being a marquess insulated him from scandal to a certain extent. The men of his generation of the *ton* generally knew about Beresford's inclinations but did not discuss them in polite society. Lark kept his interest in his own sex private, although now he was thinking about his recent tumbles with Beresford, partly because Beresford was now eyeing him in a meaningful way.

Lark sighed. "Did *you* see Canbury at the molly house?"

Beresford scoffed. "No. Nor would I go to one myself. Nor do I have any interest in donning women's clothing if that is your next question."

"You'd rather follow Brummell's instructions to the letter," said Fletcher. He tipped his glass toward Beresford. "I read that he's decided the dandy set were all to wear that exact shade of yellow this Season."

Beresford grinned and fingered the edge of his waistcoat, which was indeed a rather bold shade of yellow. "Do not shame me for following the latest fashions. I'm told this makes me quite attractive to a certain set of men who are in the know."

Lark rolled his eyes. "And dressing like a goldfinch is the very height of discretion."

Beresford shrugged. "Anyway, I also came to pay call to your little quadrangle because I wanted a word with you, Waring. May I discuss something with you without the presence of all of your friends?"

"We were having a somewhat serious conversation before

you interrupted," said Lark. His mind was still on Hugh, and he wanted to spend more time brainstorming how they might find him. Beresford was… a distraction.

"Just a minute or two of your time."

"All right."

He followed Beresford to a dim hallway out of sight and earshot from the rest of the members of the club. Beresford kissed him, fast and hard, then stroked the side of his face. "What I actually wanted to discuss was how I might find you without the presence of all of your clothes."

"An urgent business matter requiring my attention has suddenly made itself known this week, and I'm afraid I don't—"

"Surely your business obligations do not require your attentions at night."

"Anthony, I—"

"I want you however I can get you. Tonight, tomorrow, anytime. I think you want me, too. I know you don't want to get caught, and I will do everything in my power to see that we aren't." Beresford nipped at Lark's lips. "You may not think I am capable of discretion, but let me assure you, I can keep a secret if needed."

"Kissing me in the hallway of a gentlemen's club certainly seems like a good way to get caught."

Beresford smiled and stepped away. "Fair point. Come to the house on Charles Street tonight."

Beresford owned three houses in London. He had enough money to make scandals disappear as well, which Lark assumed was why he was not currently in jail or an asylum. At any rate, the house on Charles Street was the least glamorous. He kept minimal staff there, the house itself was nondescript and looked identical to three others on the block, and only a handful of people even knew Beresford owned it. Which, of course, meant Lark was hardly the first man Beresford had brought to that house, since it was ideal for secret trysts.

He grunted. "Fine. I need some time, but I will come by

tonight."

"Only if you want to."

"I want to, all right? But you must be more careful in public."

"Naturally."

When Lark returned to his friends, Fletcher gave him an odd look. "What did Beresford want?"

"Nothing of consequence. You know how he is."

"Indeed. Now, what are we going to do about Hugh?"

ADELE WAS SURPRISED when Smith moved his knight and put her king in danger.

"I thought you didn't know how to play chess," she said.

"I must have in my previous life. That knowledge seems to be rattling around in my head."

It had been like this for the last day and a half. Little dribbles of knowledge and skill seemed to be emerging from whatever veil kept them hidden from Smith, although he still could not recall his name or where he came from. Today, they'd been playing games to see what he could recall. He remembered the rules of whist but had lost several games to Adele. He'd been able to explain gambling strategies for a few card games of chance to Adele, which allowed her to picture him in a room full of cigar smoke playing cards with the men of the *ton*.

The first new set of clothes from the tailor had arrived that day as well. The new clothes fit Mr. Smith much better than the earl's clothes had; those clothes had been rather tight and had not left much to the imagination. Adele had found herself avoiding looking at him as much as possible, lest her gaze settle on his powerful thighs, his shapely calves, the curve of his behind, his... well. He seemed oblivious to her attentions, but spending time with him was a challenge. She knew he needed her help, but sometimes it was all she could do not to dissolve into girlish giggles, because she found him easy to talk to and exceedingly handsome.

The countess was still pretending he did not exist, unwilling to leave her room or have visitors aside from Adele despite authorizing the purchase of clothing for him. She may not have understood that he was likely a nobleman and not just some ruffian brought in off the street, but Adele found herself wondering at the countess's motives.

After all, Smith's manners—which he seemed unaware he was even exhibiting and were likely something drilled into him from a very young age—were impeccable most of the time, and he seemed to innately understand his place in the world, which indicated to Adele that he was no matrimonial prospect for her.

She hadn't exaggerated when she'd told him a few days before that she doubted she'd ever marry because that was not in the hand of cards life had dealt her. She'd been destined to love once and never again. But every now and then she fancied meeting some country gentleman and settling down in the relative obscurity of a modest house far from London. She wanted a child, sometimes so badly she could feel it in her belly, but she did not think she'd ever have one, so she had to be content with her lot in life. But Smith's presence was dangerous because it was inspiring hope in her once again.

She moved her king out of danger now.

Smith eyed her for a long moment and then concentrated on the board. He moved his bishop. "Checkmate," he said.

He was right. Moving her king had left her queen vulnerable. She laughed. "So that's something you remember."

"Apparently so." He leaned back from the table. "Is this how gentlemen spend their leisure time?"

"I suppose so. I don't rightfully know. That is, men spend time at their clubs. I am not permitted to know what happens at those clubs, but I always reasoned it was drinking and cards. Perhaps smoking cigars. Or men go to balls or pay social calls to women they fancy or ride horses or any number of things."

Smith nodded. "Do you think I am married?"

"You do not wear a ring, so I do not believe so, but I suppose anything is possible."

Smith looked at his hands. He turned them over a few times. "I think I normally do wear a ring. Perhaps it was stolen by whoever hit me on the head."

That simple fact should not have been disappointing, and yet Adele felt her heart sink to her stomach.

He continued to study at his hands. "A heavy ring, I think. With a... some kind of insignia on it. And a red stone. A... a ruby."

"That sounds like a signet ring," said Adele, feeling a certain amount of relief. Smith was really not husband material, and yet the more time they spent together, the more she wanted him to kiss her. Which was ridiculous. She shrugged her shoulders and said, "A ring like that might signify that you descend from an important family. It might have a family symbol or a coat of arms imprinted on it."

"Yes, that seems correct."

Inspiration struck. "Can you remember anything about the coat of arms? That may narrow down which family you come from."

He closed his eyes for a long moment. "I see... a knight holding a shield divided into four sections."

"Yes, excellent." Nearly every coat of arms appeared that way. "What else?"

"The shield has... two animals. A lion is one."

Adele bit her lip. A lion appeared on nearly every ducal coat of arms.

"And the other is a... pig. No. A boar." He opened his eyes. "Is that helpful?"

"Yes, I believe so. I think it is actually quite unusual for two animals to be on your coat of arms. The lion might indicate you are a relation to the King, or it could just be a coincidence. The boar is interesting to me, though. I don't know which family uses a boar as their symbol, but that should be something I could find easily. I will ask the countess if she knows, and if not, I will check in with the bookseller at my favorite bookshop on the morrow. He knows more about the history of the peerage than anyone I know. And if he does not know, he may have a book in which I could look it up."

"I could draw it if that makes it easier. I can picture it now."

Adele stood and grabbed a few sheets of paper and a pencil from the writing desk in the corner. She handed them to Smith, who put the papers right on the chessboard. He quickly sketched out a coat of arms with four sections. He drew three lions in each of the top right and bottom left sections, then three boars each in the top left and bottom right sections. He had to pause and close his eyes a few times as he drew, as if he were trying very hard to picture exactly what it looked like.

"I am not as good at drawing as I am at chess," he said, handing his sketch to Adele. "But that is what I see in my head when I picture the ring. The ruby is right in the center, where the four sections meet. I see an *S* also, somewhere on the ring. Maybe inscribed in the band." He grunted. "It is ridiculous to me that I can picture this ring but still cannot recall my name.

"This is still a very important clue." Adele felt nearly giddy now. "Your family name must begin with an *S*. Not Smith, but likely not far off the mark. Of course, there are probably dozens of peers with names that start with *S*. Salisbury, Somerset, Shrewsbury, Suffolk… it could be any of those."

Smith tilted his head. "None of those seem familiar."

"Those were just the first *S* names that popped into my head. The Earl of Suffolk must be older than fifty, for example, so clearly you are not him. The Marquess of Salisbury is an ancient man. Which is not to say that you may not be related to those men, I do not know. These are just guesses."

"I do appreciate your help, if I have not said. I do not believe I could figure any of this out on my own."

"You are welcome. You seem like a good man and I would

like to help you."

"You would like me out of your hair, you mean."

"Not at all. I enjoy your company. Why, we've spent nearly all day today playing games, and I've never once felt bored."

He chuckled. "Do you often feel bored?"

"I suppose. The countess cheats at cards, which is frustrating, and Hodges occasionally plays chess with me but is not very good. It is nice to have a challenge."

Smith stood. "Then I shall endeavor to make sure you are never bored when you are in my company."

Her heart began to beat harder as he approached her. "I can't see how I would be bored with you around."

"Do you think we now have enough clues to piece together my identity?"

"I certainly hope so. This is a lot right here. How many peerages can there be that start with *S* and have a boar in their coat of arms?"

"It might almost be sad to return to my old life. Although I have not felt in top physical form, I feel as though I have no particular worries. That is likely because I've forgotten them. I have a sense that I often have a lot of responsibilities piled on my shoulders. But it's almost relaxing in a way to not know what I don't know, if that makes sense."

"It does," she said, aware of how close he stood to her now.

He gazed at her face, a smile playing on her lips. "With no cares, I could almost do anything my mind was set on."

"You could."

He smelled good and emanated a warmth Adele found comforting. He was so very tall and had a certain strength looming below his clothing. He was the sort of man artists painted because his beauty was so profound they could not contain themselves.

And he was standing a hairsbreadth from Adele now, and he was very likely going to kiss her.

Her heart pounded in her throat.

"Since I am not of right mind, perhaps you will excuse me

this indulgence," he said.

Then he kissed her.

Adele had not been kissed since her late fiancé had passed, but she found the mechanics of it came back to her in a whoosh of yearning. She'd been wanting this man to kiss her for days and he finally was, and it was all she could do not to throw herself on him. She opened her mouth for a better taste, and he groaned, clutching her shoulders in his hands.

Then he wavered and stepped back.

"Oh, dear," she said.

"I apologize, my lady, I am… well, a bit dizzy, if I'm honest."

"Oh. You must sit down then."

"Was that too forward?" He sat carefully on the chair near the chess table. "Not the dizziness, the kissing."

"Well, yes, it was rather forward, but I did not mind. That is, I enjoyed the kiss."

"I probably should not kiss pretty ladies until I know for certain that I am not married or betrothed to anyone else. Still, it is somewhat reassuring to know that I still know how to kiss."

Adele sat across from him and patted his hand where it rested on the chess board. "I am growing quite fond of you," she said. "I think I should very much like to kiss again sometime."

He smiled. "I will take that under advisement."

Chapter Six

AFTER DINNER, ADELE took Smith to see the countess, who had professed earlier in the day that she was in high spirits and felt much better than she had in a week.

Adele went in first and made Smith stand in the hallway. She found the countess sitting up in bed with a book in her lap. "I've brought our guest to see you," Adele said. "But I wanted to check on you before I brought him in. How do you feel?"

"Much better. The fever seems to have passed."

"I am very happy to hear that." Adele leaned over and smoothed over the countess's hair. "You could use a little color on your cheeks."

The countess waved Adele away. "Pale complexions are fashionable, are they not? Besides, our guest knows I have been sick in bed. That is not a secret we are trying to conceal." She set the book on the side table. "Are we any closer to guessing our guest's identity."

"Not quite. The staff and I have been calling him Mr. Smith. However, he remembers a signet ring with a coat of arms on it that may help. Perhaps you can recognize it. Or you may even recognize our Mr. Smith."

"I'm afraid my knowledge of these things is seeping away like my health, but I will do what I can. Bring him in."

Adele fetched him from the hallway. The countess gave him a long look.

"My, you're a handsome one," said the countess.

Smith laughed. "Thank you, my lady."

"You do look familiar to me, but I cannot place your face. Or perhaps I knew your father. It has been quite some time since I went out into society."

"I wish I could say."

"Tell me about this coat of arms. And please sit while you do it. I don't need two tall people hovering over me."

Adele pulled over two chairs, and she and Smith sat beside each other next to the bed. "I forgot the sketch I made downstairs," said Smith, "but what I recall is lions and boars on a family crest, on a signet ring that I believe has an *S* inscribed on it."

The countess closed her eyes for a brief moment, likely trying to picture what he was describing. "I'm not connecting it with anything I remember, but then, my late husband, god rest his soul, was better at remembering those sorts of things anyway." She smiled at Smith. "I'd ask you to tell me about yourself, but you don't know much, do you?"

"I'm afraid not."

"We lead a pretty quiet existence here," said the countess. "Often Lady Adele and I read together. We play cards. She helps me with my needlepoint because the old eyes are not as sharp as they once were."

"That sounds... nice."

The countess laughed. "It sounds dull to you. We can't all lead the thrilling life of a society gentleman."

"What have you been reading today?" asked Adele, anxious to change the subject.

The countess touched the book on her bedside table and her face lit up. "It is a mystery story. A detective must find a missing person who seems to have disappeared into thin air. The story is quite enthralling, but I'm afraid it has few tips for how to solve our real-life mystery."

"Do you think you'd see something like that in a novel?" Adele asked.

"I did read about a case similar to Mr. Smith's in a novel once. The character fell from a great height and hit his head, although miraculously sustained no other injuries. When he came to, he could not remember anything. The affliction is called *amnesia*."

"How did the character solve it?"

"He got hit in the head again."

"I don't think I would like that much," said Smith. "Nor do I recall that being on the list of things Dr. Willis suggested to encourage my memory."

"Best to follow the doctor's orders, then," said the countess with a wink.

The countess gave Smith a long look again. "I do wonder now if I knew your parents in my youth. You look about the age of my son. Perhaps it will come to me."

Adele had hoped the countess would remember. Part of her also hoped Smith's family would be out looking for him, but how would they know to look for him here? She'd been checking the newspapers for stories of missing nobles but had yet to see anything. Perhaps tomorrow, she'd be able to put a name to the coat of arms and that would narrow the search enough.

Probably she could have gone to town today. Part of her was putting off the inevitable.

She felt a little guilty about that, but Smith hadn't questioned her.

"Back in my day," the countess said, "we still powdered our hair to go out. I met the earl at Lady Christie's annual ball, and my own hair was too flat, so my sister talked me into this ridiculous wig festooned with flowers and feathers. The earl told me later that he found me quite fetching, though I do not know how he did not think me a clown. Let me tell you, I was not sad to see that custom pass into obscurity."

Adele wondered what the point of this story was, but Smith said, "Perhaps my parents were hidden under wigs when you met."

"Precisely so," said the countess. "My last social season was long ago. Lady Christie is long dead."

"I have the sense that my father and I were not particularly close but that my mother and I were. Part of me wishes to see her, although I of course barely remember what she looks like." Smith sighed. "I do not wish to bring the room down. Perhaps we could play cards?"

"I'd be delighted," said the countess. "Adele, dear, there is a deck of cards in the top drawer of the chest of drawers in the corner."

MUCH LATER, SMITH escorted Adele down the hall to her bedroom, which he had not realized until they arrived was across the hall from the room where he'd been staying.

"The countess seems... lively."

Adele laughed. "She is that, most days. I worry about her lately. She has not seemed herself, although she did tonight. Perhaps she just needed some company to put forward a good face."

"She clearly cares for you a great deal."

"Thank you. We've grown quite fond of each other, I think." Adele shook her head and pressed a hand over her eyes.

"What is it?"

Adele sighed and dropped her hand. "Are you familiar with the Brothers Grimm?"

The question took him aback. "No. Are they society gentlemen?"

She laughed. "No. They are German academics who compile and publish old folktales. They released a collection not long ago that contains a story called 'Cinderella.' In the story, a young girl loses her mother, and then her father remarries. Shortly after the wedding, the father joins his first wife in heaven, and Cinderella is left in the care of her stepmother, who is not at all kind or compassionate. She makes Cinderella wait on her as a servant would. I lately feel that way. I am not a blood relation of anyone in the Sweeney family, nor am I a servant. I work for the countess, but my role is to keep her company, not make her tea or clean up her bedroom. And yet…"

"Is that why you are so unhappy?"

She winced. "I should stop being so unflinchingly honest with you or you will think me truly pathetic."

"I do not think you pathetic." Smith picked up her hand and held it in his own. He was surprised by how small and delicate her hands seemed. He smiled at her. "I appreciate your honesty. I suppose if we had met at a party, we'd have guile enough to put forth some perfect version of ourselves meant to impress each other. But I feel that I have gotten to know something of you these last few days."

She smiled back shyly. "Thank you. I believe I have found some innate goodness of you. You may not know your name or your title or where you came from, but you are… yourself."

"I hope so. I would hate to think that I've forgotten that I used to be a tyrant."

"That cannot be possible."

"And if it turns out I have no title or if I am a mere baronet without any significant wealth or property?"

"It would not matter to me. You earn a title merely by being born by the right family. A title does not speak to your work ethic or your kindness or your character."

"Well put."

He couldn't seem to stop gazing at her. She had lovely eyes, light grayish blue, with long eyelashes. Her whole face brightened when she smiled. Would he ever tire of gazing at that face?

Was this conventional? He felt drawn to her, but they'd known each other mere days.

"That is not much of a story," he said.

"What wasn't?"

"Cinderella. Her father dies, so she becomes a servant to her stepmother?"

Adele laughed. The sound rang through the hallway. "Oh, no. The story actually has quite a happy ending. You see, the king has a ball. The stepmother takes her own daughters but forbids Cinderella. Cinderella is of good heart and has befriended animals, so when she wishes with all her heart to go to the ball, birds bring her a beautiful gown to wear. When she arrives, her stepmother does not recognize her. The prince however thinks she is beautiful and will dance with only Cinderella. He falls in love with her. But she must return home before her stepmother does, so she runs away and leaves a shoe behind. The prince declares that he will marry only the girl who fits this shoe. Only Cinderella has feet small and dainty enough to fit the shoe. So they marry and she lives happily ever after."

Smith smiled, liking the story. "That's quite lovely. I'm sure that was revenge on the stepmother, who likely wanted her own daughters to marry the prince." Something about that prickled at Smith. Had he been a prince, or at least a gentleman, in the middle of a ballroom, surrounded by prospective eligible daughters? It seemed he had been.

"It is a nice story. Life does not work like that, though."

"No?"

"Of course not. I may think of myself as Cinderella some days, toiling on chores, but no prince will fall in love with me and sweep me away from here."

His heart ached for the way she'd given up. She deserved so much better than the hand she'd been dealt. He reached over and tucked a loose tendril of hair behind her ear.

"You are beautiful," he said.

"Oh." She looked down.

"Has no one ever told you that?"

"Not in a very long time."

"Someone should tell you that every day, because it's true."

"I am old and on the shelf."

"No." Smith reached below her chin and tilted her face up so he could look at her eyes again. "You are not old. Older than this year's new crop of debutantes, yes, but not too old to marry and have children, if that is what you most desire. Not too old to make something of your life. Not too old for this."

He leaned down and kissed her. The vulnerability in her eyes and the slightest pout in her lips rendered him unable to resist.

This was ridiculous and he knew it. There were any number of obstacles laying between them. But enough time had gone by that he was beginning to doubt he'd ever fully recover his memories, so why shouldn't he court Lady Adele? She was smart and beautiful and he knew he could make her happy.

She tasted lovely, too.

Dr. Willis had come by earlier that day and discussed his progress. Smith had been grateful Adele had been otherwise occupied at the time, because the doctor had asked about some basic operations of Smith's body. Smith was relieved in a way that, as he kissed Adele, as he put his arms around her and pulled her close and felt her soft body pressed against his hard one, his body responded. In fact, he was responding now for the first time since he'd first woken up in this house.

That part of him still worked. He'd been worried it wouldn't.

Although now he'd surely scare her, so he eased away.

She squeezed his hand. "I think it is quite likely that whatever flirtation exists between us will not last once you recover your memories."

"Perhaps. Or not. We can't know." He let out a breath. He should go to his room, but he couldn't bring himself to leave her side. "Perhaps if nothing else, this has shown me that life is never quite what you expect it to be."

She shook her head. "That's a nice sentiment, but—"

"If nothing else, I hope that we might be friends. If I ever go back to my old life, I'd hate to think of it without you. You've been so kind to me these last few days, and I did nothing to deserve that except fall out of a carriage onto your doorstep."

"Friends. That I can do." She glanced at her door. "I

should…"

"I will bid you good night, then, Lady Adele. Sleep well."

"Good night." She lifted up onto her toes and kissed his cheek.

When he slipped back into his room a moment later, he tried to tell himself that he was in no position to plan his future, but he wanted Adele to be a part of it in some way.

Chapter Seven

ADELE ALIGHTED FROM the Sweeney carriage and gave instructions for where the driver should meet her in an hour, figuring that was how long it would take to buy a few things for the countess and walk to the bookseller to hunt through *Debrett's* for the right family name.

She took care of the countess's tasks first. Then, on the walk to the bookshop, something in the window of a newspaper office caught her eye.

She paused to look at a newspaper headline, which said, *Swynford Missing, Presumed Dead.* Around the newspaper were a series of drawings of a man who looked very much like her house guest. She read the first few lines of the story and saw that Hugh Baxter, the Duke of Swynford, had disappeared on the same evening a mysterious man had turned up on her street.

She raced to the bookshop and found Mr. Ross, who owned the shop. She was out of breath.

"Are you having some kind of literary emergency?" Mr. Ross asked.

"I need your help." She was reluctant to tell the whole story because she did not want it to become widely known that the Duke of Swynford was likely in her house at that moment, so she paused to consider how to phrase it. "I found an object with this coat of arms imprinted on it, and I need to know the family it signifies." She handed Mr. Ross the sketch Smith had made.

Mr. Ross squinted at the sketch and then led Adele to a corner of the store. He opened a large book that clearly had all of the coats of arms of the families in England, listed in alphabetical order.

"There was also an *S* imprinted on the object," Adele said. "If that helps narrow it down."

"It does. I thought it looked like the Swynford crest, but I wanted to be certain."

He opened the book to a page that showed a drawing that showed a coat of arms very similar to the one Smith had drawn. "Swynford" was written across the bottom of the page.

"Does this answer your question?" Mr. Ross asked.

Adele nodded. "I believe I have something that belongs to the Duke of Swynford. Could you tell me where he lives so that I can return it to him?"

Mr. Ross raised an eyebrow. "Have you not heard that he is missing?"

"Oh dear. Missing?" That sounded like a poor stage performance, so she added, "That is, I saw something in a newspaper in passing, but I did not make the connection."

"I believe your best course of action is to call on Larkin Woodville, Lord Waring. He is a friend of the duke's and has been doing a poor job of being discreet while making inquiries about the location of His Grace."

Adele recognized that Mr. Ross had made a joke, so she smiled and said, "This Lord Waring would not be a good hero for the mystery stores the countess likes, then."

Mr. Ross laughed. "Indeed, no. He thinks he is the soul of discretion, but there has been gossip around town for a few days that His Grace never made it home after the Rutherford ball last week."

"Does anyone have an idea for what became of him?"

Mr. Ross shrugged. "I've heard he ran off with some woman he was sweet on, that perhaps they have gone to Scotland to elope, but I do not know if I give credence to such rumors. His

Grace is a regular customer here and has always struck me as a thoughtful man not prone to acting rashly. He has the weight of responsibility on his shoulders, and he takes his family duties very seriously."

Adele nodded, feeling somewhat validated in her opinion of Smith. Or Swynford, she supposed.

"Oh the other hand," said Mr. Ross. "He is a rather large man. He would be difficult to abduct."

"Perhaps not if he were hit on the head."

"There is that." Mr. Ross barked out a laugh. "Have you ever met the duke?"

"I can't say that I have," she said, which was true enough.

"Perhaps Lord Waring will know what to do with the object you found. What was the object?"

Searching her mind, she said, "A handkerchief."

Mr. Ross nodded. "Yes. Swynford would of course have the family crest embroidered on his handkerchiefs. Yes, I do believe you should show it to Waring. Let him know where you found it. Perhaps that will help him locate the duke."

"I sincerely hope so. His family must be so worried."

"I imagine so, although the dowager duchess would never admit as much publicly. I am certain if you asked her right now where the duke was, she would tell you he is home, safe and sound. Nothing to bring dishonor on the family."

That sounded intimidating. Adele wanted to ask more about that, but she understood that Mr. Ross was speaking off the cuff, and besides, it suddenly felt like time was of the essence. She could not wait to return home and tell Smith that he was very likely the Duke of Swynford.

Which of course meant that there was no way he would ever court Adele. As an earl's daughter, she was perhaps eligible, but even Adele knew that the Swynford name was one held above reproach. The duke had never even breathed near a scandal.

Adele was not naive. She was a spinster, her father was a politician of dubious reputation, and thus she was clearly below the Duke of Swynford in social standing.

"Thank you for your help," she said. "Before I go, the countess was looking for something new to read. Do you have any suggestions?"

"As it happens, I do. We have some new novels."

Adele let Mr. Ross show her what he had in, and she picked out and purchased a novel for the countess. Mr. Ross tried to entice her into something for herself, too, but she wanted to get to Lord Waring with all possible haste, so she promised to come back in a week. Perhaps by then, she would have overcome the unbearable sadness seeping into her body now that she knew the man she'd been spending time would leave and likely never see her again.

As she paid for the book, she considered stalling, going straight home and telling Smith she'd found nothing. That would keep him with her for longer. But perhaps it would be better to end this now, before she fell in love with him.

"Let me give you Lord Waring's address," Mr. Ross said. He walked into the back room and returned with a piece of paper displaying an address in Mayfair.

"Thank you, Mr. Ross. If you could keep this between us, I would appreciate it. I merely found a handkerchief. I wouldn't want people to get the idea that I know the duke's whereabouts."

"Of course, my dear. Do visit soon. I've heard there will be a new book by the anonymous author of *Emma* soon."

That *was* good news. "Please hold a copy for me if it comes in before I can next see you."

"Of course, my lady. Have a great evening."

"Are you in to female callers?" asked Kelly, Lark's butler.

Lark was in his study, awaiting word from Mr. Hogarth and pretending to check his ledgers. He cleared his throat. "That seems highly unusual. I was not expecting any female callers. Who is it?"

"Lady Adele Paulson."

The name didn't ring a bell. "I do not think I know her."

"She claims to have information on the Duke of Swynford."

A hundred thoughts flitted through Lark's mind. Was it possible Hugh had absconded with a woman after all? How did the woman at his door come to have knowledge about Hugh? Was she Hugh's mistress? Did she know Hugh's abductor? "Please show her to the blue sitting room. I will be there momentarily."

He did not know the woman he encountered a few moments later, although his mind registered a few things about her. She was pretty, albeit plain; she had the sort of understated beauty that clung to women who could not be bothered to fuss over their appearance but had been nonetheless blessed with familial good looks. She also seemed old for a debutante, so he ruled that out as a possibility. Lark was at a loss.

He cleared his throat. "I am Lord Waring."

She turned toward him. "A pleasure to meet you, my lord."

"And you are?"

"Yes, apologies. I am not quite myself, as I've had a shocking few days. I am Lady Adele Paulson."

"Paulson." Lark tossed around the name in his head again. It was the last name that finally clued him in. "Canbury's daughter."

"Yes."

"A pleasure to meet you. Please sit down."

She did not sit. Lark stared at her for a long moment, now wondering how Hugh had gotten tangled up with the Earl of Canbury and what his daughter could possibly be doing here. Since she insisted on standing, he remained on his feet as well.

She cleared her throat. "My lord, your name was in an article in the *Gazette* about the disappearance of the Duke of Swynford. I hope you won't think me forward, but I acquired your address because, if you are looking for him, I believe I may have some information."

Oh, lovely. Canbury was broke, so of course he sent his daughter to sniff out reward money. Lark's heart fell. For nearly a week, he'd been looking for Hugh and had come up with nothing. Worse, that newspaper article had sent him on more false leads and goose chases than he had imagined possible. It was like Hugh had simply disappeared into thin air. And here was the Earl of Canbury's daughter to send him on one more.

He tried not to betray any emotion as he spoke. "Indeed, I am looking for him. If you read the article, you know he vanished a week ago."

"Yes. Who is His Grace to you, if you do not mind my asking?"

Lark was losing patience. What an odd question. "He is a dear friend. We grew up together. I love him like a brother. Please sit and tell your tale, my lady."

She finally relented and perched herself at the edge of a settee, so he sat in the armchair across from her. She said, "You do not believe my inquiry is genuine."

"I have spent the last two days speaking to people just like you who claim to have information on Hugh's whereabouts but are really in search of financial compensation. Some lordling came by yesterday and gave me the address of where to find Swynford, and it turned out to be a brothel. His Grace was not at this brothel. And I saw things I wish I could unsee."

"I sympathize, my lord. Please be assured that I have no designs on monetary compensation. I had not considered the possibility until just now."

"Let the chase begin, then," said Lark. "Please proceed."

Lady Adele folded her hands neatly over her crossed legs. "Last week, a man was tossed out of a carriage and landed on the street near my home. The man was unconscious and had sustained a serious blow to the head. When he awoke the next morning, he could not recall who he was or where he came from. I've been working with him for the last week to try to recover his memories. Although little bits have trickled back, he still cannot recall his name or where he lives."

And suddenly she had his interest. Lark leaned forward. "A blow to the head, you say?"

"Yes. And now I have reason to believe the man in my house is the Duke of Swynford."

"How did you arrive at such a conclusion?" Lark didn't want to get his hopes up, but he believed this woman for some reason.

She produced a reticule deep from within a pocket of her gown. From it, she pulled out several folded sheets of paper. "He believed he owned a signet ring that perhaps his attacker stole. He recalls the ring had these animals on it." She showed Lark a crude sketch of the Swynford coat of arms, with its boars and lions. Lark was familiar because he had seen it in Hugh's house and on the doors of his carriages many times. The dowager duchess took great pride in the Swynford name and displayed it wherever possible.

Lady Adele went on, "He also recalls that an *S* was inscribed on the ring somewhere, so we deduced that this coat of arms belonged to a family with a name that began with *S*. I was on Oxford Street today to see a bookseller I know so that I might review a copy of *Debrett's* for some ideas on any family that might meet these criteria. On my way to the bookshop, I happened to see a drawing of the missing duke in a print shop window. I am fairly certain that the man in my house and the Duke of Swynford are one and the same."

"That is compelling evidence." He held up the drawing. "This looks like the Swynford coat of arms. And I have suspected for some time that he was abducted or attacked and did not merely wander off or run off to Scotland to elope, as some have suggested. It is very unlike Hugh… that is, His Grace the Duke, to be anywhere he is not supposed to be."

"Hugh?"

"That is his name. Hugh Baxter, the twelfth Duke of Swynford."

The woman smiled to herself. "Hugh. It suits him."

"I should like to see him right away."

"Yes, of course. The doctor suggested that being around something familiar might help encourage His Grace's memory to return, but until today, I had no earthly notion what might be familiar to him. Perhaps seeing a friend would be helpful."

"If I had more time I'd summon a few of his other friends, but perhaps we will need to introduce him to society a little more slowly."

"He is still recovering from his injuries. We'd best not overwhelm him."

"Yes. All right." Lark was eager to go, so he stood and set off for the door with the woman on his heels. "We'll take my carriage."

"What shall I do with mine?"

"Send him home."

Lady Adele let out a frustrated grunt. "My lord, if I may, my carriage is already sitting in front of your house. The horses are ready and my driver knows the way. It will save time if you come with me."

"I suppose I could take a hackney back home."

"And I understand you are eager to see your missing friend, but please be advised that while the evidence is compelling, I am not completely certain the man in my house is your Duke of Swynford. I also believe it is best to gradually reintroduce him to his old life because I do not want to shock him. He sustained quite a serious head injury and is still subject sometimes to pain and dizziness."

"All right." Something broke through Lark's worry for Hugh and he really saw this woman, who was a little aggressive and seemed protective of Hugh. Lark wondered if he should infer something about her. He was certainly curious to see how Hugh regarded her.

They walked outside. A carriage that had seen better days was indeed waiting in front of the house. The Sweeney coat of arms was painted on the door. As a devoted reader of the scandal sheets and society columns, Lark prided himself on his knowledge of everyone in the *ton*, and he could not recall how the Paulsons and the Sweeneys might have been related. Lark gestured to the Sweeney symbol.

"Perhaps I should have explained," Lady Adele said. "I am a companion to the Countess of Sweeney. I reside in her house in Marylebone, near Regent's Park."

The address surprised Lark. Had the Sweeneys fallen on hard times? But there was a more pressing question. "How did Hugh end up in Westminster?"

"That remains a mystery, my lord."

As the carriage got underway, Lark asked, "Does he remember how he came to have a head injury?"

"No. He doesn't remember much of anything before he woke up at my house six days ago. He's recovered snatches of childhood memories, but not enough to reveal his identity."

Lark nodded.

"Can you tell me much about him?"

Lark considered the question. "I'm not sure what would be best to reveal. His father, the previous duke, died about six years ago. He and Hugh were not especially close. His parents had one of those customary *ton* marriages where they knew each other for about three days before the duke offered, and once the requisite heir was produced, the duke left his family in the country and spent most of his time in London. But Hugh is quite close with his mother, despite the fact that she is a difficult woman."

Lady Adele huffed out a laugh and said, "This tells me nothing about the current duke."

Lark nodded. "I suppose if he has lost his memories, he may have lost some aspects of his personality as well. But the Hugh I know is a very proud man who performs his duties without complaint even though I know he loathes some of them."

"Give me an example."

"He hates balls for once. Don't tell him I told you that."

"Does he hate dancing?"

"No, it's not that. I think he is fond of dancing, in fact, but he will never admit it." Lark laughed softly, thinking of a discussion they had on the last night Lark had seen Hugh. "You see, as a handsome duke of good marriageable age, all of the society mamas have been throwing their daughters at him. He is the most eligible bachelor in London, you see."

"Oh. Of course."

Lark watched her face carefully for a reaction. He was not disappointed. She'd obviously grown quite fond of Hugh in the time he'd spent at her house. Lark supposed that made sense; Hugh was a good man, even if his priorities had been a little off-kilter of late. Lark worried he'd been close to succumbing to his mother's pressure and just picking some debutante at random. Hugh had always said he'd wanted more for himself than a marriage like his parents. Hugh's father's absence had made Hugh feel disconnected from his title in some ways, or so Lark had long hypothesized. He played the role of the noble duke for the sake of his mother, but some part of Hugh had wanted a quiet life and a family and none of his ceremonial responsibilities. Perhaps that was still possible; plenty of members of the peerage, even those with familial ties to the king, lived far from London and did not participate much in the rituals of society. But the dowager duchess had plans for her son.

Lady Adele clasped her hands in her lap and looked forward, as if willing herself to get home faster. Likely Lark was making her uncomfortable.

"You do not travel with a maid?" he asked, likely pushing his luck.

"I did not see the need when I left home a few hours ago. My intention had been to look up the coat of arms at the bookshop to see if I could identify from which family His Grace came. Based on his manners and the few memories he's been able to retrieve, I gathered he was a lord, although I honestly had no idea he was a duke."

"They are precious few, the dukes. Although my father is

one, so I forget that sometimes."

"Who is your father?"

Lark smiled. "The Duke of Beaufort. Hugh and I are in fact cousins of a sort. We're both descended from ancestors who married into royal family at some time. Only his relative is a great aunt and mine married a Plantagenet. My future dukedom was a weird consolation prize from Charles II. As in, sorry your family was nearly brought to ruin by several generations of Tudor rule and then civil war, but here is a title."

Lady Adele laughed, but it was reluctant. "Do you and His Grace sit around discussing English history? You just said quite a lot. I barely recall the lessons my governess taught me, although I admit I was an inattentive pupil."

"I suppose we do. It's an interest for both of us." Lark tilted his head. "We could perhaps mine his memory for any of this knowledge. He may know it somewhere deep in his foggy brain."

"Perhaps you can try that. But no need to spell it out more for me. We are here."

Chapter Eight

S MITH HAD FINISHED *Emma* and found it quite charming. This afternoon, he had chosen a novel at random from the library and was now skimming it while lounging in the gold salon. After he'd said that reading might be a pleasant diversion, the countess had told him which shelf contained her most beloved books, and he'd promised to take the utmost care of them. He now sat alone, reading *Gulliver's Travels*, which was proving to be quite familiar. He'd read this book before, he knew, even though he could not recall the plot.

Adele entered the room, still in her coat. Wilton trailed behind her and helped her out of it as she spoke.

"I have some important information."

Smith made note of the page he was on and set the book aside. "Yes?"

"I believe I know your identity."

A flutter went through Smith. He sat up a little taller, waiting to hear.

"That is, I discovered today that a certain gentleman went missing a week ago, and the family's coat of arms does indeed include lions and boars. I brought a friend home with me. That is, he is not my friend but a friend of this missing man, and I believe will be able to confirm my identification. But I wanted to warn you before I brought him in."

"Will you not tell me my name?" He was desperate to hear it.

"Lord Waring, please come in," said Adele instead.

The man who entered had dark hair and eyes and impeccable dress. Smith thought him familiar. The man clasped a hand over his mouth. "Hugh."

Hugh. Yes. That was his name. And this man was… "Lark." Hugh stood. The name had just popped into his head. "I recognize you."

"Yes, my good man. Lady Adele tells me you have lost your memories."

"Yes, I am afraid I cannot recall my surname. Or yours. But I know you are Lark and we are friends."

"Yes. I am Larkin Woodville, Lord Waring, heir to the Duke of Beaufort. And you." Lark pointed at Hugh. "You are Hugh Baxter, the Duke of Swynford."

"Swynford," Hugh whispered. The *S* on the signet ring had stood for Swynford.

"How are you feeling?" Lark asked.

"Confused much of the time. Lady Adele and the staff here in the Sweeney house have been taking good care of me, and my head does not pound the way it did a few days ago, but it is enormously frustrating not to remember things. It's like everything in my mind is separated from me by thick curtain. If I could just pull the curtain aside, I could remember everything, but I haven't managed that yet." Hugh sighed and sat back in his chair. "Instead I get little flashes of memory, but nothing like a complete picture."

Adele gestured toward the other chairs in the room. Lark took one across from Hugh. Hugh studied him for a moment. "Do I call you Lark?"

"Yes, usually. Sometimes Waring if we are at our club and other gentlemen are about."

"We have known each other a long time."

"Since we were boys. Our mothers are dear friends."

Hugh had a flash of running through a garden with a dark-haired boy at his side. Something told him he could trust Lark.

"Where do I live?"

"On Upper Brook Street near Grosvenor Square. In one of the finest houses in Mayfair."

"Who is there now?"

"Your mother, for certain. The dozen servants you keep there."

"I cannot go home yet," Hugh said.

Lark glanced toward Lady Adele, whose face displayed a befuddled expression.

"I would not think of keeping you from your family," said Adele.

"It's not that. I just need more time to prepare myself to see my mother. Am I correct that she is quite overbearing?"

"She can be," said Lark. "She is also quite worried about you. I should like to put her mind at ease."

Hugh found himself in a bit of a conundrum. Something told him that once he left Adele's house, that would be it for them, and he was not ready for it to be good-bye yet. His lips tingled when he thought about kissing her. But he did not want his mother to worry, either.

"You may be right, though," said Lark. "I had tried to postpone letting it be known that you disappeared as long as I could, but as we had no clues as to what had happened to you, I spoke to a writer I know and we ran a story in the paper. My intention had been for you to pop out of the woodwork and announce your presence, or to coax someone who knew who you were out of hiding, but instead, of course the story has ripped through the *ton* like wildfire. Should it become known that you have returned, you'd be beset by callers at all times of day, and I imagine that would be unbearable to you at this point."

"Yes," said Hugh, thankful for the rescue. "Perhaps you could tell my mother that I am all right."

Lark nodded. "Lady Adele mentioned that seeing familiar things may help bring your memories back. I assume that is true of people. Perhaps I could bring some friends here tomorrow.

Fletcher and Owen have been out searching for you, too."

The names were familiar, but Hugh could not connect faces with them. "These are friends of mine?"

"Yes. We all went to Eton together. We often meet at our gentlemen's club to talk or play cards over whisky and cigars."

He had a flash of three men sitting around him in a dimly lit room. "I wish I could remember."

Lark frowned. "Who hit you on the head and why did they dump you here? No offense, Lady Adele, but this part of London has fallen out of fashion."

"Perhaps that is why he was left here," said Adele.

"Then why not dump him in St. Giles or another slum? It occurs to me that perhaps whoever hit him on the head intended for him to die."

"He was unconscious when I found him," said Adele. "It's possible whoever abducted him already thought him dead. If his body were left here, someone might find him and make sure he was dealt with correctly. If he were dumped in St. Giles, pickpockets would likely make off with his fine clothes or anything that might identify him. Then he might be given a pauper's burial and never seen again."

Lark appeared to turn that over, but Hugh could only feel dread that someone in London wanted him dead. What had he done to inspire such a fate?

"An interesting point, my lady," said Lark.

"I've had a few days to think this over."

"Was I a bad man?" Hugh asked.

Lark turned to him quickly. "No. Of course not. You are proud and stubborn at times, but I can't see you ever intentionally harming someone. I can't think of who would want you dead. But Lady Adele's theory makes sense. If you were left here, someone might find and identify you, in which case your family would know you are dead. If you'd been left in a less savory neighborhood, there'd be no telling you from any other poor man left for dead in St. Giles. Whoever threw you out of the carriage may have wanted your death recorded."

Horror crept up Hugh's throat. "Who would want to kill me?" He felt dizzy at the thought. "Lord, what a mess. How could this be happening?"

"I'm beginning to think you are right," said Lark. "You should stay here. We don't want to alert whoever tried to kill you that you are alive, at least not until we have a stronger grasp on this situation. Will you be all right here?"

"I believe so. I am safe and well cared for here."

"Good." Lark turned to Adele. "I am grateful that you found him, my lady. I must go chase down Fletcher and Owen. I will try to get them here tomorrow or the day after so that we can devise some kind of plan. And, Hugh, I will let the dowager duchess know you are all right."

"Thank you," said Hugh.

ADELE HAD LONG stopped thinking about the rules of propriety between men and women. Society had decided she was unmarriageable, after all, which rendered her essentially invisible. If she were to be discovered alone with a gentleman, there seemed to be few consequences. These rules had long puzzled her, anyway. Men and women were not to be alone together if they were not married to each other because one or the other, likely the man, would not be able to restrain himself, was that it? Two people of opposite genders in a room alone could touch each other, she supposed, although, before Hugh, no man since her late fiancé had made overtures.

She hadn't had many occasions to be alone with a man in her life, but on the few when she was, that man had not tried to compromise her. Good men were generally capable of behaving as gentlemen, or so her own experience told her. She knew bad men took liberties, and she read the scandal sheets as everyone else did when she needed a diversion, so she did not think herself naive when it came to men, but she did not think she should fear them. If she should find herself in a room with a man, why should she fuss about it?

And yet, as she found herself alone in the gold salon with Hugh Baxter after Lord Waring left, she found herself suddenly nervous.

Hugh rubbed his forehead. "I have a name," he said softly.

"Yes," said Adele. She felt guilty for mulling over being alone with him when he was still reeling from all the new information he'd just received.

And she had to admit that his name was intimidating her a bit.

"Why do you seem unhappy?" Hugh asked.

Adele looked up and met Hugh's gaze. "Do you want my honest answer?"

"Yes, of course."

Adele didn't see much point in pretense. "Well, now that you know your identity, you will return to your old life soon."

Hugh stood and moved over to sit beside Adele on the sofa. "This worries you."

"We will not see each other again once you leave."

"What makes you say that?"

It was sometimes interesting to converse with Hugh because he seemed to know some things by instinct but there were still many significant gaps in his memory, including, apparently, the rules for how society was stratified. And Adele knew she was destined to remain a spinster; she was too old and too poor, and she'd never marry, least of all Hugh. But she said, "You are a duke and you come from a family with an impeccable reputation. I am a spinster whose father is a politician."

"Your father is an earl."

"Yes, but he made a name for himself in Parliament. Not that there is anything wrong with that, but the scandal sheets say terrible, untrue things about him frequently, and he is not well liked or respected. I wonder sometimes if this is the reason no one offered for me when I reentered society after my fiancé died. But I think the end result is plain."

"I'm afraid I still don't follow."

Adele smiled. "You are naive, then. Our lives are what they are, Your Grace. I live here and take care of an older woman. You must go back to your life where you will undoubtedly meet and marry a beautiful young woman of impeccable reputation. Where will that leave you and me? We cannot be friends. Men and women are not friends in that way. You will soon forget about me, at any rate."

"I could never forget about you."

"That is kind of you to say, but—"

"If I am this all-powerful duke, as you say, why should it not be my choice who my friends are?"

"I have no explanation for why things are the way they are. I only know there are rules that must be followed. By rights, there should be some sort of chaperone in the room with us now to prevent us from behaving inappropriately with each other, only no one can be bothered because I am so undesirable as to be invisible."

Hugh reached over and cupped her cheek. Unable to help herself, she closed her eyes and leaned into his touch. "You are *not* invisible."

"No?"

"No. Since I cannot remember all the rules, I will only follow the ones that make logical sense to me. And I see you just fine."

He kissed her. Adele felt both elation and concern over this course of events, but she kissed him back anyway, letting him slip his tongue between her lips. Heat flushed her face and her heart began to pound.

"Am I not supposed to do that?" Hugh asked.

"Likely not."

He rubbed her arm. "You are shaking."

She touched his hand. "You quite literally fell into my life, and I have enjoyed your company immensely. I love when you kiss me. It thrills me in a way I cannot explain. But it is something you should not do if you do not mean it."

"I do mean it. You have been good to me and I care for you. I cannot imagine leaving here and never seeing you again. I do not want that to happen."

"But you cannot continue to kiss me if you do not intend to commit to doing it for a long time."

"You mean if I do not marry you."

"Yes." Adele felt her heart break because she knew how impossible this situation was. She did not want him to leave, but she had to prepare herself for that inevitability. He barely knew her, and although that was not exactly an impediment to marriage, he was the Duke of Swynford and she was so far beneath him in social rank that he could never offer for her. "I'll not be a mistress, and you cannot kiss me if you are married to someone else. I will miss you, however."

"Why can I not marry you?" Hugh seemed genuinely puzzled.

She reached for his hand and threaded her fingers with his. "Because of an accident of birth, really. Your family will never agree that I am a suitable candidate for a wife for you. Besides, you only just rediscovered who you are. You cannot make a decision like that so rashly. And you cannot marry me just because you like kissing me."

"So if I am understanding you correctly, you are upset because whatever there is between us must end when I go back to my old life. However, you have grown fond of me, just as I have grown fond of you."

"You make my conclusion sound silly, but your memory is not recovered enough to understand the intricacies of British society, I'm afraid."

"It all seems terribly unfair. If we want to kiss each other, we should be allowed. If I chose to marry you and I am in a position of power, how can it not be so?"

"I suppose that depends on how much you care for the opinions of your family."

"I cannot remember my family."

Adele sighed and looked away but did not let go of Hugh's hand. "Let us not make any decisions right now. I suppose some dukes do marry for love, but it is rare, and we are not in love. We are fond of each other, yes, but we have known each other a mere week. We should... I will go to bed. Tomorrow will be quite taxing, I expect."

She had to get out of here. All afternoon, she'd felt her heart cracking. It was silly to have gotten invested in this man, but the truth was that she liked him a great deal. Nothing could ever happen between them, a fact she often forgot when she sat this close to him.

As Adele stood, Hugh stood with her. She began to leave the room, but he grabbed her hand.

"Adele, please."

"Your Grace, do not... that is, I can't..."

"If your heart hurts half as much as mine does right now, please do not leave me this way. Please do not just give up. Perhaps I can find a way."

"I very much doubt that."

"Before you found out I was a duke, you were not so reluctant to kiss me. Does a title really change who I am so much?"

"In England? Yes."

Hugh frowned but did not let go of her hand. "Then if all is about to change, I will not be satisfied without one more kiss."

Adele wanted to resist but didn't have the will. Hugh put his arms around her and pulled her close until her body was flush with his. He pressed his hands against her lower back, grabbing a fistful of her gown, and she put her arms around his shoulders. He was remarkably tall, but then, she was a little tall for a woman, and she found their shapes seem to complement each other as their lips pressed together, almost as if they were made to fit together. She sighed into his mouth, committing this moment to memory: the taste of him, the pressure of his lips on hers, the way he smelled.

When at last she pulled away, she said, "I do wish things were different."

"Me too," he said softly, his grasp lingering on her hand. He brought it to his lips.

"I should sleep. And you should, too. Your friends will visit on the morrow. They may help you recover your memories so that you no longer have any need of me."

"I suspect a part of me shall always need you."

Adele tried not to let that ring in her head as she walked up the stairs.

Chapter Nine

LARK REALIZED WITH a start that he'd woken up in the bed of Anthony Pearson, the Marquess of Beresford and that enough sunlight was streaming through the window that it must be well into the morning.

He hadn't intended to spend the night. He'd run into Anthony at the club last night when he'd gone there to tell Owen and Fletcher the news about Hugh. He'd let Anthony talk him into bed again, but he'd only meant to have sex and then leave. Instead he'd fallen asleep.

Anthony's arm was draped over Lark's middle, which was endearing. Lark liked Anthony; he was a beautiful if arrogant man with hair that was unfashionably long and piercing green eyes. Anthony was a little too sure of himself; the way he propositioned Lark always made Lark want to put up some token resistance, just to show that Anthony would not always get his way. But he always succumbed. He never regretted their time in bed together, which seemed to be more frequent lately than the occasional dalliance.

But there was no future in it.

"Lark," Anthony said softly.

Lark turned to look at Anthony. "I did not mean to stay here all night."

Anthony yawned. "I am not angry."

"I have many things to attend to today."

"I'm sure you do."

"We cannot let things like this happen. If we were caught—"

"We won't be."

"And besides, one day we'll be married, and—"

"I've no intention of marrying."

Lark let out a frustrated grunt. "I'm afraid I do not have that liberty. Nor do I relish having to explain to my future wife that I will be sleeping at my male lover's house."

"Is that really any different from telling her about your female lover. And I know you've had a few of those, too."

"Consider a gently bred woman of the *ton*. A pretty little virgin debutante like my mother wants for me. She barely knows what men and women do in the bedroom, how will she begin to comprehend what men like you and I do?"

"Why would you tell her? Plenty of married men have lovers they do not tell their wives about."

"That doesn't seem dishonest to you?"

Anthony shrugged. "This is why I don't intend to marry."

"So you would just let the Beresford title die with you?"

"It'll pass to my cousin." Anthony yawned. "You have had female lovers, yes?"

"Yes." Lark liked sharing his bed with both men and women. He'd ended an affair a few months before he started spending time with Anthony; she was an older widow who knew her way around men's bodies and had no interest in marrying again. The trick in all of these affairs, though, was to keep his heart from getting ensnared. He'd ended things with his widow when the emotional attachment had made it too difficult to leave her side, and he suspected that was becoming the case here, too. "What does that matter?"

"I'd feel jealous, but you are here with me and not one of them, so I'm afraid I only feel gratitude that I'm the one you keep coming back to."

"You make it sound like this is some lengthy love affair."

"We had an affair at Eton, did we not?"

"I highly doubt a bit of groping when we were boys constitutes an affair. And as I recall, your attentions were not limited to just me."

"No, but your enthusiasm always made you my favorite."

"Enthusiasm?"

Anthony stroked the side of Lark's face. "Let us just say that some of the boys I groped, as you so delicately put it, merely wanted their cocks stroked. You actually wanted *me*. You still do."

Lark didn't say anything, even though it was true.

"I am glad that your enthusiasm has translated into some actual skill and technique over the years."

Lark lay on his back for a long moment and then looked around for a clock. A large, ornate one stood in the corner. Lark had to squint to read the time but saw that it was still quite early in the morning. He had time to go home, change clothes, drop by the Swynford home to speak with the duchess, and then collect Owen and Fletcher at the appointed time. He sighed.

"Mentally going through your calendar for the day?" asked Anthony.

"Yes. I have several personal errands to attend to today."

"Do any of them have anything to do with the Duke of Swynford?"

Lark knew that if he said nothing, Anthony would interpret his answer as the affirmative.

"Should I be jealous?" asked Anthony.

"Never, and Swynford is missing, which I assume you know because your devotion to the scandal sheets is greater than mine. I discovered something yesterday and I want to follow up on it, that is all."

"So you don't think he's dead?"

"No, I don't. But I do think foul play is involved. And I see your expression, so I will just say that I do not know how or who and that is all I will say about it."

"Very well. I just hope you do not show Swynford the same enthusiasm you show me."

And this was the real reason why Anthony would only ever be a diversion. He reveled too much in his own nonsense. "I have never, and Swynford is only interested in women. Besides which, you have no right to be jealous."

"Don't I?"

Lark rolled his eyes and got out of bed. "You aren't my wife. We have no legally binding relationship. I could bed half the men in London and it wouldn't make any difference."

"It would to me. *Are* you bedding half the men in London?"

"No. Only you, as it happens."

"Ah." Anthony nodded as if he now understood something he hadn't before. "I guess I have nothing to worry about then."

Lark wanted to inquire about that but concentrated on getting dressed instead. He was somewhat alarmed by the fact that his clothing was neatly folded and placed on a chair, which meant some silent servant had come in while they slept and picked up his clothes from where they'd been tossed on the floor.

"Servants talk," Lark said as he slid on his shirt.

"I pay mine not to. Do you need a hand?"

"I—" Lark snapped his mouth closed, not sure how to answer. His valet normally helped him dress, but it wasn't like he was incapable of pulling on his clothes.

Anthony got out of bed and helped Lark with his buttons. When Lark was dressed, Anthony ran his hands over his waistcoat to make sure everything was smooth. Lark found the gesture sweet, though he didn't want to.

"I know a fellow," said Anthony. "He fell in love with a solicitor, of all people. They went to America, where I suppose all things are possible, or at least where his title meant nothing, and as far as I know, they are living happily ever after on some estate in Virginia."

"I'll wager your friend is not heir to a dukedom."

"Well, no. His father is a viscount, but he's the third son."

"Mm-hmm." Lark shrugged into his jacket and eyed Anthony, trying to convey that he rested his case.

"Fine. Give me a few minutes to make myself presentable and I'll walk you out."

THE CONVERSATION WITH Anthony that morning was still sitting uneasily with Lark as he collected his friends to call on Hugh.

Something about Anthony's cavalier attitude, like nothing could touch him and he could live as he pleased, made Lark worry. One of these days, Anthony would walk into a trap and great harm would come to him, and there was little Lark could do to stop it. In the meantime, Lark could feel himself becoming increasingly ensnared by Anthony and he worried he wouldn't be able to extricate himself when the time came.

But he had to set all that aside for now.

As Owen climbed into the carriage, Lark asked, "What is new?"

"Parliament business."

Fletcher, who was already seated, rolled his eyes. "Who cares?"

Owen grunted. "Lark said our dear friend is staying with Canbury's daughter. I thought what is going on with Parliament might be relevant."

"I don't think it is." Lark shook his head. "But fine. What is it?"

"Well, Parliament was indeed called to session because Prinny has some sort of urban planning proposal that involves building several new roads that slice through the middle of London, mostly to make the distance between Carlton House and Prinny's mistresses more direct." Owen rolled his eyes. "Someone please tell me why I decided taking my father's house in Lords was a good idea."

"I tried to talk you out of it, as I recall," said Lark.

"Anyway, Canbury gave an impassioned speech on the importance of better roads in London, which is fair enough, but it was clear he was trying to ingratiate himself to ol' Georgie Boy."

"Does anyone actually call him Georgie Boy?" Lark asked Fletcher.

"Not to his face."

"As I was saying," said Owen, "Canbury is definitely angling to become Lord Chancellor or gain some other government position, and he's apparently willing to kiss Prinny's shoes to win over the honor. But then!"

Lark glanced at Fletcher, who shrugged. Lark had not the foggiest idea what this had to do with anything, and apparently Fletcher didn't either.

Owen went on, "Lord Saxon got up and gave a speech about the abolition of slavery in the West Indies, to which George Baxter took great offense." George Baxter was the Earl of Collingswood, Hugh's cousin.

That did hook Lark's attention. Collingswood and Hugh had some bad blood between them.

"Of course he did," said Fletcher dismissively. "All of his money is from sugar picked by slaves on his plantation in Jamaica."

"I heard a far more devastating rumor."

When Owen did not speak more, Lark leaned forward and said, "What?"

"There was a story buried deep in *Times* a few days ago about a series of slave rebellions in Jamaica. This resulted in a great deal of property damage and many slaves running away. Some think there is an organized independence movement, like in Haiti."

"I hope there is," said Fletcher. "Slavery is a vile institution."

Owen nodded. "I agree. The rumor is that the Collingswood plantation was hit especially hard. Some structures burned down and about half the enslaved people escaped. Collingswood is out thousands upon thousands of dollars, or so the rumor goes. He is agitating for stricter laws in British territories."

That nauseated Lark. "Collingswood is a swine. That is horrific." But he was swiftly sorting through what little he knew of Collingswood. The hit to his estate could put him in dangerous territory financially. Would he sniff around his wealthy cousin to get the money he needed for repairs.

"It is just a rumor," said Owen, clearly not drawing the same conclusion Lark was. "I do not know if it's true, but either way, he opposes the abolition of slavery."

"Slavery *should* be abolished," said Fletcher. "It is barbaric."

"You are not wrong. Abolition is gaining some traction in Parliament. Saxon made a moral argument about amassing fortunes on the backs of humans, which I found compelling. I think many other MPs did, too."

"You do not own a plantation in Jamaica," said Lark.

"That is true, but I do have an estate in Wales with tenants who farm my land. I've been working with my land steward on the sheep farm for ways we can maximize profits while still treating my tenants and employees fairly. It *is* possible to turn a profit without relying on slave labor. However, that would require an ounce of cleverness, ingenuity, and organization that George Baxter does not possess."

"True," said Lark.

"I imagine Hugh would have more to say on the topic," said Fletcher.

"Perhaps not at the moment," said Lark. He shook his head. He'd known Collingswood since childhood and had never liked him. He definitely didn't trust him not to harm Hugh if it came to that. He made a mental note to dig into that at a later date.

"What do you mean?" asked Fletcher.

Lark took a deep breath. "I will warn you, Hugh is not quite himself. He still seems rather confused."

"His memory is missing, you said," said Fletcher.

"Yes. Canbury's daughter has been taking care of him, and she seems to have done a good job so far. She is quite protective of him, in fact. And I believe they may have grown fond of each other in his convalescence. Difficult to tell, but I thought I saw something in their dynamic when I visited yesterday."

Fletcher pursed his lips. "Do you think that is something we should discourage?"

"Hard to say. I spent some time with her yesterday, and I was impressed by her intelligence. She is also quite pretty, although not in a showy way."

"Why had I heard Canbury's daughter was an ugly old spinster?" said Fletcher.

"She is a spinster, but she is not very old. I did not ask, but I'd wager she is five or six and twenty at most."

"Still," said Owen, "she is Canbury's daughter. He's a farce."

"I wonder at times if someone is spreading false tales about him to discourage his pursuit of the Lord Chancellor position," said Fletcher. "He has many political rivals."

"Beresford says the rumors are not true."

Both men turned to look at Lark.

"Why are you looking at me like that?" said Lark. "You were there when he said as much a few nights ago."

"Yes," said Owen. "I never believed the rumor about Canbury wearing women's clothing. But some of the rest has a ring of truth…"

"Well. I can't speak to that."

Fletcher regarded Lark with a raised eyebrow. "So when Beresford secrets you away at the club, are you discussing this gossip?"

"It comes up in conversation sometimes," was all Lark was willing to volunteer.

"Beresford would know about the Canbury rumors," said Owen with a certain amount of disdain.

"What do you mean by that?" asked Lark.

"Nothing. Forget I said anything. Oh, look, we're here."

They had indeed slowed in front of the Sweeney house. "Behave, my friends. Since I am fairly certain Lady Adele will not leave Hugh's side, we are about to be in the presence of a lady."

"I'll behave," said Fletcher. "I can't speak for Owen."

"Get out of the carriage," grumbled Owen.

Chapter Ten

THE TWO MEN who accompanied Lark into the gold salon were strangers, although something in Hugh recognized that he'd seen both men before.

Adele was on guard. She seemed nervous. Hugh couldn't deny that their conversation the night before had stayed with him. He supposed she'd offered him reasonable logic, but he did not want to lose her. Marriage did seem rash, but how else was he to keep her in his life?

A puzzle for another time. Lark now introduced Hugh and Adele to Fletcher Basildon, Baron Fowler, and Owen Thomas, Earl of Caernarfon. When Owen said, "'Tis good to see you, my friend," Hugh heard an accent and asked about it.

"I'm from Wales, mate," Owen said as if it were obvious. "But since my ancestors betrayed their fellow Welshman and sided with the English every time they tried to invade, some old king bestowed a title on us. You knew that, back before the, er, head injury."

"I had an interest in history, didn't I?" Hugh asked.

"You did," said Fletcher. "You descend from a very old and prestigious family, so your parents drilled that lineage into you. There's a pile of bricks in Kent they call Swynford House that has a great hallway lined with portraits of the past eleven dukes, and it looks like a lot of stern-faced men in funny wigs, but you always seemed proud of it."

Adele frowned at that, which prompted Hugh to ask the question, "Was I proud of my name?"

"Not as much as your mother," said Lark, "but yes."

"Your memory is really gone?" asked Owen.

"I've recovered bits of it, but most of it is inaccessible to me. The doctor says I will recover the rest in one sudden burst, or over time in dribbles, or perhaps not at all."

Fletcher laughed. "Yes, those would be the options. Doctors don't know anything, do they?"

And suddenly this all seemed familiar. The four of them often sat in this very configuration, facing each other and talking. Lark loved gossip, Owen followed politics, and Fletcher pretended to be disinterested in all of it. Hugh gasped as he realized he knew these men.

"Are you all right?" asked Lark.

Hugh shook his head. "Until yesterday afternoon, I had no idea of my own name, but now I can recall sitting with you gents in a club, sipping whisky."

"That *is* how we spend most of our time," said Owen.

"Lord Caernarfon," said Adele, correctly pronouncing the Welsh name—it sounded like Canarvon, "are you the same man my father has mentioned who serves in the House of Lords."

"I am," said Owen. "That is, only recently. My father held the seat until his untimely death last year."

"I am sorry for your loss."

"Thank you, my lady. If your father mentioned a Caernarfon, it was probably my father. He cared far more about parliamentary procedure than I do. But I feel some obligation to maintain the seat, so I show up when Parliament is in session. I was there yesterday, in fact."

Adele looked startled by that. "Parliament is in session?"

"It was yesterday."

"That must mean that my father is in town. He did not tell me."

Lark's eyebrows shot up. Hugh made a mental note to ask

about that later.

"He is indeed in town," said Owen. "I watched him give a speech yesterday with my own eyes."

"Curious," she said leaning back on the sofa. "Usually he writes me to let me know he'll be here."

"So you have not seen the paper, then," said Fletcher, which got him an elbow in the ribs from Lark.

"I've been so busy taking care of the countess and His Grace that I haven't really looked at the papers, although I suppose there would have been an announcement of Parliament being in session there."

"Er, yes, that's what I meant," said Fletcher.

Lark rolled his eyes, which Adele didn't appear to notice.

She stood quite suddenly. "If you'll excuse me, gentlemen, I will go ask Cook to provide us with some refreshments."

"You don't have to leave," said Hugh.

She sent him a soft smile. "I shall return in short order."

When she was gone, Hugh said, "You fellows are not subtle, although I do not understand what this was about."

Lark glanced at his friends, who signaled for him to speak. Lark sighed. "Are you fond of Lady Adele?"

"Yes. She has been a great help to me this last week."

"In other ways?"

Hugh bristled.

"So, yes," said Lark. "You should probably know, and would know if you had your wits about you still, that Lady Adele's father is the Earl of Canbury. Canbury is a wily politician who, frankly, most MPs do not like. He aspires to a higher position in government and has been campaigning to earn it, which has put him out of favor with just about everyone."

Hugh supposed this filled in some gaps and gave context to some of the things Adele had said the previous night. She knew that her father's reputation was less than pristine, and she knew Hugh's friends and family would look down on her for it. "Lady Adele is not her father," Hugh said. "She is a good woman who has been nothing but kind to me."

"I'm sure that's true," said Lark. "I am just trying to give you a complete picture."

Hugh sat with that for a moment. "If I were interested in a lady before, would I have cared much about her reputation?"

His friends exchanged glances, which Hugh did not find comforting. Lark said, "Well, you have seemed somewhat resistant to marriage."

"Haven't we all?" said Owen.

"Is there a reason?" asked Hugh.

"I imagine you have a reason you haven't told me," said Lark, "but what I do know is that you wanted to live life to the fullest before committing yourself to matrimony. And you are not quite ready to be a father."

Hugh nodded. "I have the sense that I have been with women before. Do I have a mistress?"

"Not at the moment as far as we know," said Fletcher. "There was that actress, though. What was her name?"

"Marlena," said Owen. "She's Spanish."

"Yes," said Fletcher. "But you ended that a year ago."

"There was the Countess of Lefcourt," said Lark.

Owen waved his hand. "That was only a night or two. Lady Lefcourt does not bed a man more than twice."

"Do you say this from experience?" asked Fletcher.

Owen shrugged, which Hugh interpreted to mean he had.

"I suppose what I'm asking," said Hugh, "is that *were* I to marry, imaginatively speaking, would I worry much over the future duchess's reputation."

"You might," said Lark. "Your mother would care more."

"Do I worry over my mother's opinions?"

"Yes," all three of Hugh's friends said in unison.

"It's curious that this should be the case when I can scarcely remember what she looks like."

"Your mother dominates British society these days," said Lark. "Her influence can destroy and rehabilitate reputations, and she exercises that power with skill and precision. But she is very particular about who she helps and who she puts out of favor, and her orders are generally followed, even by you, despite the fact you are twice her weight and a powerful man in your own right."

"She scares me," said Owen.

Lark laughed. "She can be intimidating, that is true. She tried to come with us this morning, but I wanted to be able to candidly answer your questions without her here. There are some things a mother does not need to know."

"I should like to see her soon," Hugh said.

In the distance he heard someone wrap on the front door and the creak of Wilton opening it. He wondered where Adele had gone off to. The men continued to speak, mostly about their families, and then all at once, Adele returned with Cook and several trays of refreshments and Wilton escorted in Dr. Willis.

"I am glad to see you, doctor," said Adele. "Thank you for coming. I hope you can help us come up with a plan for reintroducing His Grace to society."

"Yes, I got your letter. The Duke of Swynford. I never would have guessed."

Lark stood and introduced himself to the doctor. "I was concerned about taking him home because it is now publicly known that he is missing, and I worried the horde would descend once it became known he was back home. That would be overwhelming."

"It would, yes," said Dr. Willis. "But I also read about a case like Swynford's in which a woman was reintroduced to her bedroom and her memory returned quite swiftly. So I think it behooves us to get His Grace home."

"Perhaps we can sneak him into the house," said Adele.

"Or," said Fletcher, "we could let it be known that Hugh was ill and recovering at his country home and had merely been a careless aristocrat and failed to inform his family and friends."

"That's good," said Lark. "I like it."

Hugh glanced at Adele, who looked troubled. He understood why. Perhaps in his former life he would not have grown so attached to a woman, but he hated to leave this one now. He said, "That is a clever idea, but there is still one other issue. We still do not know who hit me on the head to begin with. He may still be lurking about in Mayfair."

Lark frowned. "Perhaps you can hire a body man."

Hugh groaned. "Just what I need is a guard to interfere with my privacy all day long."

"You can't hide here forever," said Fletcher.

"I think it advisable for you to return home," said Dr. Willis.

"We can help," said Lark.

Hugh turned to Adele and was about to ask her thoughts when she said, "If it will help you recover your memories, I think it is the best course of action." She turned to Lark. "He does not have much in the way of possessions. Really just the clothing he came here with. If he had anything else on his person when you last saw him, whoever abducted him has stolen it."

Lark nodded. "His signet ring, of course. Hugh sometimes carries a silver money clip his father gave him. I do not know if he had it on him the night of the Rutherford ball."

Hugh didn't either. He would have to check his home. He turned to Adele. "Please do allow me to repay the countess for the clothes she bought me as well."

"That is not necessary," said Adele.

Hugh turned to his friends. "Am I wealthy?"

"Yes, substantially," said Lark. "A lot of it is family money, but you have a good head for business and have made some profitable investments the last few years."

"Then I shall pay the countess for her hospitality."

Adele nodded slightly.

"Perhaps I should move home tomorrow," said Hugh.

"Your mother would appreciate that," said Lark. "I will let her know so she can ensure your rooms are ready."

"I live with my mother?"

"She stays at your London home when she is in town," said Lark. "She lives primarily at your estate in Surrey, but she likes to be in London for at least part of the Season. She has not been to many events in the last few weeks. I worried she was in ill health, but she looked to be in fine form when I called on her this morning."

"All right," said Hugh.

"Where is the Countess of Sweeney?" asked Dr. Willis.

"She said she felt too tired to socialize," said Adele. "We managed to get her out for a short walk around the garden yesterday, but that seems to have worn her out."

"I will check in on her before I take my leave," said Dr. Willis. "I am encouraged by His Grace's progress, however. Memory aside, how do you feel?"

"The headache is gone, but I still feel dizzy sometimes," said Hugh, which was true. His head hadn't bothered him much in the last day or two, but once or twice a day, he was struck quite suddenly with a wave of dizziness.

"That may last a bit longer," said the doctor. "Head injuries can be unpredictable."

"I'll say."

"All right," said Lark. "I'll bring the Swynford coach round tomorrow to collect you and we will move you back home."

Adele stood quite suddenly. "Excuse me a moment." Then she left the room.

Hugh hesitated to go after her because he didn't want his friends to know he was so smitten with her, but then he realized that was his old self thinking. One thought he hadn't been able to escape since he'd learned his identity was that this was a new opportunity to take his life in a different direction. His mother and various family reputations were things he'd have to deal with at a later date, but he wanted Adele at his side.

"I'll go check on her," said Hugh.

ACROSS THE HALL from the gold salon was a dusty music room no one used anymore. The countess had been quite talented at the piano once upon a time but had not played in years. Old bedsheets had been thrown over the grand piano at the center of the room, but there was no disguising what it was.

Adele stared at it now from her perch on a threadbare upholstered bench at the side of the room. She had excused herself because she felt tears burning her eyes, and she felt like a lovesick child now as she wiped at her eyes and tried to school her features.

When the door opened, she turned away, guessing it was Hugh and not willing to let him see her cry.

"What's wrong, Adele?" he asked.

"You are leaving tomorrow," she said.

"You said I should."

"Because I care about you and want you to recover your memories, not because I want you to leave."

Hugh came to her side and put an arm around her. "I want to go home, but I do not want to leave you. You could come with me."

"That is ridiculous. I must care for the countess. You must return to your life."

His proximity, his strength and his scent and his very presence, were her undoing and she lost control of her emotions and began to cry in earnest. Hugh took her more forcefully into his arms, and she pressed her face against his chest.

Hugh pressed his cheek against the top of her head. "I am not willing for this to be the end of us. This cannot be our story's finale. I do not yet know what the solution is, but I keep thinking about something Doctor Willis said."

"What did he say?" Adele pulled away slightly and looked at Hugh's face, which was a model of determination.

"That I should take things one day at a time. I don't seem to have much control over how my memories return, nor did I have a plan for returning to my old life until today, so I've been taking each day as it comes."

Adele leaned against Hugh, savoring the sensation of his strong arms around her. She said, "There is still so much. Your old life. Your family name. My responsibilities here. How can we be together under such circumstances?"

"I do not know yet."

She pulled away slightly and looked up at him. "You care for me?"

He smiled. "I do. I am anxious to see my mother and return to my own house, but I am reluctant to leave you. The circumstances of my stay here have not been ideal, but you have made it pleasant. I have no regrets about anything that has occurred for that reason, except that I must leave you tomorrow. But let us not make any decisions right now. We shall take each day when it arrives and figure out what we must to ensure our own happiness."

"You make things sound easy when you say that."

"I am a wealthy duke, am I not? I should be able to move mountains, or at least pay someone to move them on my behalf."

She laughed, although it was his status as a duke that felt like the biggest impediment, like a huge, immovable granite rock between them. He perhaps did not have the memories to understand how society worked, but she did.

"And who knows?" he added. "I could perhaps be the prince who sweeps poor Cinderella out of the drudgery of her life and into a grand new world where he spends the rest of his life seeing to her every whim."

She shook her head. She knew better than to wish for that. "You should return to your friends," she said, pulling away gently.

"I suppose I should. They are undoubtedly speculating about us now."

"Does that bother you?"

He shrugged. "Let them speculate. I have nothing to be ashamed of. Do I?"

"No. I do not believe so."

"Good. Are you coming?"

"I will be there in a moment. Just give me a moment to compose myself."

After Hugh left the room, Adele walked over to a dusty mirror and peered through the grime on the surface to see if she looked terrible. She looked tired but all right.

She did wonder what exactly they had just promised to each other. Marriage? No one had ever said that aloud. Adele thought the odds long; she doubted his family would permit him to even offer for her, and even if they fell in love, it wasn't like members of the *ton* married for such foolish notions. They had strategic marriages, meant to bring together dynasties or create alliances. Dukes tended to marry pretty, convenient young ladies with the right pedigree, not old spinsters from families that had fallen out of favor. And Adele would not allow herself to be a kept mistress. She had gotten to this point in her life by her own skills and resources, and she had modest funds after her time as a paid companion, so she could make her own way in the world.

Where did that leave them? Adele didn't want Hugh to leave at all, as she'd just demonstrated in a silly, overwrought way. The fact that he did not laugh at or mock her meant he understood the depth of her affection, but it didn't much matter.

Adele knew Hugh would leave the next day and that would be the end of their acquaintance. Oh, he'd put some effort into calling on her, very likely, but it would soon fizzle as his memory came back and he realized they had no future together.

She felt tears sting her eyes again as she thought about it, but blinked at her reflection and took a deep breath. She'd come to expect this from life. She wasn't sure what she had done to offend her maker in a previous life that He should continue to dangle happiness before her just to take it away, but she should expect no less. This was her fate. No amount of hope would change it.

She took a deep breath and walked back to the gold salon.

Chapter Eleven

IT WAS GOOD that the distance between Adele's room and Hugh's was a few steps across the hallway, because a longer walk might have caused Adele to lose her nerve. As it was, she hesitated before knocking on his door. And then her fist seemed to fall upon the wood.

He opened the door wearing only his breeches and stockings. Adele was momentarily dumbstruck by the wide expanse of his finely muscled chest, his athletic body, and the dusting of hair across his torso.

He smiled.

"May I… speak with you?" she asked.

"Of course. Do come in."

Adele stepped into the room and saw that one of the earl's old trunks was open to the side with Hugh's new clothes neatly folded in it.

"You are packing," said Adele. "I did not mean to disturb you."

"You aren't. I am happy for your company. What did you want to speak to me about?"

Adele took a deep breath. Here went nothing. If he refused what she was about to ask of him, it wouldn't matter, because she would never see him again past tomorrow. And if he said yes, well, she would cherish the memory of this night for always. "I have something of a proposition for you."

He raised an eyebrow. "Indeed?"

"I have given this some thought, so I do not wish you to think I arrived at this idea on a whim." And she had thought about this quite a bit, nearly constantly for the last two days, and thought her logic infallible.

Hugh looked mystified. He sat on the foot of the bed. "What is it?"

She was nervous. She could not predict what he would say, but she would hate herself if she did not ask. "I will bungle this," she said.

He reached for her hand and wrapped his much larger one around her fingers. "I will be patient."

"I don't want there to be any expectations between us. I do not know what the future holds. If it should come to pass that we are separated permanently tomorrow, I do not want to have any regrets."

He nodded, though he still looked confused.

"We are… that is, you find me attractive."

"Yes. Immensely."

"I came to you tonight because… well, I never had a chance to… that is, I was once engaged to be married, but that relationship was never consummated. And now that I face a prospective future life in which I may never know the touch of man, well, that future is unbearable to me. And I thought that, since you are here and we both find each other… attractive… that perhaps you would…"

She looked at his face but could not read it. Her mouth went dry and she could no longer speak. She'd put all of that in the room, and he only stared. Mortified, she dropped her head.

"Forget I spoke. I will just…" She started to leave the room.

Hugh still had a hold of her hand and pulled her back. "What is it you want, Adele?"

She loved how he said her name, like she was precious to him. "This is your last night with me, and I would like for us to spend it together."

He nodded. He tugged on her hand so that she was sitting beside him. Then he kissed her softly, and she thought she'd been spared mortification. Her heart beat faster and stronger in anticipation of what was about to happen.

Hugh ran his hands through her hair and let a few strands slowly trail through his fingers. "You never wear your hair loose like this."

"No, I… it would be bold of me to… that is—"

"I like it this way." He turned his head slightly and focused his gaze on her face. His eyelids lowered, and she realized he was looking at her lips. Then he bent his head and captured her mouth with his, kissing her a little more strongly this time. He plunged his fingers into her hair and cupped the base of her head with his hand. She opened her mouth to let him in and put her hands around his neck. Then he pulled back slightly. "Are you sure? Do you know what you're asking me?"

"Yes. I'm certain. That is, I've never… but I want to experience this. I can't go to my grave without ever…" Adele struggled to even find the words. Hot embarrassment burned her face.

Hugh nodded but was quiet for a long moment.

"You have…" Adele continued to blubber. "That is, you must have some experience… er, bedding women. I know you don't remember, but…"

He smiled. "I think there is an instinctual element to it. That is, I cannot precisely remember any prior encounters, but I feel that I must have had them. More to the point, Doctor Willis warned me that I might have certain… male problems, let's say, as a result of the head injury, but I am happy to report that I am not experiencing those problems."

Adele had only the foggiest notion of what he was talking about. She'd received a cursory talk about what happened between husbands and wives from her mother weeks before her scheduled wedding, but had no clear frame of reference.

She let out a breath. "I want one night with you. That is what I am asking."

"Then one night is what you shall have." He let out a sigh. "It is less than I would have hoped for, but realistically perhaps all we have. Is that is what you are telling me?"

"Yes."

He touched her hair again. "Then I shall endeavor to make this night far surpass your expectations."

He kissed her, which was a good start. Adele didn't really have many expectations, except the few things she understood about how things should be between men and women and her own body talking to her. As Hugh trailed his fingers down the sleeve of her dressing gown, she felt warmth bloom in her chest and her heart begin to pound.

Unable to resist, she put her hands on his chest. "Is this all right?"

"Yes. Please, touch me anywhere you like." He leaned close and nipped at her jaw. She closed her eyes and leaned into his touch. As he slid her dressing gown off her shoulders to reveal her nightgown, he said, "Please do anything to me that strikes your fancy. If I do not like it, I will tell you. And I expect the same for you. If I do anything that you do not like or that does not feel good, tell me and I will stop. Is that a deal?"

"Yes," she said breathlessly.

"Good. Because a night like this should be about pleasure. I want you to feel good. Understood?"

"I understand, yes."

"Perfect."

He stood and held out his hand for her. So she stood up next to him, and as she did, her dressing gown slid off her arms and onto the floor.

"Leave it," he said. "Raise your arms as if you and I are about to waltz."

She followed his instruction and spared a thought for some fantasy world in which Hugh and Adele waltzed in a crowded ballroom with all of the *ton* looking on. In her fantasy, the crowd tittered about what a beautiful couple they made, how happy they looked together, how plain Adele Paulson had blossomed in her marriage to the Duke of Swynford. She closed her eyes and touched his chest again, sliding the palms of her hands over the hard planes of it, and hooked her hands behind his neck.

"This is not proper waltz technique," said Hugh.

"Do you mind?"

He grinned. "Not at all."

He put his arms around her and swayed gently, as if they were dancing. Then he pressed a hand against the small of her back and pressed her against him. Only her delicate nightgown separated her bare skin from his, and she pressed against him, from her breasts to her knees. He kissed her as they swayed back and forth, which made Adele feel more certain of her decision. Whatever was about to happen would be magic. She wanted to remember every second.

Her nightgown was a flimsy thing. She'd chosen to wear it because it was barely there and she thought he might find it enticing. It was a little big on her, though; she'd likely lost a little weight in the time she'd been working for the countess. But that meant that Hugh could easily slide his fingers under the fabric near her neck. He undid the buttons that went down the front of the shift like he was unwrapping a gift.

She gasped at the realization that he was about to see her nude.

"Do not feel shame," Hugh said, gently removing her fingers from where they clutched her gown closed. She hadn't even noticed she'd done that. "Never feel shame. You are a beautiful woman. And most men love women's bodies."

She raised an eyebrow. "Most men?"

"Somehow I know that some men also like men's bodies. Which is not... that is, I do not know if I am supposed to know that or if it is socially acceptable, but... well, suffice it to say that *I* love women, and what I know of your body arouses me, and I would like to see more of it. Do not feel shame."

Adele was so touched she couldn't speak. She was nervous,

but she would push any shame away. Instead she dropped her arms and her breasts seemed to burst out from between the buttons. Something changed in Hugh's gaze, darkened it. He ran his hand over one breast and her nipple hardened under his palm. He bowed his head and kissed her as he slid the nightgown off her shoulders and it pooled at her feet.

Instead of shame, she felt arousal. She'd experienced desire before, but this was something else entirely. As Hugh scooped her up into his arms, she felt her skin tingle everywhere, but especially near her breasts and between her legs. She wanted more of whatever this was, wanted it to grow stronger, wanted to go somewhere with Hugh.

He gently lay her on the bed and gazed at her for a long moment before his hands went to the placket of buttons at his waist. He leaned down and a little awkwardly removed his stockings and tossed them aside, then began to unbutton his breeches.

Adele stopped breathing.

She'd never seen a naked man before, but what she could see of Hugh was already striking. He had wide shoulders and a torso that narrowed like an inverted triangle. The rounded muscles of his arms seemed to flex as he moved. She liked everything she saw, from the hair on his chest to the shape of his bare ankles and she wanted to touch him everywhere. But right now, all she could think about was what was under his breeches.

She resisted the urge to touch herself and instead focused on his hands as he undid those buttons. The act probably took a few seconds, but it felt like an eternity as her heart sped up watching him slide each button through its corresponding buttonhole.

And then he moved and pushed his breeches down his legs and stood before her in all his glory. He did not look entirely as expected, but she felt flush everywhere as she gazed on him.

He climbed onto the bed with her. She was almost glad that they were no longer displaying themselves for each other. She looped her arms around his neck and kissed him, and she felt him smile against her lips.

"Does this… make you happy."

"Immensely," he said. "You are still sure about this?"

"Even more than I was before. But I do not know what to do."

"Let me show you."

He slid his hands over her body, a leisurely exploration of her curves and planes. She was somewhat surprised when he planted kisses all over her chest and then took one of her nipples into his mouth. She'd never expected a grown man to do something like that, but it felt so good she didn't care. She pushed her fingers into his hair and was surprised by how soft it was. She was reminded that he'd given her permission to touch him wherever she wanted, so she did, feeling whatever skin she could reach. His body was a little slick with sweat, but she was surprised again by how soft his skin felt against his hard muscle.

"How did you achieve the body of an athlete?" she asked.

He lifted his head and smiled at her. "I'm afraid I do not remember. Through any number of gentlemanly pursuits, I expect. Riding. Boxing." He shrugged.

"I like it," she said. "You are so strong. I feel safe with you."

"I am very glad of that. You will always be safe with me."

Adele put her arms around him and hugged him close to her. She did trust him. She knew he'd never do anything to deliberately hurt her; that just wasn't in his nature. But she did not trust that her heart was safe with him. He would leave tomorrow and take her heart with him.

But that was why this moment was so important. She kissed him and was not shy about it. She touched him where she wanted to touch him. She took what she could while he was here, while he was hers.

He slid his fingers between her legs and groaned. "You are already wet."

"Is that bad?"

"No, my dear, it is very, very good. It shows that you want me. And it will… ease the way. Here, touch me."

He took her hand and brought it to his... member. She wrapped her hand around it and felt his warm skin there. "It is so hard," she said.

"That is how much I want you."

They kissed and she stroked him, tentatively at first and then with more pressure, and the tingle of her skin, the warmth in her chest, and the arousal between her legs that was so intense it bordered on pain all continued to grow.

"I cannot bear this much longer," she said.

"Me either. Let me show you what happens next."

She parted her thighs almost by instinct and he settled between them. They kissed and she pressed her chest against his, and then she felt the blunt head of his cock at the entrance to her body.

"Please tell me you are still certain," he said. "Because once I push forward I cannot take it back."

"If you do not push forward, I think I shall die."

He laughed softly. "Yes, I know a little about that. But if you should find yourself with child..."

"There are ways to prevent that, are they not?"

"There... yes. There are."

"I trust you."

He began to slide inside her. He groaned as he did it. There was a brief moment of searing pain and she cried out, but her body quickly adjusted.

"Are you all right?" he asked.

Her heart cracked a little whenever he asked her if she was certain or all right. She was and she wanted this, but it touched her that he was leaving so much up to her. She felt powerful, like she was in charge, and this was on her terms. She could never regret anything they did for that reason.

"I am very all right. It feels strange but good."

"Good. I will make it feel even better."

He began to move, sliding in and out of her body, slowly at first and then with increasing speed. It felt like everything in her body was rushing to the space where their bodies connected.

As he moved, she touched him. She moved her hips up to meet his. She loved the sounds he made in reaction to her. He practically yipped when she pinched one of his nipples, but didn't say to stop, so she reasoned he liked it. They kissed, and with every kiss, she felt herself growing closer to him, like they were coming together to create a kind of magic.

As they moved together, she felt something building in her. She wasn't completely sure what it was, but it was like she was moving inexorably toward some conclusion. She gasped as the pleasure spread through her body.

"Surrender to it," Hugh whispered. "Let go."

So she did, and it felt like her body exploded. The tingly sensation between her legs ran through her whole body and she stopped seeing or feeling anything but Hugh for a very long moment.

As her senses returned, she felt him jerk suddenly, and then he slid out of her. She felt something warm on her abdomen and looked to see him spending on her belly. She shivered, excited by the sight of that.

Hugh rolled onto his back, out of breath. But he reached for a handkerchief on the night table and gently cleaned her up.

Adele's heart still pounded as he settled in bed beside her and pulled her into his arms.

"Did you… that is…" she started to ask.

"It was marvelous," said Hugh. "You are marvelous."

"I feel marvelous."

He chuckled softly. "I hope I have not disappointed you."

"You have not. I will remember this for a long time. Thank you, Hugh."

"Thank *you*."

She yawned, feeling sleep pulling at her. "I should return to my room."

"Please stay a little longer. If you fall asleep, I'll be sure to wake you before the servants do their rounds."

She put a hand on his chest, feeling proud and brave for what she'd done. She'd been right; this was something she needed to experience. She often worried life was passing her by and she was missing essential experiences, but now she at least had this. How she would live the rest of her days without experiencing it again, she did not know, but she supposed she'd have to manage.

Now, though, his warmth and his scent and the safety of his arms were lulling her to sleep, so she closed her eyes and succumbed to it.

HUGH FELT THE moment when Adele surrendered to sleep.

He'd felt it when she'd surrendered to *him*, too.

Lark had said Hugh hadn't been eager to marry in his previous life, but perhaps that was because he'd never met anyone he wanted to marry. It was true that he had not known Adele very long, but he could feel that she had depths worth exploring should they spend more time together. And if nights with her were like this… he could still feel her tentative hands exploring his body, could feel the moment when her curiosity got the better of her and she touched him with confidence.

Something in him wanted to hold her, care for her. She'd said she felt safe with him, and pride warmed his chest. He wanted her to feel safe; he wanted to keep her safe.

Perhaps these were the thoughts of a besotted fool, but he didn't care. He *was* besotted. Why shouldn't he offer for Adele?

On the other hand, he still had not regained his memories. He had snatches, but no clear picture of who he'd been before someone had struck him on the head. Maybe he owed it to himself, to Adele, to recover his memories before he made any decisions that would impact the rest of his life.

If he could recover his memories.

She had long tresses of shining blond hair that were now

splayed across his chest and pillows. He touched the ends now, careful not to do anything to wake her. He loved her hair, had loved running his hands through it as they'd kissed. He loved her body, love its softness, loved the pink undertones of her skin. He'd loved the earnest expression on her face as he'd asked him to be with her tonight, and he'd loved the ecstasy on that same face as she'd come apart in his arms.

He'd been with women before. Clearly he had. But nothing rattling around in his mind now told him he'd ever been with a woman like *this*. The fact that she'd come to him almost seemed remarkable.

And he'd wanted to say no. He knew it was wrong to bed a lady who might someday marry another man. It was wrong of him to have ruined her as he had. But he hadn't been able to resist her, not when she'd had that earnest, pleading look on her face, not when he'd seen traces of her beautiful body below that flimsy shift and dressing gown. It had taken every bit of strength he had to pull away from her body at the critical moment, because he'd wanted to bury himself in her and lose himself there. She seemed certain they would not see each other after tomorrow. So he could not risk them conceiving a child. Nor did he want this to be the last time they lay together, because this night had been a taste but he wanted a full meal.

But did he want to marry her?

His instinct said yes, but also that he should not make a decision just yet.

He must have drifted off to sleep, because the next thing he knew, he was in bed alone. He acutely missed the feel of Adele's body against his, but as he roused, he saw that she'd left a note on the pillow beside him.

It said: *Thank you. I shall never forget this. —A*

Hugh folded the note, got out of bed, and tucked the note into an inside pocket of the formal coat he'd been wearing when he arrived at this house. That seemed the safest place for it.

He looked out the window. The sun was high enough in the

sky that Hugh guessed the time to be about seven in the morning. He was excited to be going home and looking forward to seeing his mother. He was hopeful being back in his home would help him recover his memories. But he could not overcome the sinking feeling that he would not be seeing Adele again, and that *this*—this moment, this week, this woman—was perhaps the memory he needed to cling to most fervently.

Chapter Twelve

HUGH ENTERED THE house and was at first struck by the familiarity of the front hallway. It was painted a deep olive green, with paintings in gold frames on the walls. Most of the paintings seemed to be still lifes of flowers or fruit, although Hugh paused before a portrait of a man that he recognized but could not name.

Stand up straighter, my boy. You must never let them forget who you are or where you come from.

His father. The portrait was of his father. And his father was no longer alive, which was how Hugh had come to be the duke.

Hodges cleared his throat. He clearly knew Hugh was coming, because he was calm as he allowed Hugh back in, but Ventnor, Hugh's valet, gasped as he hurried down the stairs.

Hugh knew his valet's name was Ventnor.

"Your Grace, what are you wearing?" Ventnor asked, smoothing the front of Hugh's jacket.

"You are not elated to see me then?" said Hugh.

"Of course I am. It is most agreeable to see you in what appears to be good health. But these clothes are not befitting a duke of your wealth and stature."

"I am certain you will rectify that at my nearest convenience. But first, I should like to see my mother."

"Of course, sir. She is in the red room."

Hugh looked down the hall. In between the paintings were a

series of doors. Hugh could not remember which led to the red salon.

"I will escort you," said Hodges. "Mr. Ventnor, perhaps you can see to His Grace's luggage."

"The formal suit I wore to the Rutherford ball is at the top of the trunk. It has already been laundered, so please just hang it in my closet."

"Of course, sir," said Ventnor. He turned on his heel and walked away.

Hugh followed Hodges to one of the doors, which he opened for Hugh. Hugh walked inside and saw an older woman in an elaborate day dress seated on a settee with needlework in her lap. She stood as soon as he walked in.

"Oh, gracious. Hugh!" She immediately crossed the room and pulled him into a hug.

This was his mother.

You look so handsome, Hugh. Soon you will be full grown and getting ready for a wedding of your own. I will undoubtedly cry. I can only pray that you visit me often while you are married. I do adore you, my son.

"Mama," he whispered.

"I have worried about you so. Are you all right?"

"I am still missing a lot of memories, but I can already feel things coming back to me now that I am here. But I feel all right, except for the occasional dizzy spell. The doctor I consulted with says it is normal for head injuries and will go away in short order."

"While I am not happy to hear you are still missing memories, I am elated to have you back in good health. I was so worried."

Hugh closed his eyes for a long moment and then looked around the room.

This was the room the Duchess of Swynford used for family. He knew suddenly that there was a more formal room closer to the front of the house that was used for social calls.

He could see himself running around the room with Lark or one of his cousins. The scar on his knee, which he'd noticed while bathing a few days prior, had been caused by his running into a low table at the center of the room. He could see his father reading while lounging on the settee off to the side. He could see his mother working on her needlepoint or writing a letter to a friend. This house was not very old, Hugh suddenly knew; it had been purchased by his father when Hugh had been a boy.

"You recognize me and this room," said the duchess.

"I do, suddenly. I feel more things coming back to me. Images, memories. Did there used to be a blue chair right here?" He gestured at a space on the rug.

"You and Lark broke it when you were about ten by climbing on it. That was twenty-five years ago."

"There does not seem to be much rhyme or reason to when things return." Hugh sighed and sat on a chair. "Things may return in dribs and drabs. Or I will never recover my memories. There is no way to know."

Lark entered the room then. Hugh looked up and saw his friend as the adult he was now and not only as the child he was starting to remember. Lark had accompanied him home but had busied himself making sure the carriage and horses were taken care of before coming inside.

Hugh understood that Lark was handsome, but in a different way than Hugh. Where Hugh was athletic, Lark was almost dainty. Tall but thin, with long eyelashes and long fingers. He had an elegance about him, even now as he took off his gloves and walked into the room. They'd grown up together but had diverged at some point, too. Hugh wished he knew why.

"I am glad you found your mother," Lark said.

Another memory hit Hugh then. He stared at Lark. "We had a conversation in this room about two weeks ago."

"We did, yes."

Hugh closed his eyes.

Mother says I must marry soon, although I do not understand her rush.

She wants grandchildren. And she is not getting younger.

The same must be true of your mother, and yet she is not exercising that same pressure on you.

I am not a duke.

But you will be if heaven forbid something should happen to your father. Do you intend to marry?

When I must.

I cannot fathom committing myself to some chit just to satisfy my mother.

"What did you discuss?" asked the duchess.

"Hugh's allergy to wedlock," said Lark.

"I think," Hugh said, "that it is not an aversion to wedlock per se but a reluctance to marry one of the empty-headed debutantes I had met this season."

Lark grinned. "Ah, there you are. That is exactly the sort of thing your old self would say."

Hugh nodded. He had not seen Adele that day. She'd sent word through Wilton that the countess needed her attention, but Hugh knew she was avoiding him. He had felt quite disappointed by that; he'd hoped to see her one last time before he left.

Had he bought into her thinking that last night really had been the last time? He had meant it when he'd say they'd take each day as it came because the thought of never seeing her again was unbearable.

"Are you all right?" his mother asked. "You looked quite pained just then."

"I apologize. I feel all right, but this situation is very confusing. There are some things I know and some things I once knew that still seem to be hidden from me. Putting it all together to create an understanding of who I am and what my life is... it is a unique challenge."

"I can only imagine," said his mother. "Perhaps a meal would help. I can call on Mrs. Fairchild to fix up a meal."

"I am a bit hungry," Hugh conceded.

After they ate, Lark offered to escort Hugh on a walk to

Grosvenor Square for some fresh air. He explained as they left the house that they would undoubtedly run into people who knew about Hugh's disappearance, but Lark had spent the better part of the last thirty-six hours leaking that Hugh had merely been under the weather and adjourned to the country to recover. "So expect to hear many men greeting you by saying they are happy to see you in good health."

"I supposed it is not even largely untrue. But what about how I came to be a convalescent to begin with? Are we any closer to finding out who hit me in the head?"

"No, but I am hoping your presence at home again will lure him out. I have not told your mother this, but Owen and I hired a fellow he knows to guard your house. He is a former royal guard and is very good at hiding in plain sight."

"A royal guard? Aren't those the fellows with the red uniforms?"

Lark grinned. "You remember that?"

"Apparently."

"Owen assures me this man will be discreet. He should be arriving at any moment. Oh, here he is."

A man on horseback stopped in front of Hugh and slid off his horse. Lark snapped his fingers and a groom appeared.

"Michael, would you please see to Mr. Sedgwick's horse?"

The groom nodded and led the horse away. Mr. Sedgwick, a man about Hugh's age with thick brown hair and drab, nondescript clothing, shook hands with Lark.

"Your Grace, may I present you with John Sedgwick, the man I was just telling you about. Mr. Sedgwick, this is Hugh Baxter, the Duke of Swynford."

Hugh shook Sedgwick's hand.

"Sedgwick, you may go inside and let Hodges know who you are. I've asked the duchess to order a room prepared for you if you need it."

"That is not necessary," said Sedgwick. "Does this gate lead to the garden?" He pointed at a wrought iron gate next to the house that Hugh had not noticed before.

"Yes," said Lark.

"I shall be fine."

Hugh found this behavior puzzling, but then he did not know how a guard did his job.

"His Grace and I are going for a quick walk in the square. We shall return shortly."

"Not a problem."

Hugh shook his head and focused forward as Lark led him toward the square. There was a fence around a massive garden full of colorful flowers. Men and women walked slowly through the square in groups of two or three.

Something about the fence was familiar. It was…

It was the last thing Hugh had seen before being hit on the head.

"Oh, god."

"What?" asked Lark.

"The Rutherford ball. I was walking home from the ball, and it was right here." Hugh took a few steps forward and stood where Upper Brook Street met the edge of the square. "I was thinking about how Mayfair couldn't really be very dangerous at night since the only people on the street were likely to be drunk aristocrats when a red rose caught my eye through the fence. As I looked at it, I thought I heard someone call my name, but I wasn't certain so I didn't look. Then someone I did not see hit me in the head."

Lark leaned forward. "Can you recall anything else?"

Hugh closed his eyes. "I can picture it clearly, but I did not see the man coming. I just recall pain at the back of my head and then waking up at the Sweeney House."

"I supposed your recalling the man's identity would have been too easy. But you heard someone call your name. Did you recognize the voice?"

"I'm afraid I didn't. I was certain I'd imagined it, but I wonder in retrospect if I did not."

A woman appeared then. "Your Grace! It is wonderful to see you in good health!"

This woman was… no, Hugh could not recall her. Suppressing a sigh of frustration, he said, "I thank you. I am nearly recovered."

"Glad to hear it."

"I would linger to speak with you, but I'm afraid I am still occasionally prone to dizzy spells. Lord Waring and I are merely out here walking to get some fresh air, but I must return to my home very soon."

"Of course, Your Grace. I hope I shall see you at the Wakefield ball next week?"

"I have not yet attended to my social calendar, but should I be available, I shall be there."

"I look forward to it. Good afternoon, Your Grace."

When she was gone, Hugh asked, "Who was that woman?"

"I am not entirely certain. One of the Sackville daughters, perhaps? I see your manners have not deserted you, however."

"She is a prospective wife, I suppose."

"You have a few of them."

As Hugh realized that several similar women were headed his way, he said, "I believe we shall take our leave before this gets out of hand."

"An excellent suggestion."

ADELE HADN'T LIED when she'd conveyed to Wilton that he should tell Hugh that she was attending to the countess.

The Countess of Sweeney had woken up feverish. She seemed disinterested in eating, but Adele fed her some broth and a little bit of bread. That seemed to help the countess regain some of her energy.

Still, Adele could have stolen five minutes to say good-bye to

Hugh. She just couldn't bring herself to face him. And it wasn't that she felt any shame or regret—she didn't—but the very idea of saying good-bye to him broke her heart.

The house was small enough that she heard the Earl of Waring arrive. She heard Hugh ask after her. And since all of Hugh's possessions fit inside an old trunk, she heard them leave in short order. Then Wilton came upstairs to convey that about five minutes after they left.

"I am sorry, my lady," said Wilton.

"For what?"

"You seem sad. I know you had grown quite fond of our guest."

"Yes, well. We knew it would be short-lived. And I am happy that he may soon recover his memories."

When the countess fell asleep a short while later, Adele planned to return to her room so that she could contemplate resuming her normal life as it had been before Hugh had arrived. The prospect saddened her. She hadn't realized how gray and dull things had become, how much of her daily life was drudgery, until Hugh had fallen at her feet and turned everything upside down. She didn't relish in righting everything.

However, as she left the countess's rooms, Wilton appeared and said, "The Earl of Canbury would like to see you in the gold salon."

Adele was tired, but she went to the gold salon and found her father sitting there.

"Hello, Papa. I heard Parliament was in town."

"It is, yes. Very important business." He stood and looked her over. "Oh, my girl, you seem tired. Are you well?"

"I did not sleep well last night and the countess has needed a lot of my attention today, so I am a bit tired, but I am all right."

He crossed the room and folded her into a tight hug. Then he stood back and grasped her shoulders. "Good. I wanted to let you know I am renting rooms at an inn on Haymarket Street and thought to give you the address so that you might call on me there should you have time."

She stepped away and motioned for her father to sit. "Yes, I would like that. Why did you not write me to say you would be in town?"

"Time got away from me, I'm afraid. I gave a very important speech in front of Lords a few days ago. The Prince Regent is working with a small coalition of us to develop a new urban plan for London so that the streets are more direct and not the winding cow paths we all know now."

"That sounds promising."

"I have spoken with the Prince Regent extensively while I've been in town."

"What an honor!"

"Indeed. That is part of why I have not come to see you until now. I've been quite busy with this project. I believe if we accomplish the Prince Regent's vision, I could be handsomely rewarded with either a leadership or diplomatic position."

Adele knew of her father's ambitions, and service to the Crown was what he'd always most aspired to, but lately, titles seemed to matter more. That was, he wanted to be Lord Chancellor or Prime Minister or Chancellor of the Exchequer. Likely he was working with the Prince Regent with the hope of earning an honorary title as well. To what end, she did not know; if he were elevated to become a marquess or duke, he had no clear heir. Well, Adele had a distant cousin who would be the likely recipient of any titles Adele's father acquired.

As far as Adele could tell, the only real purpose of a hereditary title was to pass it on to a son. Well, her father had a few ceremonial duties and a piece of entailed property outside London where he lived when Parliament was not in session. But it seemed to Adele that all these titles were meant to create artificial ranks within society. After all, how were she and Hugh different? Hugh had a higher rank than Adele's father—Adele had no rank at all because she was a woman—but until Adele had known Hugh's identity, he could have been any man. But now, just because he was a duke, they would probably never see each other again.

And for what purpose could her father be trying to accumulate all these honors except as a means to gaining power and money.

She pushed it aside. Her father had called on her and she should give him her attention, even if sometimes she found his ambition gauche.

"I will likely be in town for a few more weeks while we develop this planning project," said the earl. "But you know how I do not care much for London. I hope to return to Canbury as swiftly as possible. But while I am here, perhaps we can have dinner."

"Yes, I would like that."

"And perhaps you would like to accompany me to a little fete next week."

"I would be happy to as long as I am not needed here. The countess's health has been failing for some time."

"Yes, the butler mentioned as much when I arrived. I do hope it is not too serious."

Adele nodded. "She seems to have already greatly improved today. What is this fete?"

"Do you know the Marquess and Marchioness of Wakefield? They are the hosts."

"I know them by reputation but I do not believe we've met."

"Wakefield is an old school chum of mine. He heard I was in town and sent me an invitation to the ball he and his wife throw annually. It might be quite the crush. Wear your best evening gown."

Adele nodded. She hadn't been to a ball in a number of years, but she still knew how to dance and did own one gown that would be appropriate. She and the countess were sharing a ladies' maid at the moment, but perhaps Adele could borrow Mary the evening of the party to help her do her hair.

"I hate to make this visit so short, but I have urgent business," said the earl. "I wanted to see you as soon as I was able."

"Thank you, Papa."

"You are all right here? The countess is taking good care of you?"

"I am taking good care of the countess, but the staff here is wonderful and I want for nothing."

"Very good." He kissed her cheek. "If you need anything, please ask and I will do what I can."

"I will."

As she walked him out a few minutes later, it occurred to Adele that she'd lied. What she wanted was Hugh, but of course, no fatherly intervention would bring him here.

Chapter Thirteen

ESTATE MANAGEMENT WAS a struggle when Hugh could only remember about half of what his secretary insisted was a great deal of knowledge and experience. Killingworth, Hugh's secretary, had given up on having Hugh solve complex mathematics equations. "Your solicitor, Mr. Hogarth, has also requested a meeting to discuss some parcel of land in Kent," said Killingworth.

"Very well. Set up the appointment."

Killingworth now turned his attention toward sorting through the vast number of social invitations he'd received in the last week.

"I don't know if I am up for a ball," said Hugh.

The dowager walked into his office then as if summoned. "A ball?"

"Mother, I can't possibly—"

"Listen to me, my darling. You do not have to accept every invitation that has been sent, and in your prior life, you would have only gone to perhaps one out of five of these events, so your behavior will be viewed as typical and no one will feel slighted."

"How can people not feel slighted if I don't attend many events? Why waste paper on me if I don't plan to attend?"

"Because you are the Duke of Swynford."

Hugh sighed.

"Did I ever tell you, I have an ancestor who married the Duke of Lancaster? This was back when the Lancasters and Yorks were trying to steal the throne from each other."

"I imagine you have told me this, but I do not remember the particulars." He had, at his mother's insistence, been reading a heavy tome on the history of England, and he'd just gotten to the Wars of the Roses, so at least he had a frame of reference. And if his ancestor had married the Duke of Lancaster, that ancestor had lived some 350 years ago. He wondered how this could possibly have relevance now, but he supposed she would tell him.

Which she did. Helena Baxter swept into the room with all the regal stature of a duchess descended from kings. "She was a common ancestor between your father and I. Imagine my consternation as I pored over one of those huge tomes at Swynford House that included the Baxter family tree. And there it was, the name of the woman who was both a many times great-aunt to me and a direct ancestor of your father's. And it is precisely because we can trace our lineage back to these great dukes and duchesses of the past, and indeed to royalty since your Aunt Katherine married Prince William a few generations ago, that we are considered important. It is that lineage that makes everyone want you to attend their parties. The very history of Britain moves through your veins. Not to mention, you are handsome and wealthy and any woman you meet would be a fool to refuse your attentions."

"Thank you for spelling that out, Mother."

"You see, it does not matter if you turn them down because they live in hope that one day you will accept. But that is only because you do attend some parties, so everyone remains hopeful. Therefore, I shall choose which parties are best for you to attend. Hand me those invitations."

Hugh was not certain why he was dreading all this. Partly, he was tired; Killingworth had been bombarding him with information all day and it was exhausting to try to process all of it.

Killingworth passed the dowager a thick stack of invitations. She sorted through them and tossed a great number on the floor.

Hugh tried to see the names on them as they fell. He did not know most of them.

"Ah, here. The Marquess and Marchioness of Wakefield are having a coming out party for one of their daughters. The Marchioness and I have long been great friends. I shall even accompany you to that one. I should like to see Amelia again." She placed the invitation on the settee beside her. "Oh, and dinner with the Sackvilles. Baron Sackville is a marvelous art collector and his dinner parties are always a hoot, so that should be quite pleasant." She tossed a few more invitations on the floor. "And the Duke of Ardmore is having a party to celebrate the arrival of some friends from Paris by the looks of it. You must attend that. Do you remember Ardmore?"

"I don't."

"The duke himself is a fusspot, but his family is delightful." Helena tossed the remaining invitations over her shoulder. "There, that's sorted. These are the only events worth being seen at. And I promise, you do not have to stay long if you get dizzy. But we must keep up appearances if we are to make everyone believe you merely had a spot of illness and were not seriously ill or residing with the Countess of Sweeney."

The way his mother wrapped the name "Sweeney" in disgust surprised Hugh. "What is wrong with the Countess of Sweeney?"

"Well, she's nearly broke, for one thing. And her son is very good at losing at cards. So good, in fact, that he hardly shows his face in London anymore because he owes quite a bit of money to some unsavory characters."

"Does the countess know that?"

"I do not know how it would be possible that she doesn't."

Hugh considered. "It never came up in conversation while I was there. I did not meet the earl. I was told he was at his country home with his family."

"Is it true the countess has some old spinster as a paid companion?"

"No. That is, she has a paid companion who is an unmarried

daughter of an earl, but the countess's companion is not old. She is six and twenty."

"And homely, I take it, if she's still on the shelf."

Hugh did not want to have this conversation with his mother, but he said, "Lady Adele is a respectable woman who took good care of me while I was out of sorts."

"As well she should have, given who you are."

"She did not know who I was when I arrived on her doorstep, since *I* did not know who I was. I could have been any stranger, a man with no wealth or title. And she took me in and cared for me anyway. Do you not think that shows some strength of character?"

"I suppose it does."

Killingworth gathered up the discarded invitations and dumped them in a wastebasket. "Well, Your Graces, if there is nothing else, I will respond in the affirmative to the chosen invitations. Shall I indicate that you will both be attending all three events."

"Yes, I think that best," said the dowager. "Now that I have Hugh back, I find myself reluctant to let him out of my sight."

Hugh rolled his eyes. He loved his mother, but he found he did not like her controlling his life. "Please excuse me for the next few minutes, at least," he told her.

"Dinner in an hour."

"Yes, of course. I was just going to go dress for it."

Helena patted Hugh's shoulder and took her leave. So Hugh walked to his bedroom. He shrugged out of the jacket he'd been wearing. Ventnor appeared as if from nowhere and took the jacket from him.

"This linen will wrinkle," said Ventnor, walking to the closet. "Really, Your Grace, you cannot just discard your clothing on the floor."

Hugh felt tired suddenly. "I dressed myself during my convalescence."

"Yes, and it was abundantly clear when you walked back in

here. What would you like to wear for dinner, Your Grace."

"Remind me why I cannot wear my day clothes to dinner?"

"It is not done. Also, Lord Rutherford is coming to dinner at Her Grace's request, so there will be company. I think the black formal jacket will do nicely. Perhaps the blue waistcoat."

"Whatever you think, Ventnor."

A few minutes later, Hugh was dressed properly enough to please Ventnor. He recognized his jacket as being the one he'd worn the night he'd landed on Adele's doorstep, which of course made him think of Adele. Ventnor ran a brush over it to remove any lint.

"I suppose the family you stayed with did an admirable job of cleaning this coat," said Ventnor. "I have always liked it. I would have been sad if it had been permanently damaged."

"I imagine it must have picked up some dirt from the street."

"Perhaps. But here we are, good as new." As Ventnor smoothed the front of the coat, his hand caught on something. "I believe there is something in the pocket, Your Grace."

Hugh reached into the pocket inside his jacket and found a folded piece of paper. It was the note Adele had left him on his last morning at the Sweeney house. He read it and reread it. Then he refolded the note and left it on top of a chest of drawers.

He knew he must see her again.

So resolved, he said, "Nothing to worry about, Ventnor. Do I look presentable enough for dinner?"

Ventnor smirked. "You'll do."

LARK LOOKED BOTH ways as he snuck out of the empty cloak-room. Bless the warm weather outside; no one wanted to check their coats at the door.

He checked his hair in a mirror before he returned to his friends, still ensconced in their usual spot near a fireplace. Lark was elated to see Hugh laughing with Owen and Fletcher as he approached.

When Lark was just a short distance from his chair, Anthony caught up with him. Anthony's long hair had fallen out of the ribbon he'd used to tie it back. Lark's fingers itched to run through it, but he instead shoved his hands behind his back.

"I meant to ask, will you be attending the Wakefield ball?"

"Looks that way. Swynford is making his grand reentry into society after his brief illness and has asked me for moral support."

Anthony tilted his head. "Is Swynford's health still poor?"

"No, he's perfectly fine. But you know how he loathes balls."

Anthony nodded. "That is because the mamas of the *ton* throw their daughters at him like dockworkers throwing cargo from a ship. Cultivating a reputation for being the sort of man who may or may not indulge in certain unspeakable acts allows me to avoid most of that."

Lark shook his head. "You are going to get yourself hanged one of these days."

"If I am, it will have been worth it." Anthony grinned, then said, "Do you suppose that when you have the cover of a respectable wife, you will still find the time to bugger me in cloakrooms?"

Lark pressed his lips together, bothered by the many layers of implication in the question. "Doubtful."

Anthony winked at Lark and then looked over his shoulder toward Lark's friends. "You don't suppose party-averse Hugh would—"

"No." Lark shook his head. "He's got his eye on an entirely inappropriate woman, though."

Anthony clapped his hands in delight. "I love it. Who?"

"The Earl of Canbury's daughter."

Anthony's eyes widened. "There's no way the dowager duchess would ever let Swynford near anyone even associated with Canbury."

"I know."

"The rumors about Canbury wearing women's clothing in public are falsehoods, but I've heard he has a male lover. I actually suspect a spurned lover is responsible for the clothing rumors. And who knows, perhaps Canbury likes to wear a silky chemise in the bedroom."

"I'd rather not contemplate that," said Lark, unwillingly allowing a mental picture of the beady-eyed Canbury in a woman's undergarments.

Anthony chuckled. "All right. I will stop hoarding your time. I need to go out of town for a few days to attend to a tenant issue at my estate in Surrey, but I will be home in time for the Wakefield ball. I shall see you there, yes?"

"I imagine you will."

As Lark sat down with his friends—from what he could tell, Fletcher was telling a story about a trip to his tailor on Savile Row, one Lark had already heard—he smiled at everyone. When Fletcher wrapped his story and Hugh laughed as he was supposed to, Hugh turned to Lark and asked, "Who was that?"

"Anthony Pearson, the Marquess of Beresford," said Fletcher, sounding irritated. "He's been paying you a lot of attention lately, Lark."

"He snared me on the way back from the retirement room to ask my advice about something," said Lark, which had been true enough. Although the question Anthony had asked was, "Do you think anyone would walk into the cloakroom if we spent a few minutes there?" And Lark's response had been, "Let's find out."

"Is he a friend of yours?" asked Hugh, looking puzzled. "My gut tells me I do not like him. He's quite… foppish."

Lark laughed. "He's a lot to take, that is true. I suppose he has his charms."

"Lark can be foppish," said Owen. "And yet we keep him around."

"That is not precisely what I meant," said Hugh.

"Even understanding that, my answer does not change," said Owen.

Lark rolled his eyes and picked up his snifter of whisky. He took a healthy sip and let the liquor burn his throat pleasantly on the way down.

Under different circumstances, Lark would have gleefully related the rumor that Canbury had a male lover because it was just the sort of gossip his friends seemed to eat with a spoon. But given that Owen seemed to already be implying that he knew Lark and Anthony were lovers, and given that Hugh seemed sweet on Canbury's daughter, it seemed ill-advised to mention it.

"Beresford told you something, didn't he?" asked Fletcher. "Some bit of rumor you are reluctant to share for some reason."

"If you must know, I asked Beresford about Canbury."

That definitely caught Hugh's attention.

"I know you are fond of Lady Adele," Lark said, "but you should know, her father is something of a laughingstock. Beresford thinks someone with ulterior motives is the one spreading rumors and nothing said about Canbury in the scandal sheets is true, but people believe the rumors anyway, so the damage is done."

"It is true he aspires to a position in the king's government," said Owen.

"Oh. Yes," said Lark. "That is true. The ridiculous rumors about dressing as a woman are pure imagination, however."

Hugh guffawed. "People are saying that?"

"Everyone in the *ton* is an unrepentant gossip," said Fletcher.

"Remember that MP caught up in a similar rumor maybe ten years ago?" asked Lark. "What was his name?"

"Miller, I think," said Owen. "Ah, Lord Broward."

"That rumor was also false, as I recall," said Fletcher.

"No, it wasn't," said Lark. "He showed up for that year's Rutherford ball in a gown. I saw it with my own eyes. He was a hideous woman."

"Oh," said Fletcher. "But the Canbury rumors are false?"

"This is only conjecture, but the rumor has two possible sources," said Lark. "A spurned lover looking for revenge or one of his political rivals who wishes to discredit him so that he does not get a position in His Majesty's government."

Hugh had stayed thoughtfully quiet through this conversation. He glanced at Lark as he reached for his whisky. "It is these rumors that make Lady Adele unmarriable, aren't they?"

"In your mother's eyes, certainly," said Lark.

"Lady Adele believes it is because she spent her best years betrothed to a man who died and that she is too old now."

"Stranger things have happened," said Fletcher. "Wakefield's wife was nearly thirty when they married."

"Well," said Owen, "she spent a few years in Paris doing God only knows what before returning to England to marry Wakefield. You can't say that wedding did not raise some eyebrows."

"But Wakefield is too important to snub," said Hugh. "As I would be if I married Lady Adele."

"Hugh, don't get foolish ideas in your head," said Owen. "She's a pretty girl, I agree, and your mother is most eager for a grandchild, but being associated with Canbury will certainly ruin your reputation."

"To what end?" asked Hugh.

Hugh's post-amnesia naïveté was only charming to a point. The old Hugh would have understood what his friends were trying to tell him.

"Well," said Fletcher, "it could limit the number of people willing to do business with you."

"It would certainly limit the number of social invitations you receive," said Owen.

"That might be a blessing," said Hugh. "She is a good woman. Morally upright. Very clever. Her only flaw seems to be that society does not like her father."

"Your mother would *never* approve," said Lark.

Hugh sat back. He'd been back home long enough to learn what a force of nature the Dowager Duchess of Swynford was, even if he could not remember on his own. No one in her orbit did anything without her permission.

"Best to forget all about her, mate," said Owen.

Hugh did not look convinced.

Chapter Fourteen

M ARY, THE SWEENEY residence's lady's maid, slid the last pin into place and admired her handiwork.

"You look lovely, Lady Adele," said Mary.

Adele stood and walked to the mirror on the other side of the room. She did look... better than usual. Mary had taken a hot iron to Adele's hair to help it curl in the fashionable way and had pinned it up in artfully, with a few loose tendrils framing Adele's face. Adele's formal gown was perhaps a year or two out of fashion, but it was one of the few things she'd saved from her wedding trousseau. It was a gorgeous gown of pale-yellow silk with lace trim around the sleeves and neckline. Adele had always loved this dress. And, indeed, as she looked at herself in the mirror, she thought she looked the most beautiful she ever had.

Wilton came to the door. "Your father is here, my lady. He is waiting for you at the base of the stairs."

"Let us not keep him waiting much longer," said Adele. "How do I look?"

"Splendid, my lady."

Adele smiled to herself, feeling giddy. It had been a long time since she'd gone to a ball. She often told herself she did not miss these sorts of events, but in all honesty, she had quite enjoyed prettying herself up to mingle with her social betters with the hopes a handsome man would ask her to dance. She doubted anything like that would happen this evening, but perhaps her father would ask her to dance and he'd inspire one of the men there to take his place.

She descended the staircase. Her father was waiting there with a smile on his face. His clothes were a bit over the top; he'd dressed as a dandy but was perhaps too old to pull it off. He wore formal breeches with crisp white stockings, though the breeches had buttons at the hem covered in red-and-white striped fabric. His jacket was bright red and he wore a ruffled shirt with a high collar that masked the sides of his face. The proportions were exaggerated, although the jacket seemed well-fitted.

"Papa, is this the latest fashion?" She flicked a finger at one of the ruffles near his neck.

"The Prince Regent was dressed just like this the last time I saw him at a formal event, although his jacket was, naturally, in the military style. He had gold buttons and epaulets." The earl gestured at his shoulders. "You look quite pretty, my dear."

"Thank you."

He offered his arm. "Shall we be off?"

"Yes." She smiled and took his arm.

The Wakefield ball was clearly the event of the week. The Canbury carriage was caught up in the traffic building around the Wakefield residence. It took them nearly a half hour to reach the red carpet that had been laid out to welcome the guests to the ball. Adele tried to school her face so that she looked like she felt like she belonged, when really she was in awe. The women entering the Wakefield home were dressed impeccably, with beautiful gowns and perfectly coifed hair and sparkling jewelry. Adele felt plain by contrast, but she was enchanted by how beautiful everything was.

They arrived at a grand entryway and followed the crowd to the ballroom. They entered a balcony before a short staircase where each arrival was announced.

"The Viscount and Viscountess Hayes! Lord and Lady Morrow! Baron Fielding and his son Lord Berkley! The Earl of Canbury and his daughter Lady Adele!"

Adele's father offered his arm again, so she took it and let him escort her down the stairs. She had been so long out of society that she hardly recognized anyone. She turned to begin a conversation with her father, hoping he'd keep her company, but he was already engaged in what looked like an intense conversation with another man.

"I shall find some refreshments for us," she said.

He nodded and returned to his conversation.

With a sigh, Adele crossed the ballroom and found a servant ladling cups of lemonade. She waited behind a line of party guests and examined the other fare offered at the table. She'd had dinner before leaving for the party and was grateful now, for there was not much in the way of food aside from some tiny cakes.

"Lady Adele?"

Adele turned and found Larkin Woodville standing beside her. She gave him a shallow curtsy and said, "Lord Waring, it is refreshing to see you."

"Agreed. You are waiting for lemonade?"

"Yes. It is quite warm in here and I thought to bring some to my father." She turned to look for her father and saw that the group of men around him had grown. "I suspect he's forgotten all about me."

"Government business undoubtedly."

It was finally Adele's turn. She motioned to Lark to ask if he wanted anything. When he shook his head, she took one cup of lemonade. She stepped away from the table and took a sip. The lemonade was warmer and sweeter than she would have liked. She looked up and saw that Lark still stood beside her.

She smiled at him. "You don't have to keep me company, although I would be much obliged if you spoke with me for a few minutes. I haven't been to a crush like this in years and I do not know many people. I assumed my father would introduce me, but he's clearly engaged in other business."

It occurred to Adele then that Lark's presence at this ball meant Hugh might be there somewhere as well. She'd known that was a possibility but had been trying not to think about it. She was about to ask where he was when she heard the announcement from the balcony.

"The Duke of Swynford and the Dowager Duchess of Swynford."

Adele turned and saw Hugh standing with an older woman—his mother presumably—on his arm. He escorted her down the stairs, but as soon as his foot hit the main floor of the ballroom, a crowd descended on him.

"That all seems to be in order," said Lark. "His last social event was the Rutherford ball the night he turned up on your doorstep. It may be some time before he can escape."

"I didn't come here to see him. My father invited me."

Lark nodded. "I assumed as much. I think he will be glad to see you, though."

"Do you think so?"

"Your name has come up in conversation a few times."

Adele shook her head, feeling embarrassed. "I'm afraid I did not leave things well. That is, I did not say good-bye to him the day he left. I merely left him a brief note."

"Did you not want to say good-bye?"

"No. That is, of course, that I wanted to see him off, but I was feeling sad about his departure. I did not want him to leave. So I took a coward's way out." She pressed a hand over her mouth. "I should not have said that much."

"It's all right. I seem to be everyone's secret keeper of late. I will not breathe a word."

"I appreciate that." She glanced about. "You mentioned the night he ended up in my company as the last time he attended a ball. Have you come any closer to determining how he ended up with his head injury? Does he remember?"

"No. I've paid a guard to keep an eye on him because I fear danger might still be about. It bothers me that we still do not know what happened."

"Indeed, I've been worried about his safety. It is some consolation that he is guarded."

The string quartet set up near the dance floor struck up the opening notes of a country dance. Adele tried not to look too wistful.

"May I have this dance, my lady," asked Lark.

"Yes," she said and let herself be escorted to the floor.

She did not think Lark was interested in her in a romantic or matrimonial way. He seemed to have his own interests. She at least recalled the simple steps of the dance while facing Lark and wondering at his motives here. He could have been dancing with her as cover for something, or to be nice to her, or just for the pleasure of dancing.

It wasn't that she didn't trust Lark exactly. He had only ever been honest with her. It was more that she knew he had his own agenda. He followed the steps of the dance with practiced ease, but his attention was clearly elsewhere. He looked Adele over, as if he were evaluating her dancing abilities, but then his gaze would shift elsewhere in the room. Sometimes he looked at the other dancers, sometimes he looked across the room. Adele couldn't begin to guess what he was thinking.

Not that her attention was fully on the dance. She tried not to think about Hugh, but it was like she could feel his presence in the room, even when her back was to him.

When the country dance ended, she curtsied to Lark again and he shot her a smile she did not know how to interpret. When the quartet began to play a waltz, Adele decided she'd go get one of the little cakes from the refreshment table, mostly just for something to do. A woman snared Lark's arm and pulled him to the side for a conversation, leaving Adele quite alone again.

But when she turned to head that way, she found her way blocked by a broad chest. She gasped when she looked up and saw Hugh gazing back at her.

"I claim this waltz," Hugh said, his voice not leaving room for argument.

Adele was so baffled by this that she couldn't do much more

than stammer, "Surely every woman in the room has you on their dance cards."

"No." He held out his hand for her.

Dazed, Adele took it.

IT WASN'T SO much that Hugh was jealous because he'd recognized what Lark was trying to do. And it wasn't like there was much intimacy in something as perfunctory and chaste as an English country dance. And yet something about seeing Adele take steps with Lark had pulled Hugh across the room.

And now he had her. She felt good in his arms, like she fit there, like she belonged there. Being in her presence soothed something in Hugh. He was reminded quite suddenly that the last time she'd been in his arms, they'd been making love.

She looked spectacular tonight. The yellow of her gown made her skin look bright and warm. Her hair had been curled and pinned upon her head in a way that made Hugh's fingers itch to pull out the pins and run his fingers through it. The only other adornment was a delicate silver locket at her neck. She was dressed far more plainly than most of the other women in the room, and yet Hugh thought her the most beautiful.

Something in Hugh wanted to drape her with fine jewels and fabrics. The gown she wore now had a sheen to it, and he guessed it was probably the finest one she owned. But she should have diamonds and emeralds and sapphires and fine gowns and hats and hairpins as befitting a duchess.

She should be *his* duchess, he realized. He didn't mind how plain she was; she had a fine beauty that anyone in the room could see, diamonds or not. He wanted to give her the world, because she deserved it. She had such a good heart. She spent her life taking care of others, and now he wanted to take care of her.

"I've missed you," said Hugh, leaning close to her.

She sighed and he felt her chest move against his. "Are you certain this is smart?"

"Yes. If I could, I'd dance every waltz with you, just as the prince did with Cinderella. Do you not want to dance with me?"

"Of course I do. I just worry that people will think—"

"It doesn't signify."

"Surely enough of your memory has returned by now to know that's not true."

Hugh was reluctant to admit he understood, primarily because he thought that, if he wanted to be with this woman, he should be able to be with her. If he wanted her as his wife, why shouldn't he choose her?

A lot of his memory had returned, but not all of it. In the week since he'd been home, things came back to him in dribbles. He knew enough to recognize most people and handle his business affairs, but there were some things that were still behind the curtain. He often found himself in the position of needing to answer a question and picturing the answer clearly without being able to attach a name or a word to it. He found that experience frustrating and worried those things would remain hidden from him until given the opportunity to ambush, but on the other hand, he felt like he had a new lease on life. His mother kept commenting that things he would have objected to before his head injury were things he was willing to let go now, like she'd detected a change in his personality. He couldn't say whether her assessment was accurate, but he cared less as each day went by. He wasn't certain that his priorities before the head injury had been correct.

The dance ended. Hugh bowed and kissed Adele's hand.

They weren't two steps from the dance floor when a group of overdone women approached him. He recognized one of them as Eugenia Sackville, who clutched his arm. Adele turned and walked away. Hugh's heart sank.

He looked around the room. He could not avoid his social obligations, but he felt an urgent need to tell Adele how he felt.

Instead, he saw Fletcher out of the corner of his eye.

"Ladies, will you excuse me for just one moment?"

He snagged Fletcher's arm as he walked by. "Can you please do me a favor?" Hugh asked.

"Find an escape route?" Fletcher said as he eyed the crowd of ladies.

"Will you please see to Lady Adele? I will never get across the room without being accosted by others, but I wanted her to know that I do not mean for our one waltz to be the end of our acquaintance."

Fletcher nodded, and the smile on his face told Hugh he understood. They shook hands and Fletcher walked toward the refreshment table.

As Hugh reengaged with the group of women, his mother appeared at his elbow and said, "Lady Eugenia, it is a delight to see you."

Hugh had recognized Eugenia as the woman who had stopped him in the park on the day he'd returned home, but had not been able to recall how well they knew each other prior to that. He'd gotten pretty good at faking it when people he spoke with clearly remembered more than he did, and currently only his friends, mother, and Adele knew his memory had been so severely injured. But the familiarity with which his mother greeted Eugenia set off alarm bells.

"Hugh, dance the next waltz with Eugenia," said Helena.

Eugenia was a pretty enough girl, he supposed. Eighteen if she was a day. Her curly reddish-blond hair was piled high on her head and festooned with flowers and her gown was a deep red, well-made, and expensive. She wore rubies at her throat and hanging from her ears. Lord Sackville had earned a ceremonial title after he'd set his textile mill to the task of making uniforms for His Majesty's army, and said textile mill had earned him enough money to drape the women in his family in jewels and fine linens. Hugh interpreted Lady Eugenia's dress as a clear signal that Lord Sackville was offering a substantial dowery to the man who took his daughter off his hands.

As they spoke, Eugenia wrinkled her nose, and Hugh remembered quite suddenly that he did not like her; he found her rude and judgmental. Indeed, now she said to her friends, "Did you see Winifred Parker dance with Lord Hinton? Her dance steps are as horselike as her face." The other women giggled in response. Hugh glanced at his mother, as if he could mentally ask her if she really thought Eugenia was a suitable romantic prospect, but her face looked serene.

Thus he was somewhat chagrined when the waltz started and he had to escort Eugenia to the floor.

"Who was that plain girl you danced with before?"

"Lady Adele Paulson."

"Paulson? She is… Canbury's daughter."

"Yes."

"Papa loathes Lord Canbury. I overheard him say, quite inappropriately I might add, that Canbury spends so much time kissing Prinny's feet that he does not have time to do anything of worth in Parliament. Of course, as a lady, I do not need bother with the goings on at Lords, but I get the impression Papa is not alone in his feelings."

"She does not live with him," Hugh said. "She is a companion to the Countess of Sweeney."

"Hardly more than a servant, I hear. Quite ignominious of her, isn't it."

He was reminded of Adele's lament that she had so few options. She had come to his bed because she genuinely thought she'd never know the touch of a man otherwise. Adele deserved so much more than scraps.

"I disagree," said Hugh.

"You are softhearted then, Your Grace."

"Perhaps." But he didn't view that as a character flaw, the way her tone implied.

After the waltz with Eugenia, his mother took up the strings as if he were a marionette, and had him dance with a series of young ladies, until he worried his feet would fall off. Each lady seemed more empty-headed than the last, striking up conversations with him about fashion or music or something similarly shallow. By the time he finished a country dance with the younger sister of the Duke of Ardmore, he recognized that he wasn't being fair; each of these ladies was probably perfectly nice and reasonably intelligent and would make some man of the *ton* a delightful wife, but he didn't want any of them because he only wanted Adele.

Eugenia Sackville circled back around to him just as he was looking for Adele again. If he could not escape this room—and indeed, he hadn't managed to venture father than a few feet in front of the dance floor—he would at least seek Adele out again. But Eugenia hooked her hand around his elbow and said, "Father wanted me to mention that he is interested in acquiring a parcel of land in Shropshire, and since you are the foremost authority on how to best negotiate land sales, he would like to speak with you on the matter. Just to gain your insight."

There was no way Hugh could have carried on such a conversation without the aid of Killingworth, but he nodded. He understood as well that Sackville was invariably throwing his daughter at Hugh with the aim of gaining access to perhaps even more land, or creating some kind of alliance. The realization disgusted Hugh, even while he knew that this was how the *ton* worked. Marriages were not for love, but rather for land and property, financial gain, or the continuing of a line.

"Tell your father he may schedule an appointment with my secretary if he would like to discuss."

"I am sure he will be happy to hear that, Your Grace," said Eugenia.

Hugh watched Fletcher lead Adele to the dance floor for the next country dance. They smiled at each other, and Hugh knew that Fletcher was merely doing what Hugh had asked of him, and yet Hugh struggled to tamp down the hot acid of jealousy rising in his throat.

"Forget about Lady Adele," said Eugenia, clearly following Hugh's gaze.

But Hugh knew he could not.

LARK WANTED A drink.

He snared a glass of champagne as it went by on a tray, but as he tasted it, he remembered that the Wakefields watered down their wine. He sighed and downed it anyway.

Adele and Fletcher were engaged in conversation about some novel they had both read recently. Fletcher seemed to be succumbing to her charms. Not in a way that would anger Hugh, of course, but more Fletcher was beginning to see what Hugh saw in her. Lark found her quite charming as well. She was intelligent and kind and had no ulterior motive, which was refreshing.

"Who is the woman Hugh is dancing with?" Lady Adele asked Fletcher.

"Lady Eugenia Sackville."

"She's pretty," said Adele.

"She's a monster," said Lark. "The old Hugh detested her. One of the worst gossips in the *ton*."

"That is saying something coming from Lark," said Fletcher. "I would not feel jealous, my lady. I am certain Hugh is dancing with her to appease his mother."

"What makes you think I am jealous?"

"The expression on your face," said Lark. He sighed. "I believe you are much on his mind."

"True," said Fletcher. "He sent me to make sure you knew he wanted to see you again."

"But to what end?" she asked. "Will he cease being a duke?"

Lark appreciated her understanding of the reality of the situation. Hugh was too besotted and used to getting his way to understand that this would not end as he expected it to. But Adele knew her place in the world. Lark did not see much wisdom in letting them pine after each other, although he supposed it was too late now.

Adele frowned. "He sent you to protect me, didn't he?"

Fletcher shrugged.

"I suppose that is significant," she said. "It does not change our circumstances, though."

Lark spotted Anthony walk across the room. "Will you excuse me for a moment?"

Fletcher engaged Adele in conversation while Lark went after Anthony. He found Anthony amiably greeting Lord Wakefield. When Wakefield moved on to greet another guest, Lark approached.

"You sought me out this time," Anthony said.

"I wanted to greet you."

"Until three weeks ago, you acted annoyed that I was even in your presence, and yet now you come to say hello like we are good friends."

"Are we not good friends? Are you irritated with me?"

Anthony smiled. "No, not at all. Just making an observation." He motioned for Lark to follow him and they left the ballroom and entered a hallway. A few other men were about, which led Lark to conclude that Wakefield had set up a room for cigars and cards down this way. Indeed, the Marquess of Blandford passed Lark and entered the room down the hall. He was greeted by a masculine cheer and then the door was closed again.

Lark sighed. "I would very much like to leave this place, but I think I may need to keep an eye on the object of Hugh's affection."

"Canbury's daughter?"

"Indeed."

"I saw them dance together earlier." Anthony raised an eyebrow. "You know, you never told me exactly what happened while Hugh convalesced."

Lark cursed. He hadn't intended to divulge Hugh's secrets to Anthony—whom he trusted, but whose tongue wagged more than Eugenia Sackville's—but he'd let his guard down.

"Don't beat yourself up too much. I inferred based on your inquiries about Canbury and Hugh's absence that he actually spent a week with her instead of in the country."

"It's not how it sounds. It is, in fact, entirely chaste. I will tell you, but you must not tell a soul."

"I would never."

Lark didn't believe him, but he said, "Hugh sustained a head injury that caused him to lose consciousness. Lady Adele discovered him much out of his senses and brought him into her home."

"And now he's infatuated with her."

"Precisely."

Anthony nodded. "I've heard of this kind of thing happening before. A school mate of mine took a shot to the leg at Waterloo. He has since married the battlefield nurse who brought him back to health."

"So you think it might just be an infatuation based on the fact that she took care of him when he was ill?"

"It's possible. It may be more than an infatuation. I imagine he's developed a *tendre* for her. Just as I'm sure you have a softness for certain past lovers. The first woman you ever bedded. The first man."

Lark frowned at that. He did remember both vividly. He'd never imagined himself in love with either, as he now suspected Hugh considered himself with Adele. "Surely he must know that a softness for the woman who cared for him while he was ill is not the basis for a sustainable marriage."

Anthony rolled his eyes. "I know *you* would never do anything so sentimental as to fall in love. But some men do not have your iron disposition."

Lark knew he was being teased but refused to respond. "The dowager duchess would never allow it."

"I know."

"I don't think Lady Adele would allow it either, frankly. She is too practical."

Anthony rocked on his heels. "Remind me again of her position?"

"She is the Countess of Sweeney's paid companion. I believe she feels loyalty to her mistress and will not leave her even if Hugh does something so daft as to propose."

"I heard it from Lord Melvin who heard it from John Sweeney that the countess is at death's door. Hasn't gotten out of bed in three weeks."

Lark crossed his arms. "Earlier tonight I called Eugenia Sackville the biggest gossip of the *ton*, but you have her beat. How did you come to be speaking to Lord Melvin about the Earl of Sweeney?"

Anthony laughed. "Are *you* jealous?"

"Hardly. It was just a question."

"If you must know, I ran into Melvin at the club a few days ago. We were catching up on the comings and goings of our various mutual acquaintances. He mentioned Sweeney is on his way back to town in anticipation of his mother's demise."

"Charming."

"Sweeney is rarely in town these days, so it must be serious."

"I don't really know Sweeney."

"He's broke, for one thing. Likes to bet on cards and rarely wins. Not to mention, I've heard his estate is not terribly profitable these days. His wheat crop failed on account of this cool we're having."

Lark's own main line of income came from the tenants who lived on the country estate he'd purchased with family money a few years before, and he stood to inherit the rest of his family's holdings when he inherited the dukedom now possessed by his father. This was how most of the British gentry made money these days; England's greatest asset was land, after all. Hugh himself owned five estates, two of them entailed. And when land ran out in Britain, some aristocrats had turned to British colonies. And thus Hugh's cousin owned a plantation in Jamaica, and he was hardly the only British lord to own land in the Caribbean.

"Enough of this nonsense," said Anthony. "Will you come home with me tonight?"

"My mother is here. I must escort her home."

Anthony looked around. "'Tis a pity this hallway is not more private. Perhaps there is a cupboard or somewhere we can hide."

"I should get back."

Anthony leaned against the wall and looked wistful. "Imagine if I were allowed to freely show you affection without the risk of being hanged."

"Even if one of us were a woman, it would still be inappropriate."

"I saw you waltz with Lady Matilda when I arrived." Anthony looked down. "I would have given anything to be in your arms instead of her."

"She's my cousin, you know."

Anthony shook his head. "That wasn't my point. I do not anticipate you taking up with Lady Matilda. I knew she was your cousin. But I should like to waltz with you sometime."

Something in his tone wrapped around Lark's heart and squeezed. "Anthony…"

Anthony's gaze went to Lark's lips and Lark worried for a moment that Anthony would kiss him just as a number of other men walked down the hallway. But instead, Anthony said softly, "I'll be at the Berkley Square house tonight."

Lark sighed. "I'll be there once I see to my mother."

Anthony nodded.

The Duke of Rutland walked by then. He was Lark's first cousin, the son of his father's sister and only three years older than Lark. They'd been close as boys, though did not see much of each other these days. Now he paused to greet Lark and Anthony. Then he said, "Who invited Canbury?"

Lark braced himself for whatever was coming. Anthony

chuckled and said, "I imagine Wakefield felt obligated. I believe they are school chums."

"He is pretty deep in his cups," Rutland reported. "Hamilton is trying to at least steer him out of the company of women."

"What is he doing?"

"Well, it started with him mostly bragging about his relationship with Prinny, but now he's telling bawdy stories to a crowd of interested young men. The Dowager Duchess of Swynford registered her disgust before asking Lady Wakefield to ask him to leave, although neither she nor Wakefield has budged to make him. I think Wakefield is, in fact, enjoying his bawdy stories, despite how inappropriate they are in mixed company."

That was certainly terrible news. The dowager witnessing Canbury's bad behavior herself would not make her much disposed to Lady Adele.

Rutland shook his head. "I've heard he devotes the time he used to give his wife to Parliament."

"Caernarfon tells me as much," said Lark.

Rutland smiled. "Ah, yes. I forgot he took his father's seat. Lord help him."

"I think he secretly enjoys parliamentary procedure. We all need a hobby."

Anthony put a hand over his mouth but was clearly laughing.

"And what of Swynford? I read in the papers that he vanished for a week, and yet here he is."

"He was ill, it turns out. Forgot to tell his mother he was leaving town to recuperate at his country home."

Rutland nodded. "Ah, yes. I once forgot to tell my mother I was escorting my wife to the opera, and it was one of those nights that the opera had a guest *prima donna* from Sweden. I can't recall her name, but I understand she is quite famous on the Continent. Well, anyway, the crowd that night was even more of a crush than usual and my wife and I were detained trying to leave. Mother was hysterical by the time we returned home. She thought we'd been kidnapped and murdered." He chuckled.

"This is what I get for letting my mother stay with us while our children are young. Let that be a warning to you."

Lark exchanged a glance with Anthony, who still looked amused.

"How are you fellows?" Rutland asked. "Headed for Wakefield's cigar room?"

"I will momentarily," said Anthony. "I saw Camden go in there and I am eager to relieve him of a few of his coins."

Lark raised an eyebrow.

"What? Camden won a hundred pounds from me last week at the Effington fete. It is only fair."

"Right. I would like to check on Swynford." To Rutland, Lark said, "The society mamas have been quite all over him tonight. He may be in need of rescue."

Rutland laughed. "That doesn't stop until you say 'I do' to the vicar, alas. Having been through it a few seasons ago, I do not envy Swynford."

Lark said farewell to his cousin and Anthony and then steeled himself to go back in the ballroom.

Chapter Fifteen

B EFORE ADELE HAD even finished descending the staircase for breakfast the next morning, Wilton was upon her and said, "Come with me at once, my lady. I'm afraid the countess had taken a turn."

"She what?"

Adele hurried after Wilton toward the countess's room. When they arrived, Dr. Willis sat beside the bed as the countess lay there with her eyes closed. She seemed unconscious, though her breathing was labored.

"What has happened?" Adele asked.

"The countess started to struggle to breathe last night. We think it's pneumonia."

"Pneumonia?" Adele struggled to process this. "Last night? Why did no one alert me when I arrived home?"

"I did not want to bother you, my lady," said Wilton. "You needed your sleep."

"But she…" Adele shook her head, knowing from the countess's pallor and the wheeze in her breaths that the end was likely to arrive soon. "We'd best send for the earl."

"He sent word that he was already on his way two days ago," said Wilton. "He should arrive today."

Dr. Willis reported in a soft voice, "She has a high fever and her lungs crackle. A younger woman might overcome this, but a woman of the countess's age, who was already in ill health…"

As the day wore on, a steady stream of the countess's friends and family members arrived to say good-bye. Adele kept a vigil at the countess's bedside until John, the Earl of Sweeney, arrived. He ordered Adele removed from the room, so she stewed in the gold salon waiting for word, furious that the earl was keeping her away, especially since it had been Adele caring for her these last few months. He hadn't even bothered to visit.

Keeping vigil only of the old clock in the corner gave Adele too much time to think. If she had been here last night, might the countess's prognosis be different? Would she have been available to call Dr. Willis sooner? Would she have been able to see to a need that would have prevented the countess's current decline. Had the countess caught pneumonia because of Adele's neglect? Adele had grown somewhat resentful of the countess as Adele's duties had shifted away from companionship and more toward those of a servant, but she had tried not to let that affect how she treated the countess, and she was fond of the woman, after all.

And for what had she gone to the ball? To wear a pretty dress and drink lemonade? To indulge in some superficial pleasures? She *had* seen Hugh and managed to dance with him twice, but when they were not dancing, he'd barely been able to speak to her. She would treasure those two waltzes for the rest of her days, but everything else had been superficial and silly. It hardly seemed worth it if she could have been here to help the countess.

The earl's wife and children arrived at the house as the sun began to set. She took the children up to see their grandmother after exchanging only a few clipped words with Adele. Adele tried to sit patiently and wait for news, but guilt ate at her.

Wilton appeared at one point with a dinner tray, although Adele could not bring herself to eat.

"I should have been here last night," said Adele.

"No, my lady. There is nothing you could have done."

"But if I'd been here attending to the countess instead of dancing and letting... frivolities, and..."

"Hush, my lady. No. You work very hard for the countess

and have been a wonderful companion to her. You deserved a night away. It is just her time. It would not have mattered if you'd been here or not."

"But, Wilton, surely if I'd—"

"No," Wilton said softly. "You know as well as I do that the countess has been preparing to leave us for some time. Dr. Willis says this is just God calling her home. Nothing you did or did not do affected when this would have happened."

Adele still had not eaten her dinner an hour later when the earl's wife solemnly walked into the room and stopped the clock.

HUGH WAS IN the morning room indulging in a large breakfast while his mother flipped through a newspaper. He let his mind wander to the Wakefield ball and how wonderful it had felt to have Adele in his arms. He thought back to Adele's retelling of Cinderella. The prince in the story had taken one look at Cinderella and known he'd dance all his dances with her from then on. Hugh only wished he could have done the same with Adele at the ball.

He *would* marry her. He just had to figure out how to tell his mother.

"That old crone finally left us?" said the duchess.

"Which old crone, mother?"

"It says in the paper that the Dowager Countess of Sweeney died on Sunday."

Hugh dropped his fork.

"Hugh, really. Be more careful."

Hugh swallowed the bit of bacon in his mouth and it felt jagged going down. Adele had lost the countess. What must she have been feeling?

"I met the Countess of Sweeney. It was her home I stayed in while my memory was gone."

"Right, of course." Helena turned her attention back to the newspaper.

"Lady Adele is the countess's companion. I wonder what she will do now."

Helena lowered her paper and glared at Hugh over the top of it. "Lady Adele is the plain girl you danced with at the Wakefield ball. Canbury's daughter." Her tone was not approving.

"Yes."

Helena lifted the paper back up. "I imagine there is some other wilting socialite in need of companionship. Or a child who needs a governess."

"You would relegate an earl's daughter to a governess position?"

"Canbury is clearly not supporting her if she has to take such positions. What an improvident man! You saw him carrying on at the Wakefield ball. I doubt he gave one thought to the poor girl after handing her over to the Sweeney residence. He's too busy shoving his nose up... well. I apologize, that was rude of me. He wants to be Prinny's right hand man and behaves abominably to achieve that end."

Hugh sighed. "Yes, I recognize that. Still, the fact remains that Lady Adele is not responsible for her father's behavior, and I find it insulting that you would have her be a governess rather than rising to the life to which she is deserving."

The dowager lowered the paper again and stared at her son. "Life she should be deserving? What life does any woman have apart from her father or husband? Since her father is not interested in taking care of her, she needs a husband, but who would marry her?"

Hugh rubbed his head, a headache forming. Had his mother always been this haughty? He found her company quite repulsive now, although he'd come to realize in the weeks since he'd come home that he loved her as any son loves his mother, but their relationship was complex. He did things for her out of family obligation more than love at times. She was stubborn and could be mean. And yet he had no doubt that she cared for him deeply and had doted on him when he'd been a child. It was hard to separate the woman who had held him to her bosom when he was sick or injured as a boy and the woman who now said disparaging things about other members of the gentry.

"I remain surprised that the Countess of Sweeney was even still alive to be declared dead in the paper today," said Helena.

"What makes you say that?"

"She hasn't been seen in years. Had you seen her before ending up at her house?"

"I'm hardly in a position to know."

The dowager frowned. "You still have holes in your memory."

Hugh nodded. "I spoke with Doctor Sanderson yesterday. He believes this is… just how it will be. I may continue to recover things, but there are some things that may just be gone."

"Whoever hit you in the head belongs in a cell. Who would do such a thing?"

"I wish I knew, Mother. I think about it every time I can't remember something. But no one has acted hostile toward me since I arrived back at home, so perhaps the danger has passed." There'd been no reports of trouble from Mr. Sedgwick, the guard, either. All had been quiet.

Hugh was not truly convinced he was out of danger, though. Whoever had done this to him was laying low, perhaps, but was still free. Until Hugh could either puzzle out or remember what happened, he'd never feel completely safe. But he didn't want his mother to know that.

Helena nodded, but Hugh did not believe the danger had passed, nor that the man who had gone to such lengths to injure him would have given up so easily. Likely he was biding his time, or he'd been spooked by Mr. Sedgwick's presence. Hugh had been trying to put it out of his mind, but he never went out alone, and if he came home from the club late at night, he made his driver bring him right to the door and wait until he was inside.

But worrying about what danger might befall him was maddening, so he tried not to dwell on it.

Hugh went back to his breakfast and wondered now what really would become of Adele. Was she still staying in the Sweeney home? Was she at her father's home? Did she have another position lined up? And how could he find out?

He spent part of the rest of the day focused on that. He did not know the address of the Sweeney residence, just that it was somewhere in Marylebone. But when Hugh got out a map, he saw that Marylebone was actually a fairly large area of London. So he called on Lark instead.

"I'm busy," Lark said when Hugh walked into his office.

"I won't take but a moment of your time. I need to know Lady Adele's address."

Lark sighed. "I have grown fond of the girl, too, but this is folly." And yet he reached for a piece of paper.

"Mother remarked that Canbury made quite the fool of himself at the Wakefield ball, but I did not witness that for myself."

"No, I suppose you wouldn't have." Lark wrote something on the paper, but paused to say, "Canbury had too much to drink and was telling bawdy stories in mixed company. Everyone, including the Wakefields, seemed delighted, but the old guard thought his behavior... inappropriate."

"Inappropriate?"

"We must protect the delicate sensibilities of our debutante class, I suppose. I think his offense is relatively minor in the scheme of things, more a faux pas than a status-ruining event, although your mother already does not like him, and this did not endear him to her, I would imagine."

"No, she had some unkind words for him."

Lark finished writing down the address and brandished the paper. "Which is why this is folly. Your mother will never allow you to court Adele."

Hugh reached for the paper and grabbed it from Lark's hand. "I am not asking her permission. Last I checked, I am the duke and a grown man at that, capable of making my own decisions."

"It's not just your mother. Canbury has a lot of enemies. You'd be aligning yourself to him, which could have disastrous consequences for your businesses and will undoubtedly affect your reputation. Not to mention, you still have not fully recovered your memories. You should not be making these kinds of decisions under the circumstances."

"What harm is there in courting the girl?"

Lark sighed. "Well, you clearly aren't listening. What harm is there? Besides turning the wrath of Canbury's enemies on you? Besides the fact that some villain likely still has designs to harm you?"

"Yes, besides that."

"You could fall in love." Lark laughed. "Look, I am sympathetic to your plight, as I too have found my heart pulled toward exactly the wrong sort of person. And I like Adele, I do. But you must know this cannot happen."

"Then why did you give me her address?"

Lark sighed. "I am just as foolish as you, I fear."

Hugh took his own carriage to the Sweeney house. When Wilton answered the door, he said, "Hello, Your Grace. It is agreeable to see you looking so well."

"Is Adele in to callers?"

"I'm afraid she is not. She left this morning and I do not know her whereabouts nor when she will return."

That was certainly bad news. "Left? Not for good, I hope."

"No, not quite, but it is my understanding that Lord Sweeney is determined to remove to the country at his earliest convenience and we will be closing down the house." Wilton leaned close. "I will tell you, Your Grace, that I overheard Lord Sweeney discussing a new position with Adele, but I do not know the outcome of that."

"Is Sweeney in?"

"No, sir. He and his wife had some business to attend to. I am not certain when they will return, either."

Disappointed, Hugh said, "I thank you for your help, Wilton. Do let Adele know I stopped by and wished to speak with her. And offer my condolences to the Sweeneys."

"I will, Your Grace."

It felt like a dead end. Hugh walked back to his carriage, worried now that he would not be able to track down Adele. He did not have the wherewithal to hunt all over London for her today, but perhaps he could set a few surrogates on the task.

As he climbed into the carriage, he was hit with a dizzy spell and thought perhaps it would be better to go home and nap for a while. But then he would devise some sort of plan to find Adele again before she completely slipped through his fingers.

Chapter Sixteen

HUGH WALKED INTO his club and was so relieved to see Lark and Owen in their usual spot that he nearly cried.

"Where is Fletcher?" he asked as he sat down.

"Obligated to take Lady Louisa to the opera," said Owen.

There was something here that Hugh had once known, but he couldn't quite recall it now.

"He's making that face," said Lark.

Owen nodded knowingly.

"What face?"

"You get a wrinkle in your forehead whenever you are struggling to remember something you think you should know." Lark leaned forward and pressed his thumb against Hugh's forehead, presumably where the wrinkle was. "What is it you cannot remember? Who the Lady Louisa is?"

Hugh closed his eyes for a moment. "She is… sister of the Marquess of Landsdowne. Whom we know from school. What is Fletcher's connection beyond that?"

"The Landsdowne siblings were his childhood friends," said Lark. "Lady Louisa is not yet married, but she loves the opera, so she asks Fletcher to take her when her brother is not available."

That piece of information clicked into its proper place in Hugh's brain and he nodded. "Yes, I recall that now. Lady Louisa's father was a prime minister, which is how he came by his title. And Fletcher has no romantic designs on Lady Louisa, but enjoys her company in a friendly way. And he likes the opera, though he will never admit that."

Owen chuckled. "Precisely."

"Well, regardless, I am glad to see you gents. I need some… subterfuge."

Lark sighed. "Which secrets am I to keep now?"

"You know secrets?" asked Owen. "Any you have not told us?"

"Several."

"We must rectify that swiftly."

Lark shook his head. "I'd be a terrible secret keeper if I went around divulging all I knew to whomever would listen. What do you need, Hugh?"

"I'd like to find out where Lady Adele is now that the Countess of Sweeney has died."

Owen sat back in his chair and crossed his arms. "You should let this go, Hugh."

But Hugh was tired of having this argument. "Can any of you tell me what flaw Adele has? Not her father, not her income, but what grave character flaw she possesses that makes everyone so certain I should stay away from her."

Owen looked taken aback. "It's… it's not done."

"What isn't?" asked Hugh.

"These sentimental novels the women are reading, they show this world where aristocrats who own these grand estates fall in love with their governesses, and that's just… it's not how our world works."

Hugh didn't quite follow. He turned to face Lark, who looked stricken. Then he recovered and said, "I believe what Owen means is that the marriages of titled gents are generally strategic, not romantic. You're a duke, so you marry the daughter of another duke so that you can produce future dukes. And if you're a Duke of Swynford, you do nothing that may bring shame or scandal to your family, because your father was one of the most respected men in England and you aspire to his legacy."

"Right. It doesn't matter if you love her," said Owen.

The Marquess of Beresford appeared then with a snifter of whisky in his hand, which perhaps explained the expression on Lark's face. He walked over to Lark's chair and leaned on it with one elbow resting on the top of the chair. "If you love who?" Beresford asked.

Hugh was not comfortable speaking about Adele with a relative stranger. He opted to ignore Beresford and said, "You do not need to explain it. I understand the circumstances. I am just expressing frustration is all."

Beresford narrowed his eyes at Hugh.

"None of you have married," Hugh said, genuinely angry now. "What right have you to lecture me?"

"We aren't telling you anything you don't know is true," said Lark.

"I take it you are *not* discussing Miss Sackville," said Beresford.

"Who?" said Hugh, although he recalled her from the Wakefield ball. He'd just temporarily forgotten in his single-minded focus on Adele.

Beresford laughed. "You should know, Eugenia Sackville has told her mother who told the Duchess of Claybourne who told everyone in London that you were *quite* taken with her and will make your intentions known by the end of the week."

Hugh balked, hardly believing what he was hearing. "*I* was taken with *her?*"

"Indeed. As I heard it from Claybourne, you waltzed with some mysterious wallflower who may or may not have been Canbury's daughter, but everyone knows you would never *marry* such a chit, so the fact that you also waltzed with the Sackville girl is practically a marriage proposal."

"Oh good lord," said Hugh.

"Do not blame the messenger," said Beresford. "I find Miss Sackville horrid."

"You are practically the same person," said Lark. "Like you, she also survives mostly on judgment and gossip."

Beresford grinned. "Aye, but I drink more whisky," he sipped his drink. "Also, I have a sense of humor, which I assure you, Miss Sackville does not."

"I barely know her," said Hugh. Asking after her parentage felt a bit like asking after a horse he was interested in buying, but he plowed forward. "What is her pedigree again?"

Beresford fielded this question, too. "Her grandfather was a banker who made a great deal of money fleecing London's most gullible out of their money, and her father is absurdly wealthy and also, I think, cheats at cards, although I have not been able to prove it. Yet."

"You disgust me," said Lark, shaking his head.

"You love a scandal as much as I do," said Beresford. "If you'd saved all the coins you spent on scandal sheets, you could buy a house."

"*Anyway*," said Lark. "The Sackvilles donated some of their money to a few of His Majesty's urban improvements, so Lord Sackville is much in Prinny's favor at the moment, and I can imagine your mother smiling upon your courtship, but I do agree with Anthony. She is wretched."

"I don't disagree," said Hugh. "She has spent nearly all of our acquaintance either complaining or saying cutting things about her social peers. I have no desire to court her."

"Because you love Canbury's daughter," said Beresford as if it were fact.

"Did you tell him?" Hugh asked Lark.

"I inferred it," said Beresford. He crossed the space and took the fourth chair usually occupied by Fletcher. "You and I are not friends, not really. But Lark is my friend, and he has been concerned for your welfare since the night you disappeared. So he told me about the head injury, and you may not believe me, but I swear I have told no one that you convalesced at the Sweeney house. I saw you dance with Lady Adele at the Wakefield ball and concluded that you may have developed some fondness for her during your recovery. Am I far off the mark?"

"No, that is accurate." Hugh supposed it couldn't hurt to tell Beresford the rest. "And I was considering formally courting her but had made no decision because everyone keeps trying to talk me out of it. But now that option is taken away, because the Countess of Sweeney has died and I do not know where Lady Adele is. I went to the Sweeney house today, but the butler knew only that Sweeney intends to close down the house."

"I imagine he'll sell it," said Lark.

"So," said Beresford, "you want to make some discreet inquiries as to her location or where she intends to go next."

"Precisely."

Beresford nodded. "Leave it to me. I am very good at finding people."

"How's that?" asked Lark.

"I find you all the time, do I not?" Beresford shot Lark a pointed look before turning back to Hugh. "I will find her without raising suspicion."

"How will you do that?" asked Hugh.

Beresford shrugged. "I am used to operating in the shadows."

Hugh wanted to ask what he meant by that but thought better of it. "All right. And please find out if she is all right. She must be devastated by the countess's death."

"I have some time tomorrow. I shall endeavor to learn what I can and report back with all possible haste." Beresford grinned and stood up. "I must be off, but try not to have too much fun without me."

When Beresford was out of earshot, Owen said, "Why do you like him?"

Lark shrugged. "That is a difficult question to answer."

ADELE WAS NEARLY packed, although she had no particular

destination. She knew not what John Sweeney intended to do with the house, but she figured he'd sell it. He'd been keeping it mostly for his mother and did not spend enough time in London to justify the expense of its upkeep.

John was kindly letting her stay, but she understood he wanted her to move out just as soon as she could find another position. Or sooner.

She'd written to everyone she could think of inquiring about possible places to work or live but had received only negative responses so far. Her father was renting a small room at an inn on Haymarket Street and had no room for her. Her Aunt Martha, the only other family she had in London, was not in town because her home was currently undergoing a significant renovation after it had flooded during a rainstorm a few months before. Her options were starting to look like either moving back to Canbury House in the country—where she would at least have a roof over her head, although nothing to do and no purpose to her life—or find a position or lodging in London. She did not have enough money for a long stay at an inn, and that was not a sustainable solution anyway. So she had no idea what she would do.

The glare John's wife, Eliza, shot Adele as she sat down to breakfast one morning was harsh enough to make paint peel, and Adele knew she needed to leave soon.

"I say," said John, oblivious to the daggers in his wife's eyes, "it was Swynford who stayed here for a few days, was it not?"

"Yes," said Adele. She'd had time to practice the story without a whiff of impropriety. "He'd hit his head and stayed here while he recovered from his injury."

"It says here in the paper that a Duke of S is courting a Miss S. Swynford is the only *S* duke I can think of who is not married."

"Is that the paper or the scandal sheet?" asked Eliza.

John shrugged. "What's the difference?"

Eliza sighed. "There are other *S* dukes. Somerset?"

"His wife just gave birth."

"Sussex?"

"Married. You met his wife at Covent Garden just yesterday."

"Then I suppose we've used process of elimination. But who is Miss S?"

John scoffed. "You care more about this nonsense than you pretend, wife. I do not know about this Miss S. There are probably a hundred women in London with a name like that."

It was clearly not Adele Paulson, however. Adele's heart sank. Hugh was courting someone. Not that Adele had any right to him, and of course he would find another woman to court, but she had not imagined he would move on so soon.

Eliza leaned toward her husband, though she shot Adele another scathing look before she said, "I had heard he paid Miss Eugenia Sackville a lot of attention at a recent ball. Bethany mentioned that to me yesterday."

"You were gossiping about Swynford yesterday?"

"No, we were gossiping about Miss Sackville, if you must know. Bethany went to the Wakefield ball and said Miss Sackville's behavior was positively ghastly. I've run into her a few times, so this news did not surprise me. She is the daughter of Baron Sackville, but she hardly seems gently bred. No one ever taught that girl manners. But I suppose she is pretty if you squint."

Adele's mind had swirled through this entire conversation. She connected the name to the woman Hugh had waltzed with at the Wakefield ball. That woman had been quite pretty. That Eliza didn't like her hardly signified; Eliza didn't like anyone.

Regardless, it was likely Hugh had found a potential bride who was far more favorable to his family than Adele would have been. Adele's father held a higher rank than Baron Sackville, but a much weaker reputation. Adele knew of Baron Sackville and knew the Crown had given him the title for some good deed he had done. He was also absurdly wealthy, which likely also boosted Miss Sackville's prospects; her father was likely offering a generous dowry.

Eliza went on at some length about various young women in the *ton* and how much she disliked them. John mostly flipped through the newspaper while saying, "Mmhmm" at appropriate intervals to make his wife think he was listening.

Adele focused on her breakfast and willed the rest of the meal to pass quickly. She did not want to betray her emotions where Hugh was concerned, and she chastised herself for feeling so gutted that he was giving attention to another woman.

John set the newspaper aside. "Oh, Lady Adele, I nearly forgot. The Marquess of Winchester is looking for a governess for his younger children. I can secure a meeting for you if you're interested."

Adele understood implicitly that she had no choice in the matter. "I am much obliged, my lord."

Chapter Seventeen

"THIS, MY FRIENDS," said Beresford, "is a cognac Mr. White just got in from France. I should like to share it with you all."

Fletcher shot Lark a questioning look, and Hugh had the sense that there was something about this situation he knew but could not recall. He wondered, not for the first time, if Lark and Beresford were lovers, but it seemed rude to ask. And besides that, Hugh was anxious to hear what Beresford had learned about Adele.

He waited for Beresford to pour five glasses and settle himself into a chair around the table. Lark and Owen had been eating dinner when Hugh arrived and each man was a good way through a substantial beefsteak. Hugh had eaten before leaving for the club and hadn't been hungry at any rate. He looked around and realized that they were seated a fair distance from all of the other gentlemen in the club, probably by Lark's design. At least they could speak freely.

Hugh tried the cognac and found it rich and a little sweet with a woody flavor. He liked it. But he felt like Beresford was using this as a delaying tactic. Rather than waiting for Beresford, Hugh said, "Did your discreet inquiries yield any information."

"Yes," said Beresford.

Hugh leaned forward in anticipation. Fletcher sent him a questioning look, but Hugh ignored him.

Beresford grinned. "The Earl of Canbury does not own a house in London. When Parliament is in session, he stays at an inn near Carlton House. As such, he does not have room to house his daughter. Lady Adele has an aunt, the earl's sister, who is not at present in London. Lady Adele has just been offered a position in the household of the Marquess of Winchester but has not officially accepted yet. For the time being, she is still at the Earl of Sweeney's house, but he's made inquiries about selling his house and intends to decamp back to his estate in the country as soon as possible."

"Why the rush?" asked Lark.

Beresford whistled. "He must sell his house to settle his debts."

"Of course," said Lark.

"What sort of position?" asked Hugh.

"What?" said Lark.

"With the Marquess of Winchester. What sort of position was Adele offered?"

Beresford frowned. "As governess to Winchester's youngest child."

Hugh shook his head. He had no doubt Adele would excel in such a position, but it bothered him all the same.

"There's something you're not saying," said Lark said to Beresford.

"I presented you with the facts. The rest is rumor and innuendo."

"Let's have it," said Lark.

"Well, the inn is just across St. James Park from Westminster, which is only logical. Canbury has only to walk a short distance to be at Lords. He has a more or less permanent room reserved there, but again, it is only a room and does not leave space for Lady Adele."

"But?" said Hugh, growing impatient.

"But it is also around the corner from a well-known molly house where the members are known to don the clothing of the opposite sex. Now, you know I think the rumors of Canbury being caught in public in ladies' clothing are all made up by his political enemies, but if he'd been seen near that molly house, that might explain why the rumors have persisted."

"Is Canbury a *member* of this molly house?" Owen asked.

"I have not been able to determine that," said Beresford. "There are rumors, but it's hard to sift through what's true and what is just nonsense made up by his rivals. And let me assure you, Canbury has a legion of enemies who likely sit around half the day wondering what nonsense they can make up to destroy him."

"Could you not go into the molly house yourself and inquire?" asked Lark.

"I would *never*," said Beresford, though he was grinning. "Anyway, it doesn't signify. The rumors are what they are."

Hugh was still stuck on the position Adele had been offered. "She is an *earl's daughter* and yet she is being made to work."

"I know, but her options are few. Canbury has spent the last thirty years spending faster than he earns money and doesn't have enough left to support his daughter. And so, if the Earl of Sweeney wants her out of the house, he has to find another place to put her."

"She should stay with me." The words were out of Hugh's mouth before he could think it through, but the idea had merit. Why, he'd go down to the Sweeney house tomorrow morning and tell her to pack. If Sweeney wanted Adele out of his hair, Hugh would take her.

"What are you going to do?" asked Lark. "Have her stay with you as a guest?"

"That is a good way to get the scandal mill going," said Beresford.

"My mother lives with me," said Hugh. "What scandal?"

"You can't just keep her in your house indefinitely," said Lark.

"Then I'll marry her."

Everyone groaned. "You don't know this woman," said Owen.

"I know her well enough. I know that she is good and caring. I know she wants children even though she has essentially become a spinster. I know she can play chess. I know she reads a great deal and is intellectually curious and we have many things to talk about. This is more than most gents know about their wives when they marry."

"Just make sure you are thinking through your decision," said Fletcher.

"Do you fellows object to my marrying Adele or marrying at all. Did we have some kind of pact not to marry before I got hit on the head?"

"It's really a matter of priorities," said Beresford. "How much does this sort of thing matter to you?"

"Associating himself with Canbury will harm Hugh's reputation," Lark said, "which until now, as you full well know, has been sterling. There's a reason women are falling over each other to get his attention and that he has until now been so successful in business. All of that changes if he marries this girl."

"All right. How much does that matter to you, Swynford?"

Hugh wasn't entirely sure. How much had it mattered before he lost his memories? He didn't want to disappoint his mother, but he thought the prospect of grandchildren would win her over. And Adele was still an earl's daughter, not a commoner, which should have placated her and the rest of society. The fact that her friends kept talking about Canbury as if Adele were the daughter of a leper was confusing and alarming to Hugh now.

Did society's approval matter? Would it affect his business? Hugh couldn't see how; based on the conversations he'd had with his secretary, Hugh made money from tenants on his various estates and a little bit of real estate speculation. There was a new real estate deal in the offing, but he couldn't see how the seller would care about who Hugh's wife was. He suspected that his wealth and title would trump whatever reputation loss he suffered from marrying Adele anyway.

Did his mother's approval matter? That was a more complicated question.

Did he love Adele? He didn't know. Maybe not. But he liked her more than any woman he'd met before. He dreamed about that night they'd spent together sometimes. He cherished the memories of sitting with her and talking, of walking around that little garden behind the Sweeney house, of the affectionate look on her face as she took care of him, of the feel of her in his arms as they danced. He couldn't shake thoughts of her most days. Was that love?

"None of you have ever been in love," Hugh said.

"So you're an expert?" Lark asked with a sardonic expression on his face.

"No. I don't know if I know what love feels like, and none of you do either, so maybe you should not judge me."

"I was in love once," said Beresford.

Lark's eyebrows shot up.

Beresford sighed. "I was young. The details are not important. And it hardly signifies, since the object of my affection is no longer among the living."

"How did you know it was love?" Hugh asked, genuinely curious, although conscious of the series of emotions playing out over Lark's face. This reinforced Hugh's suspicion that Lark and Beresford were lovers.

Beresford shrugged and said, "I just knew."

"That is not even a little helpful," said Hugh.

"There was a moment, I suppose. I was nineteen years old, hardly more than a boy, and the two of us were up at Oxford taking a stroll together near the river, and I looked at my love's face and *I love you* just popped into my head. But I knew, deep in my soul I knew, that I loved this person. I don't know if it's like that for everyone, but that is how it was for me."

Hugh considered that. He had not experienced a moment like that with Adele, but maybe it was only a matter of time. "That sounds lovely," Hugh said.

"It was rather. Except, you know, for the death part."

"I apologize. I did not intend to bring up bad memories."

"It is all right. I volunteered. But… I think love is not something to be trifled with. And I think also, if you care for this woman? Society be damned. Marry her if you like."

"That's not how things work," said Lark.

"No, Beresford is right, much as it pains me to say so," said Fletcher. "Is not our main reservation to Hugh's marrying this woman just that we worry about what society will think? Well, are *we* not society? Welcome to the nineteenth century, lads. Hugh deserves to marry for love."

Hugh found that encouraging. "It seems to me that the only obstacle between a powerful man and the woman he wants is whether or not she agrees, no?"

"You're determined to do this, aren't you?" asked Owen.

"Yes. I will marry her."

"Godspeed," said Lark.

LARK LAY HIS sweaty forehead against Anthony's chest.

Tonight, Lark had invited Anthony back to his own home. He knew from experience that he could count on the discretion of his household staff, but he'd been reluctant to take Anthony home. There was something too intimate about having a man in his house, but something within Lark had finally broken.

It was the expression on Anthony's face when he talked about falling in love. That was what did it.

Lark was still out of breath after spending inside Anthony. He intended to roll to the side but instead collapsed on top of Anthony, who was also out of breath.

"I think I saw God that time," said Anthony, before thrusting his fingers into Lark's hair and tugging on his hair until Lark lifted his head. Then Anthony kissed him hard, like his life depended on it.

As his faculties returned, Lark asked, "You were really in love?"

Anthony sighed, his chest rising and falling under Lark's cheek. "I wondered when you'd ask about that."

"I haven't been able to stop thinking about. Well, except for a few minutes there when I could think of nothing at all."

Anthony chuckled and put an arm around Lark. "Well, if you must know, he was a young fellow at Trinity College studying some obscure Tudor playwright who was not as good as Shakespeare. He was so beautiful, Lark, which I tell you not to make you jealous but to explain how besotted I was. I would sneak into his office at night and we'd talk into the wee hours of the morning about books and my own studies. I even explained to him once that I was mostly at university as a lark since I intended to live a life of leisure once I ascended to the marquisate, and he did not dismiss me but rather saw something in me and cultivated it. And that day, we took a walk by the river and we were discussing an idea he had about this playwright he studied, and I stopped to look at him because he was so smart I was intimidated by it. And I looked into his eyes and I realized I loved him."

"Did you tell him?" Lark asked, his voice barely a whisper. He wasn't jealous, but he was caught up in the story now.

Anthony frowned deeply. "No. For the next week, I tried. I wanted to. But I couldn't seem to get the words out. And then he..." Tears sprung in Anthony's eyes. "He caught a fever. No one really knew why. Something he ate or just random chance or I don't know. And I couldn't go to see him while he was ill, because why would some random student go to see a young teacher, let alone one as prodigal as I was, and I couldn't say good-bye because he ended up in the infirmary under the constant guard of nurses. I went to the infirmary one day on the pretense I'd heard one of my friends had been there, and I tried to see him, but he was quite insensible with fever. And then a few days later he died. I only found out because it was in the newspaper."

"Oh, Anthony. I'm so sorry."

Anthony wiped his eyes. "Men like us, we don't get to mourn properly. I wore a black armband the week after he died, but everyone did. I could talk to no one about him and I was… I was devastated. I hadn't imagined that we would have much of a future, but maybe I could have become serious about my studies and become an academic, or I at least could have bought a house for us in Oxford and happily lived a quiet life. But I was robbed of that chance and I never… I couldn't even mourn him."

Lark closed his eyes and put his arms around Anthony. Lark had very little firsthand experience with death. His grandfather, he supposed, and Hugh's father's death had been quite sad, but no one he was very close to had died. And here was Anthony, this man who put forward a public face like he cared about nothing, but he'd experienced this great loss and likely never spoken of it with anyone before.

This depth in Anthony was not something Lark had expected when they'd first started spending nights together.

"I didn't mean to force you to talk about it," said Lark.

"It's all right. I've never spoken about it to anyone. It actually feels nice to talk about him."

"What was his name?"

Anthony let out a little gasp before he said, "Simon. His name was Simon."

Lark ran his hand across Anthony's chest.

"Are you jealous?" Anthony asked.

"No. I am… humbled, in a way. I can tell by how you speak of him that you loved him, and it's a great tragedy that you mourn him still and no one can know. Except me, I suppose. I've never fallen in love that way. And I didn't know you had experienced that."

"It's easier to pretend that nothing matters."

"But these things do matter. The people we love, they matter. The people we mourn matter, too."

"I will never forget him, but as time goes on, I think of him less often. And for a while I did not intend to fall in love again, because that way heartbreak and madness lie."

"Have you changed your mind?"

"Perhaps. One thing your friend Hugh reminds me is that everything can vanish in a moment. He hides it well, but he makes a face sometimes that indicates he is confused or can't remember something, and it makes me wonder what I would do if I suddenly forgot everything I ever knew."

"I've noticed that face, too."

"And it makes me think about losing these things I've experienced. Sometimes I think my life would be easier if I hit my head and forgot I loved Simon or that I'm attracted to men in a way I should be attracted to women, but these things are so essentially a part of me that losing them would be a nightmare. I would be truly lost."

"Yes," said Lark, unsure of what else to say. When he'd become an adult, he'd been somewhat surprised to learn that not all people were attracted to all sorts of people, regardless of gender. But Lark had not met many other than himself. In some ways it felt lonely, but in some ways it was liberating. He moved in secret rooms most in society knew nothing about, rooms full of beautiful people and desire and love, and he would drink his fill before committing himself to an obligatory society marriage.

"Lark," Anthony said softly.

Lark picked up his head and met Anthony's gaze.

"I do treasure the time we spend together," Anthony said. "We tease each other a great deal, and perhaps you still view whatever this is between us as just sexual release, but—"

Lark placed a finger on Anthony's lips. "I believe we've moved past that now."

Anthony smiled. "I knew the moment you sought me out at the Wakefield ball that my interest in you was reciprocal."

"So what is happening between us?"

"I don't know. I enjoy it. I hope it lasts for a good while. I'm not so delusional as to think we will have some sort happy ending like the prince and princess in a fairy tale, but we have this now and I am happy for it."

"Yes. I agree."

Anthony smiled. "Do your friends know we are lovers?"

"I haven't said anything, but I believe they suspect."

"We are not very coy, are we?"

"No, but maybe it doesn't matter. I don't know precisely what happened in that week Hugh was lost to us, but he cares for that girl and will use every bit of power and influence he has to make any scandal around her go away. In theory, we could do that, too. Be together and ignore society and throw money at any problems that arise."

Anthony laughed. "This surprises me, that you'd be willing to take a risk like that. You seem to want to keep me a well-hidden secret."

"Well, I do, but I find I care less with each passing day. Keeping secrets is… bothersome."

Anthony laughed. "Bothersome?"

"You know what I mean."

"I do, darling, I do."

Chapter Eighteen

"**L**ADY ADELE?"

Adele turned when Wilton called her name. She was packing the last of her things before leaving for her new position the next day.

"The Duke of Swynford is here to see you. I've put him in the gold salon."

"The Duke of…" Adele's heart seized. "Yes, all right. I will be there in a moment."

She was shocked that Hugh would come to this house. Surely he'd forgotten about her by now. But she had no delusions that he was here to see John, so he must have been here to see her. But why was he here?

When she walked into the salon, she found him looking around. He was unbearably handsome in his fine clothing, with his hair styled just so. He smiled broadly when he saw her.

"Lady Adele. It is delightful to see you."

"Hello, Your Grace. It is agreeable to see you."

"Agreeable? Is that all?"

She sighed. "I don't wish to be rude, but I've still got some packing to do and I'm running out of time. Was there something you wanted to discuss with me."

"There is, yes." He rested his hands behind his back and began to pace across the room. "I understand you've been offered a position with the Winchesters, is that right?"

"Yes. I accepted and intend to leave tomorrow morning."

"To be their governess, yes?"

"That is correct."

Hugh nodded. "I have come to offer you an alternate position."

Adele balked. An *alternate* position? She had no earthly idea what he had in mind. "Where, Your Grace?"

"In my house," he said.

"In your…" It was like a slap in the face. After everything they'd been to each other while he'd recovered from that injury, she thought she meant more to him than as a potential servant. She cycled through the possibilities. Did he want her to be a paid companion to his mother? Or, worse, did he intend to marry Lady Sackville and make her the governess to his children?

No. She could not do it. She stared at him now, took in his fine dark hair and his square jaw and his strong shoulders. She remembered the one night they had spent together, the way he'd told her never to have shame about her body, the way their lovemaking had been so perfect and beautiful. She remembered dancing with him at the Wakefield ball and the perfect way she fit in his arms. She knew beyond all doubt then that, despite everything, she loved this man, and she could not be a mere employee to him. That was a point she would not compromise on.

"Adele, you deserve so much more than a position with the Winchesters. I know also that the Earl of Sweeney intends to sell this house, so you cannot stay here any longer, either. And I thought perhaps the best way to rescue you from an undesirable fate was to offer you a position with me."

Adele stared at Hugh in disbelief. He thought he was rescuing her? "You said once that you wanted me to be a part of your life once you recovered your memories."

"Yes, I did say that."

"And now you are offering me a position in your house?"

"You say that like these things are in opposition. Where is the contradiction?"

Was he serious. "You want me to have a position in your house. So, what, I can be governess to your future children? No, Your Grace, I cannot do that. I will not."

He pressed his lips together. "Why do you say that?"

Tears sprang to her eyes. "Because somehow, against all odds, in the weeks that I've known you, I've fallen in love with you. I could not live in your house with your wife and your children and pretend that this is not true. My heart would break. Every day." She was too hurt to be embarrassed, too angry that he would even make this offer to feel any shame at her admission. And it was out there now. So be it.

His face was unreadable. "I think you misunderstand my intentions."

She turned to leave. She could not let this continue. He was destined for some other life, not this one, and she would… well, she'd find some quiet place to mourn him and then she'd figure out some way to pick up her life and move on. She'd done it before.

"No, Adele, please. Let me explain."

She stopped and turned around. "Very well."

He suddenly stood right before her. He reached over and cupped her cheek in his hand, then used his thumb to wipe away the tear that fell. "The position I'm offering you in my home is as my wife."

"You… what?" Adele could not believe what she was hearing.

"I've come to ask you to marry me."

"You… are you serious?"

"You just said you love me. If that's true, then you cannot doubt me. I do not jest. And my friends will tell you I've thought of little else from the moment I left this house weeks ago. I believe they are quite tired of discussing it."

"But the newspaper said you plan to offer for the Sackville girl."

Hugh frowned. "Really? She's dreadful. I've never met a

more mean-spirited girl. I danced with her at a ball, but I did not propose. We danced at that same ball, you'll recall, where I danced with you twice."

"But what about… that is, society will…"

"I've given that a lot of thought, too. I don't care what society thinks. Do you?"

She couldn't help but smile at that, and then it started to hit her that he was serious. He had come here to ask for her hand. A giddy thrill went through her body, although she didn't dare indulge in it yet. "I do not," she replied.

"I have not spoken to my mother about this, nor have I asked your father for permission. I thought it important to speak with you first. If you were not willing to be my wife, then I figured I would spare myself those awkward conversations."

Adele was sympathetic. Those were bound to be difficult conversations. "I suppose that could be an issue."

"Adele?"

She met Hugh's gaze. "Yes?"

"You have not answered my question."

"I haven't?"

"Lady Adele, will you marry me?"

She gave in to her feelings, then. Joy made her feel like she was floating. "I will," she said. "Of course I will."

Hugh grinned and then broke into laughter. He swept her up in his arms and spun her around. She was dizzy when he put her back down, but she did not mind at all.

What he'd just said hit her, then. She imagined this conversation would replay itself in her memory many times. "Hugh, I do not believe my father will be an issue. He may not offer much of a dowry, but he will be so elated to have a man of your standing offer for me that I cannot imagine he would protest. Based on some things Lord Waring said, however, I do fear your mother's reaction."

Hugh nodded. "I cannot deny that I fear her reaction as well. Which is why I figured I would speak to you first. If you would not have me, then I needed not tell my mother."

"How would you have felt if I'd said no?"

"I would have been devastated. And I would have argued most ardently in favor of my suit. I am somewhat relieved I do not have to do that."

"Oh, I don't know. I should like to hear some ardent arguing."

Hugh gave her a soft smile, and she liked the way his skin crinkled near his eyes. "I would have said that I have never met a woman who makes me feel as you make me feel. I've never met anyone as beautiful or intelligent or kind as you are. I have thought of you nearly constantly since the moment we met, and I am overjoyed that I may have you by my side for the rest of my life. And, again as my friends will tell you, I've never met anyone who made me think matrimony might be a joy and not a reluctant obligation."

She recognized that he did not say he loved her, but that was all right. He clearly cared for her and was offering a happy life. She would take it for now, although she wanted his love in the future. Perhaps soon, he'd be able to say it, and Adele trusted him enough to know that when he did tell her he loved her, he would mean it with all his heart.

"Kiss me," she said.

"What?"

"Kiss me. Promise me."

"With pleasure."

When Hugh pressed his lips to hers, it was not a chaste kiss but a hungry one. He groaned like a man eating his first bite of food after a long fast. She put her arms around his shoulders and clutched his coat like he might escape otherwise. The kiss warmed her, made her skin tingle, aroused and excited her. All kisses should be like this, she thought, or no kisses should be because then everyone would just kiss all the time.

She laughed, and broke the kiss. Hugh shot her a happy but befuddled look. "What is it?"

"I was just thinking that if all kisses were as wonderful as that one was, everyone would just kiss all the time. Then I pictured what that would be like."

"No one would accomplish anything," Hugh said, a chuckle in his voice.

"Indeed."

"I won't keep you from your packing, but I will send my coach for you tomorrow. I can speak with Lord Winchester if you like."

"No, that is all right. I will do it."

"You shall move into my home. I'll have one of the spare rooms readied for you. Mother and I keep bedrooms at opposite ends of the house, but for propriety's sake…"

This was all happening so fast. "Yes, of course. But what if your mother says no."

Hugh grimaced. "I do not know. I hope it does not come to that." He waved his hand. "It is of no matter. I will speak with her this afternoon and hopefully make her see that you will be a wonderful daughter-in-law. She may even enjoy planning a wedding."

Adele giggled despite herself. She hadn't even met the dowager duchess, but she was intimidated by her.

Hugh took one of Adele's hands between both of his own. "Do not worry. We will find a way. I promise."

Adele had doubts, but she smiled. "Are you sure?"

"Yes. But now I must go and you must finish packing, and then we will have the rest of our lives together. How does that sound?"

"It sounds wonderful."

HUGH RETURNED HOME knowing he could postpone the inevitable no longer.

He sought out his mother and found her in one of the first floor sitting rooms, working on some elaborate needlepoint. "Mother, I need a word with you."

"Of course, darling. Please have a seat."

She smiled at him as he crossed the room and sat in the high-back chair across from her. She must have sensed his tone, and she set aside her needlework and turned her full attention on him.

He suddenly felt nervous. "I've made a decision," he said.

"Yes?"

"I'm ready to marry," he said.

The dowager sat up straighter. "You are? Oh, I can't tell you how happy you've made me. I may yet see grandchildren before I go to my grave. Do you have a wife in mind?"

"I do."

"Who is it? Not that Sackville girl. I regret pushing her toward you. She's pretty, but she's got a mouth on her and does not know when to keep it closed."

"No, not Miss Sackville." Hugh took a deep breath and with as much confidence as he could muster, he said, "I intend to marry Lady Adele."

Hugh had expected some token resistance, but had assumed his mother would be so happy he was finally marrying that she'd be relieved or happy for him. But instead, she stared at him, her mouth agape, for a long moment. Then she shook her head. "No, I forbid it."

"You forbid it?"

"You have some sickbed infatuation with this woman that will pass. She is not a worthy Duchess of Swynford. She is too old, she is too plain, and her father is a laughingstock."

"None of these things signify. They don't speak to the quality of her character. And she is *not* too plain. I find her beautiful."

"I will not have the Swynford name associated with that family."

High rolled his eyes. "Welcome to the nineteenth century, Mother," he said, remembering what Fletcher had told him.

"Shouldn't my happiness take precedence over some outdated notions about who is worthy in your eyes? And at the end of the day, she's the daughter of an earl and she'll be taking *my* name."

"It's out of the question, Hugh."

"Is it not my choice? Lady Adele is kind and caring and smart and beautiful. I think we suit each other quite well. And she and her father barely have a relationship, from what I can tell. Why should I not have her as my wife? She is who I choose."

His mother's eyebrows rose. "You can't be serious."

"I am."

She shook her head and stood up. "Absolutely not. She is not an acceptable wife."

When she started to leave, Hugh said, "Where are you going?"

"I am so furious with you that I am leaving the room. This is ridiculous. There are a hundred more suitable women in London. If not the Sackville girl, then the Townsend daughter... or the Huntley girl... or—"

"You don't even know their names. I know absolutely nothing about any of these women. They could be mean-spirited gossips like Miss Sackville. They could be women who want only my title and fortune but care nothing for me. Would you really have me marry a stranger from a better family over someone I know and care about? I know Adele and I know she is a good person and I know she's who I want to marry. Why can you not be more accommodating?"

"Because you are the Duke of Swynford. Because there are eleven previous Dukes of Swynford looking down on you to carry on the nobility of the name. Because my father was the Duke of Grafton. Because you are related to King George by marriage and descend from King Charles II on my side of the family. Because you, Hugh Baxter, the twelfth Duke of Swynford, are among the most wealthy, most powerful men in England, with the greatest pedigree, and I will not have you besmirching that name with the likes of Adele Paulson. I don't care if you love her. Marriage is not about love."

"I do not see how marrying Adele changes any of that. I will still be Hugh Baxter, the twelfth Duke of Swynford, after I marry."

"But your children would be related to the Earl of Canbury."

Hugh stood. "So is that all you care about? Names and reputations? What about happiness? What about the potential for healthy grandchildren? What if, in a generation or two, titles don't matter anymore?"

"I've given you my answer, Hugh. I do not wish to debate this any longer." And with that, she left the room.

Hugh sat back down. The more his mother had fought him on this, the more he felt determined to marry Adele.

Chapter Nineteen

HUGH ARRIVED AT the Sweeney house the next day having made what was likely a rash decision. He was greeted in the front hall by the earl, so Adele must have explained the circumstances. And then Adele came down the stairs looking perfect. Her dress was modest, a simple blue muslin with no adornments, and her hair was back to its severe knot at the base of her head, but her smile went straight to his heart. He could not help but smile back.

"I'll have a footman bring your trunks to His Grace's carriage," said the earl.

"Yes," said Hugh. "The carriage is right out front. My driver can help as well."

"That will not be necessary, but thank you, Your Grace."

Hugh turned to Adele. "Hello, my lady."

"Hello, Your Grace." She laughed. "I hardly even know what to say."

He took her hand and kissed her knuckles. "I am happy to see you."

The earl chuckled. "When Adele told me why she had chosen not to take the position with the Winchesters, I almost did not believe her, but I see now that it was true. I will see to your luggage."

He walked away, leaving Hugh and Adele essentially alone in the house's foyer.

"I am happy to see you as well," she said. "I dreamed of you last night."

"Did you? Was it a good dream?"

"Yes. It was lovely. I never…" She looked away and pressed a hand over her mouth. Then she said, "I never thought this day would come. You have… you have given me a second chance, Hugh."

He was touched by that. He knew that he was changing the course of her life, and he wanted to do right by her. But he also knew the road ahead would not be easy. "Hold that thought. We may yet encounter some obstacles."

"Such as?"

"I will tell you when we are on our way."

A series of footmen carried Adele's trunks out to the carriage. She did not own much. He'd arrived in his largest coach in anticipation of the great number of trunks for all the many things most ladies of his acquaintance had, but there seemed to be only three that carried everything she owned.

The earl appeared again with his wife in tow this time. Adele shook hands with each of them and said good-bye, but it seemed to Hugh much more of a business transaction than anything else.

At last he escorted her outside on his arm. They were far from Mayfair, but Hugh spared a thought for who might see them. He wondered if commoners in London ever thought about seeing and being seen. His neighbors were too close and too nosy for him to enjoy much anonymity in Mayfair, but sometimes he craved it.

When they arrived at his carriage, Hugh grasped Adele's waist and lifted her onto a seat. He climbed in after he and she smiled at him as he settled into his seat.

He couldn't breathe, though.

She was so beautiful. He'd hire her a lady's maid who could do her hair in a less severe style, and he'd buy her more dresses than she could ever wear, but those things would only serve to heighten the beauty she already had. She met his gaze now and he thought he might get lost in her blue eyes.

And because they were finally alone with each other and because he could stand it no longer, he kissed her.

He was rewarded by her soft lips parting and he thought he might never get enough of her taste. That helped confirm that he'd made the right decision. To hell with what anyone said, Adele was his choice.

Without breaking the kiss, he knocked on the roof of the carriage.

Adele pulled away gently as the carriage started to move. "I think the earl is happy to be rid of me."

"Then he does not appreciate you. I think I shall never want to be rid of you again."

She grinned and reached over to touch his hand. "I can hardly believe this is happening."

"Are you happy, Adele? Do you have any regrets?"

"I am very happy. I regret nothing."

He laughed and kissed her cheek, happy to have her by his side.

She looked out the window and must have realized that they were headed north instead of west toward Mayfair. She turned and gave Hugh a quizzical look. "Where are we going?"

"Scotland."

"Scotland?" She nearly shouted the word.

"We must elope."

"What?"

Hugh didn't like the startled expression on Adele's face. He explained, "My mother disapproves. But it is of no consequence. Once we are married, there won't be much she can do to—"

"Absolutely not."

Hugh grunted in surprise. Lord save him from obstinate women. Why would none of them just do as he wished. "I thought you wanted to marry me."

"I do. But I will not do it in secret in Scotland. I will not mire myself in further scandal. If we go to Scotland, everyone will assume that you behaved inappropriately during your convalescence, or that I seduced you, or something like that. They will assume we are marrying because we must. They will assume that I am some…" She looked up, as if she were thinking for the right word. "They will assume I am a harlot out to ruin you. No. We will not be eloping. If we marry, it will be in a church, here in London, with many witnesses."

"You are serious."

"Yes, I am serious. When we spent that night together, you told me to never feel shame. Well, I do not feel shame and I won't be made to feel shame over some… accident of my birth. I assume that is the main reason your mother disapproves. I'm sure she said I was too old and reminded you that my father is a joke to the *ton*."

"Well, yes, but—"

"Hugh, I am sorry, but I cannot marry you in Scotland."

That did present Hugh with something of a dilemma. Because if they did not go to Scotland, then Hugh would have to take Adele home, and he'd have to explain her presence to his mother. The fact that the reason for his haste was that Adele was about to take a position as a governess was unlikely to win her any favor with the dowager duchess.

But his mother would have to get used to the fact that this was what Hugh wanted. He rapped on the roof of the coach and waited for it to slow.

"Stay here," he said. "I'll order the coach to bring us to my house. I hope you have thick skin."

"I just cared for the countess. I can handle a stubborn older woman."

"You say that, but you have not met my mother."

THE DOWAGER DUCHESS of Swynford was probably the most

proud woman Adele had ever met.

Hugh had introduced her as "my mother, Helena," but Adele felt awkward calling her by her given name.

"Lady Adele will be staying with us until the wedding," Hugh informed his mother.

The dowager was polite, but icy. Hugh ordered a servant to set up one of the guest bedrooms, and once that was prepared, he encouraged Adele to rest before dinner.

He put her in a sumptuous bedroom with large bed made of dark wood, with violet bedding and curtains. It was much larger than her bedroom at the Sweeney home had been. Adele noticed that her trunks had already been placed in the room, so she busied herself unpacking and then lay on the bed, hoping to nap. Instead, she watched the second hand on the bedside clock and gave up.

Hugh had told her to make herself at home. She'd barely seen any of her new home, so she decided to explore it.

Even just the second-floor hallway was clean and elegant. The walls were painted a bright white and a dark-red carpet lined the floor. A huge painting of a country estate hung on a wall near the landing by the staircase. A small plaque at the base of the frame indicated it was Swynford House in Kent, the ancestral home of the Dukes of Swynford.

Slowly, Adele descended the stairs, noting that the railing was sturdy and looked recently polished. Servants buzzed around below her, likely preparing for the evening meal. As Adele reached the first floor, Hodges, the butler she'd been introduced to when she arrived, said, "Good afternoon, my lady. Is there anything you need?"

"No, I am just looking around the house a bit. Do you know where His Grace may be found?"

"I believe that he and the duchess are in the red room. That's the third door on the right down this hallway."

"Thank you, Hodges. Much appreciated."

"Of course, my lady."

Hodges walked off to do whatever his duty might be. She walked to the end of the hall and opened the door there. The door opened to a staircase, and based on the sounds and smells rising up from below, Adele guessed this was the kitchen. She noted that and decided she'd take a look later. The door closest to the kitchen was a well-appointed formal dining room. It was masculine and a little dark, with blue walls and a grand mahogany dining table. Across the hall was a morning room, not quite as formal or ornate, but with a huge window that let in a great deal of natural light.

The next door Adele found was an empty sitting room. Adele peeked inside and saw that there was a massive fireplace on one wall with a massive family portrait of Hugh's parents and Hugh when he was about thirteen or fourteen. The woman in the painting was clearly the dowager, although much younger and with less white hair. The man looked quite a lot like Hugh, though his hair was masked by a powdered wig. The boy was unmistakably Hugh, but a thinner, slightly gawky version of him.

The furniture in the room was beautiful. Adele was starting to feel the extent of Hugh's wealth and the prestige of his family. The room wasn't showy, but the quality of the items in it led her to conclude that it had cost a great deal to decorate. Adele opened a cabinet off to one side and saw it contained several bottles of whisky and wine. There was also a writing desk that had been used regularly, as a shallow box of fine paper lay open, a stoppered ink bottle beside it. Everything here was in good condition; nothing was dusty or worn or scarred the way everything in the Sweeney house was.

When Adele returned to the hallway, she heard voices and followed them.

"I cannot believe you brought her here," the dowager said. "What were you thinking?"

"I was thinking that she needs a place to stay. Sweeney is selling the house, and her father does not own property in London. What would you have me do?"

"You should have left well enough alone. She does not belong here."

"I intend to marry her, Mother. And I refuse to keep having this argument. Is this not better? You will have time to plan a grand wedding as befitting a Duke of Swynford, which I know you have long wished to do. I could have taken her to Scotland and married her quickly and not given you a say in the matter."

"But this woman?"

"You do not even know her, Mother. I think that if you get to know her over the next few weeks, you will like her immensely."

Adele leaned against the wall outside this sitting room and pressed a hand to her chest. She greatly appreciated Hugh's defense of her, but the fact that the dowager still disapproved bothered her a great deal.

"I could arrange a more suitable wife for you," said the dowager.

"You will do no such thing. I've made my choice. And I do not want to argue this point anymore. You are my mother, and I love you and value your opinion, but *I* am the Duke of Swynford, and so I have the final word here."

Adele was startled by the forcefulness of his tone. She'd never heard him use a tone like that before, but it was confident and left no room for argument. Adele imagined he'd be quite intimidating in a fight.

Apparently the dowager did not feel she could argue either. Hugh went on, "Adele will remain in the violet bedroom until after the wedding, and then she will move to my rooms. I ask that you stay here until after the wedding for the sake of propriety, but if you cannot accept Lady Adele, you can remove to one of the country houses. Although not Swynford House, for I intend to go there once the season is over."

"You would throw me out?"

"No. I'm giving you a choice. Accept Adele or leave."

"But what will your friends think?"

"My true friends will support this marriage. The rest of society can object all they want. It does not signify. Adele is a wonderful woman and I care about her a great deal. Marrying her will make me happy. The Marquess of Anglesy married a commoner a few months ago and did not become a social outcast."

"I will *not* have the Swynford name sullied by that woman."

"Then you have a very poor understanding of what it takes to sully a name. And, I repeat, if you do not like it, you can leave."

Adele heard footsteps and ducked into the nearest empty room. She heard the dowager grunt with frustration as she fled the room. After she heard the dowager walk upstairs, Adele crept into the sitting room where Hugh sat staring up at a portrait of a man Adele did not recognize.

Adele cleared her throat.

Hugh turned and gave her a startled look. "Adele. How much of that did you hear?"

"Enough."

Hugh nodded. "She will come around. It will take some time, but… she will come to see how good you are and will cease this useless protest."

Adele walked into the room and sat beside Hugh on the sofa. "I will admit to a certain amount of naiveté regarding what makes the reputations of members of the *ton*. Will marrying me really hurt your name that much?"

"No. I… how much do you know of your father's reputation."

"He is a politician and people do not like him. I have seen some of the ugly rumors in the scandal sheets."

Hugh nodded. "My friends think most of the stories told about Canbury are false and made up by his political opponents in order to ruin his reputation."

"Father is ambitious."

"Yes. And that level of ambition is generally frowned upon by the gentry. I do not much begrudge it."

"Have you spoken to him?"

"Not yet. Owen—that is, the Earl of Caernarfon—is also a member of Lords and is trying to discern Canbury's schedule so that I can meet with him."

Adele nodded. "I don't want to do anything to hurt you or your reputation."

Hugh smiled. "You are not. Men marry women whose fathers have dubious reputations all the time. A woman's father does not matter so much as the woman herself. And so many *ton* marriages seem little more than financial transactions anyway. Why, I believe Viscount Benton married the daughter of a wealthy commoner so that he could use her dowry to pay off some debts. I believe my reasoning for marrying you is far more sound for a successful marriage."

Adele's heart pounded. She reached over and took his hand. "And what is that reasoning?"

"I care about you. I enjoy spending time with you more than I do with any other woman of my acquaintance. When I think about our life together, I can picture it clearly."

But do you love me? Adele wanted to ask. It was not often that men and women of their stations married for love, but it wasn't a completely foreign concept.

Hugh answered her unasked question by leaning forward and kissing her softly. Adele sighed into the kiss. She loved the pressure of his lips on her, loved the warmth that spread through her body.

"I put you in the violet room because it is adjacent to mine," Hugh said. "Mother's rooms are at the other end of the floor upstairs."

"Are you implying you'd like for me come to you at night?"

"I most assuredly would, but it is your choice. If you want to wait until the wedding, I shall endeavor to endure our nights apart."

Adele smiled, cheered that he was giving her a choice. She

needed a little time to adjust to the fact that she would be with him. They would be married! "We have our whole lives ahead of us."

"That we do, my lady."

Chapter Twenty

GEORGE PAULSON, THE Earl of Canbury kept an office in a squat, two-story building on College Street, close to Westminster Palace. He generally spent his time away from Parliament there, taking callers and appointments with various officials.

Nicholas Vansittart, the Chancellor of the Exchequer, stood in the office now. He and George had been friends since Oxford.

"I can put in a good word for you," said Nicholas, "but I don't know if the position you're after is attainable. If you want to be Leader of the House of Lords, you'd be replacing Liverpool, which I only picture happening over his dead body. The Lord Chancellor may be aging, but he seems determined to hang onto the position. There may be a few secretary positions opening in the state department, but your most likely appointment will be as a diplomat, perhaps to Europe or maybe even India."

"I'd hate to be that far from my daughter. I'm all she has, you know."

"Prinny likes you, which works in your favor. However, those scandal sheet rumors…"

"None of those are true," said George. That was, since the death of his wife, George had taken it upon himself to explore the full range of human sexuality which meant that, yes, he'd taken a male lover from time to time, but he never wore women's clothing in public. More to the point, he'd been extremely careful for the last year or two, not doing anything that could jeopardize his chances of winning a position. His ambitions had clearly struck a nerve if his enemies were planting these ridiculous rumors in the newspapers. "You can't believe the things they say of me in the papers."

"I don't, but they do considerable damage to your reputation. We shall see, I suppose. And, to be clear, my job is not available."

George chuckled. "No. Perish the thought."

There was a knock on the doorframe. George looked up and saw his secretary standing there. "My lord, the Duke of Swynford is here to see you."

Nicholas's eyebrows shot up. "Swynford? That's... unexpected."

"Agreed, but I admit I am curious. Show him in, Drake."

George couldn't imagine why Swynford was coming to see him, although he had just enough time to get excited about his presence here. Swynford was wealthy and powerful and related to the king, after all. George felt his heart flutter with excitement wondering what Swynford could want.

George's secretary brought Swynford to the door. George had forgotten what a big man Swynford was. He was tall and athletic, but more than that, he had the sort of confident presence that made him seem even larger.

George stood. Swynford met his gaze and then turned toward Nicholas. Nicholas introduced himself and then said, "I'd better be going. I have a meeting with Lord Castlereigh about some spot of bother in Ireland." Nicholas saw himself out.

Swynford approached George's desk. "My lord, I've come to you today because—"

"Please have a seat, Your Grace." In truth, Swynford had about eight inches on George's height and two stone on his weight, which made him nervous. At least when they were seated, they were close to the same height.

Swynford sat across the desk from George and waited for a moment before he said, "This feels more awkward than I expected it to."

George was confused now. "I apologize, Your Grace, but I am at a loss as to why you are here. Are you certain you meant to meet with *me*?"

"Yes. I've come to speak about Lady Adele."

That had not been what George had been expecting. What could a man like Swynford possibly want with Adele? Did his mother need a companion? "She is not at present available for a new position, since she just accepted one with the Winchester family."

"Actually, she rescinded that invitation."

"She what?" George could not imagine Adele doing anything so foolish. And how did Swynford know that?

"At my request. My lord, let me cut to the chase. I wish to offer for LadyAdele's hand in marriage."

George could not believe what he was hearing. Was Swynford jesting? He did not appear to be. But how would Adele and a man like Swynford have even met?

He quickly shook that line of thought off. *Swynford* was offering for Adele? That was incredible. That was the kind of pedigree George most definitely wanted to be related to. He still could not quite wrap his head around how this could have happened. But perhaps he should not question it. Because there was a major issue.

George took a deep breath. "I must say, I am of course honored by this request, Your Grace, but I must also apologize as I am rather cash strapped at the moment. I cannot offer much of a dowry for Adele."

"That is immaterial," said Swynford. "I have no need of money. I merely want to marry Lady Adele. Do I have your permission?"

The Duke of Swynford wanted to marry George's daughter and he didn't need a dowry? Not to mention, if Adele were married, George would feel less guilty about taking a diplomatic position overseas, should His Majesty see fit to bestow one upon him.

He'd be a fool to say no.

"Yes, you absolutely have my permission. I am truly honored you have chosen my Adele, although I have to admit, I find this surprising."

Swynford laughed softly. "Yes, I imagine you would. I find it surprising at times." He shook his head. "I do thank you for your permission, my lord. In the interest of keeping you fully informed, I asked Adele to turn down the position with the Winchesters. Since John Sweeney intends to sell his house, I have brought Adele to live at my home on Upper Brook Street. My mother also lives there and is acting as chaperone until the wedding, which I intend to have at St. Paul's two weeks from tomorrow."

"That is a brief engagement!"

Swynford frowned. "Yes. And please be assured that the only reason for my haste is so that we can be married and remove to my home in the country by the end of the season. Nothing... inappropriate has occurred between us."

George nodded. He wouldn't have minded if it had. This was Swynford, after all. "Yes, all right."

"That is, I have not... my mother is keeping a close eye on us, let us say."

"It's all right, Your Grace. I trust you. Or I soon will, as far as my daughter is concerned, I'm sure."

"I do thank you. The announcement shall be posted in the paper as soon as I've secured St. Paul's. And, fair warning, your daughter has asked for quite a large wedding."

That seemed out of character. "My Adele has?"

"My suspicion is that she worried no one would believe my intentions were genuine unless we put on a little spectacle. So, if all goes to plan, the ceremony will be followed by a wedding breakfast at my home. Then we will stay in London another week or so before leaving for my estate in Kent."

"I suppose that makes sense. Adele is usually quite modest. I would not have expected her to want an elaborate wedding. I would not have expected her to marry a duke, though, either." George shook his head, still unable to quite believe any of this was happening. "What can I do?"

"She will need a trousseau, so any funds you can spare should go to that. It can be modest. She is already living in my home, and she will want for nothing, but money for a few new gowns or some jewelry would be most welcome."

George sighed. "Yes, I will see what I can pull together. She deserves great things, my Adele. She deserves this. She cares only for others, never for herself. She's been like that her whole life. My wife died about ten years ago, and Adele sat at her deathbed, always making sure she was comfortable and had enough to eat. Never worries for fashion or her own comforts. She is good-hearted and honest and… she told you of her previous fiancé, I hope?"

"She did, yes."

"She was devastated. I worried for her. Most of the reason I found her positions was so that she would have something to do, something to care about. When she lost hope of ever marrying, I'm afraid I did, too. But she… she will be such a good wife and mother. Have no fear about that."

Swynford smiled. "I have no fear about that at all."

"Good, good. I must say, I am overjoyed to be gaining a son, especially one from such a prestigious family as yours. I know my own flaws and how they must reflect upon poor Adele, and I am grateful you have overlooked them. Not everyone in your position would."

"Yes, I am acutely aware. Not to put too fine a point on it, but several people have tried to talk me out of this marriage. But I'm afraid the more people who tell me it is a bad idea, the more stubborn I feel about seeing it through."

George chuckled. "I knew your father a little, and he struck me as being quite similar. Some of the other peers in Lords referred to him as the Mountain of Swynford because he was often quite immovable."

Swynford tilted his head as if this story confused him, and George worried he might have offended the man, but then he laughed and said, "I don't believe I've ever heard that before, but that lines up with how I remember him."

"I shall not try to talk you out of this because I am very pleased with the match."

"That is most kind. I must be off to make some arrangements, but please do not hesitate to contact me at the Upper Brook Street house should you need anything. And you may, of course, call on your daughter any time you wish."

"Thank you, Your Grace. Sincerely. Likewise, you may reach me here most days, and if I am not here, my secretary usually knows where I am."

"Very good."

After Swynford left, George sat in his chair thinking this over for a long moment. He was thrilled for Adele for making such a smart match. He hadn't exaggerated; Adele had spent her whole life caring for others, and she deserved an easy life in which she was well cared for in return. Swynford could give her that. On top of that, having his daughter marry into the Swynford family would certainly raise his profile and might impress His Majesty and His Majesty's cabinet.

Yes, yes, this was good news all around. George hopped up from his chair and decided he'd call it an afternoon and celebrate at the nearby pub where many politicians tended to cavort. On the way out, he said to his secretary, "Let us find a pint of ale. My daughter is getting married."

"Excellent news, my lord," said Drake. "To Swynford, I gather."

"Yes. I can hardly believe it. This calls for… two pints."

Drake laughed. "All right. Let me get my coat."

IN THE WEEKS before the wedding, Adele found herself as something of a curiosity.

Once the wedding was officially announced in the newspaper, a parade of callers, most of them female, came by the house on the pretense of congratulating Adele but mostly, she felt, to gawk.

This was far from her first social season, so she was able to play her part, becoming the very picture of poise and politeness.

One of the women who arrived to call on her introduced herself as Lady Louisa Petty. "My brother is the Marquess of Landsdowne. Although in all honesty, I am here at the request of Baron Fowler."

It took Adele a moment to recall that Baron Fowler was the title of Hugh's friend Fletcher. She wondered if Lady Louisa had been sent to check on her. "How do you know Baron Fowler?" she asked conversationally as they sat together in the red sitting room.

"We are old childhood friends," Louisa said with a smile. "My parents want us to be married, but neither of us has feelings like that for the other. I view him as a brother."

"Really?"

"Yes. If you want the truth, I've had my eye on Lord Waring, but, well, Fletcher says he has some lover now that he's quite taken with, and I don't want to compete with that."

Adele wanted to ask, but didn't want to pry. Since it was just Adele, Louisa, and one of the servants laying out food, Adele asked, "I know Fowler and Swynford are good friends. Did he... are you here to check up on me?"

"Not in the way you're implying. That is, Fletcher—Baron Fowler—is worried about Hugh rushing into this marriage, but no one questions your integrity, if that's what you mean."

"I would be willing to wait. I am not the reason for the haste."

"No, I suspect your father and Swynford's mother are the reason for the haste."

Adele nodded because she agreed, on a number of levels.

"You must understand how this looks," said Lady Louisa. "I am not much interested in scandal or gossip, but the fact that Swynford has chosen to marry the daughter of an earl of dubious reputation has set tongues wagging. I've known Swynford a long time, and he has never been one to make hasty decisions, so I assume his intentions are good in this case. But Fletcher is worried. I don't even know what concerns him specifically. He seems to think you've bewitched Swynford."

"I tried to talk him out of pursuing me."

Louisa nodded. "These last few years, Swynford has seemed dead set against marriage. He understands his duty, but has seemed bored or irritated by most of the ladies of the *ton*. I think… I think perhaps something has changed in him."

Adele had worried about that. His memories seemed determined to only return in trickles rather than all at once, but she'd been worried he'd wake up one morning with all his memories returned and he'd remember something that made him not want to marry her.

"I see the worry on your face," said Louisa. "I think it is a good change. He's ready to settle down. He never has been before."

"Please know that I am not interested in him because of, well, all this," Adele said, gesturing around the room. She could not deny that the fine furnishings and the beautiful home were wonderful things, but she would have loved Hugh if they'd live in a far more modest house. "I imagine that's what the scandal sheets are saying. I genuinely care for him."

"I believe you. Hugh can smell a woman after a man's money from a great distance. Fletcher jokes it is a magic power of his."

Adele wondered sometimes what she'd gotten herself into by agreeing to be with Hugh. She hoped that, once the wedding was over and they went to the country and it was just the two of them, this low-level uneasiness she felt would go away. "I don't want to ruin him, either."

"You won't. Our parents' generation is more concerned with

names and titles and reputations than we are, and we are the ones taking over the country. A number of lords have married commoners. The Marquess of Downshire married an *American* last year. Everyone was out of sorts about it for about three days, and then we all collectively moved on to the next scandal. This will be like that. People will talk for a bit, but who cares? If you're happy in your marriage, the chatter of the gossipmongers doesn't matter."

Adele nodded. She agreed, but she couldn't shake the concern that something would go wrong. Would Hugh lose the respect of his peers? Would the enemies of her father, who seemed determined to ruin him, try to ruin Hugh as well? It was hard to set all that aside.

Lady Louisa seemed honest and candid, and Adele thought to ask her opinion on this, but before she could, Hodges knocked on the doorframe. "Apologies for interrupting, my lady, but this just came for you." He handed her a large envelope.

She opened it. Inside was a letter from her father folded around several bank notes. He congratulated her on her pending nuptials and explained that the money was hers to spend on her trousseau.

"That's exciting," said Louisa after Adele explained. "We must go shopping. Please allow me to take you to my modiste. She makes beautiful gowns and she works fast."

Adele couldn't help but get caught up in her excitement. "Yes, all right."

By the time they arrived at the modiste for Adele's appointment three days later, she and Louisa had become fast friends.

As they waited for the modiste to finish her previous appointment, Adele asked, "When Swynford pulled you aside as we were leaving, what did he say?"

"I am to tell Madame Auguste that if there is something you desire beyond your means, His Grace will cover any shortfall."

"No," said Adele, mortified. "My father gave me a great deal of money. Surely it can cover a few dresses."

"Yes, it can. I am just relating what the duke told me. He can afford it, by the way."

"I know. But he should not have to… that is, I don't want…" Adele shook her head, flustered.

Louisa laughed. "It is your choice, of course, but need I remind you that you are about to be the Duchess of Swynford. You should look the part."

That was the first moment when it really hit Adele that she was to be a duchess. She'd been looking forward to marrying Hugh, had fantasized what their life might be like, but had somehow skipped over the part where she'd be a *duchess*.

"Oh god."

"Ah, yes," said Louisa. "My friend Prudence got that same look on her face three days before she married the Duke of Huntley."

A seamstress invited Adele to the back. Adele stood as the seamstress took her measurements while two other women brought out bolts of fabric. Madame Auguste appeared and gave Adele a long look. "This blue, it is a good color for you, but this fabric is terrible. I think also… yellow. And violet."

"Two dresses are all I need," said Adele. "Some formal gowns to accompany the duke to society functions."

Madame Auguste pursed her lips. "And what will you wear when you marry the duke."

"Oh." Adele hadn't thought about it. "I guess I will need…"

"Lady Adele has some money," said Lady Louisa, stepping forward, "but please bill the Duke of Swynford for whatever she cannot pay for today."

Madame August winked at Louisa.

"My father gave me this money for my trousseau," Adele said weakly, recognizing how futile this was becoming.

"Let your husband buy you some gowns," said Louisa.

"I know *exactly* what you need," said Madame Auguste. "You are a pretty girl, but I can make your betrothed's heart stop when you walk down the aisle. Are you ready?"

Adele let out a breath. "Do your worst."

Chapter Twenty-One

PERHAPS THE GREATEST challenge to Hugh in the lead up to his wedding was going to sleep at night knowing Adele was in the adjacent room.

His London home was compact in a way Swynford House was not. He had a sense of that, at least. He lay awake one night a little over a week after Adele had moved in and tried to picture his home in Kent but could not.

It didn't quite work as a distraction. Adele was tantalizingly close. He kept picturing the expression on her face when she'd come apart in his arms that one night they'd spent together. He pictured the long lines and curves of her body, the rise of her breasts, the roundness of her hips, her beautifully formed legs. Having her in his home made him want to touch her nearly constantly, and he'd been sneaking in touches, but women wore a great deal of clothing, and Adele seemed to have put a wall between herself and Hugh.

Why was an important question. Did she not want him?

Well, he would have her on their wedding night without shame or fear of his mother's reprisal. Because Adele must know by now that she had nothing to fear from him, but she was likely quite intimidated by the dowager.

He lay in bed, unable to sleep, painfully hard. He grunted and got out of bed. He walked to the library thinking he'd find a book that might distract him enough to make him sleepy, but when he arrived, he saw the row of books on one of the shelves, ten volumes bound in yellow leather describing the history of the Dukes of Swynford. That gave him an idea.

Perhaps something here could help jog his memory.

The ten-volume history of the Swynfords was likely just the sort of dull reading that would put him to sleep, but a large volume that said "Swynford House" on the spine caught his eye. He slid it off the shelf and sat at the table in the middle of the room. The book turned out to be the family's records regarding construction and renovations at the Swynford ancestral home. He could not remember what it looked like, but he had a sense of its size. He flipped through the book's pages and found drawings and diagrams of the house.

It started to come back to him.

According to the book, the house had been built in the fifteenth century by one of Hugh's Baxter ancestors. The first Duchess of Swynford was primarily responsible for a large renovation in the 1670s that reinforced and expanded the house. Dukes of Swynford throughout the eighteenth century had renovated and modernized the house. Then there were a series of notes in Hugh's own hand indicating that, in the time since his father's death, Hugh had been working on his own improvements.

He closed his eyes and tried to remember the house. A lot of it was still hidden behind the curtain, but then he had a sudden memory of approaching the house in a carriage and was overwhelmed by the feeling of coming home. He could see now the long row of manicured shrubbery on the path to the front door, the house's blond brick facade, the columns that framed the door. The house itself was four stories tall and quite imposing as one approached it.

He looked at a diagram of the floor plan. The house had an H shape, which made Hugh recall referring to the vertical parts of the H as the east and west wings.

According to the floor plans, there was a grand suite of rooms on the third floor that included bedrooms for the master and mistress of the house, connected by his and hers dressing rooms and a grand tiled room with a bathtub. A separate room for bathing had been one of Hugh's own improvements the previous year, according to the notes in his handwriting, intended to keep mold from getting into the floor. There was a nursery on that floor as well; some previous Duchess of Swynford had wanted to care for her children rather than just handing them off to nannies and governesses, so the nursery was close to the duke's quarters.

Hugh's mother had been that way; he'd had a nanny and a governess and a tutor who taught him basic business, but spent most of his time before leaving for Eton with his mother. Portraits of her as a younger woman had brought those memories back to him. She'd doted on him, spoken with him often, and snuck him sweets when his father wasn't looking. It was why he felt so guilty for defying her now; he knew she loved him. She never said the words, but he knew it somewhere deep in his soul. But her insistence on the integrity of the Swynford name over all other things was... well, maybe something else was going on here, now that he thought about it.

He made a mental note to follow up on that later.

He was still looking at diagrams and floor plans when he heard a small sound behind him. He turned and saw Adele standing in the doorway to the library, wearing only a flimsy dressing gown over her nightgown.

"I didn't expect anyone to be here," she said.

"I couldn't sleep."

"Nor could I. I thought to come to the library and find something to read. Daisy mentioned that the duchess has been collecting Sir Walter Scott's novels, so I thought to try one of those."

"I had a similar thought and then fell into reading the Swynford House records. I'm trying to remember the house, but there are parts of it I cannot picture in my mind."

"Have you spent much time there?"

"Yes, I believe so. Most of my childhood. According to the book, I made a number of improvements just last year and bought some new furniture as well. But I can't picture a single piece of that furniture. It's all still hidden behind the veil of my broken memory."

"We'll see it soon enough, won't we?"

"Yes. It is my intention to return to Swynford House shortly after the wedding. We'll be more comfortable there when the weather turns warm. And, given that my assailant is still at large, it may be smart to get out of London. I just wish I could picture my home."

"Are you still worried about being attacked again?"

"I just wish I knew what happened. Until I know, I can't shake the feeling that danger still lurks about."

"You've got a guard outside."

"And he may be successfully deterring whoever means me harm. Getting out of London would, I think, ease my mind."

Adele held up a candle and walked along the row of books opposite where Hugh sat at the table. The way she held the candle allowed him to see the outline of her body through her flimsy nightclothes. He tried not to stare.

As if she sensed what was happening in his body, she asked. "Why could you not sleep? Are you worried about danger?"

He sighed, but then smiled at her. "Well, no, actually. If you must know, a beautiful woman sleeping so close to my room was a distraction."

She nodded. "I will admit, I suffered from something of the same affliction. I can't help but remember that night that we… but then I think about how I would feel if your mother caught us. She already detests me."

"She does not detest you."

"Well, she is not fond of me, and I do not want to give her more reasons not to like me."

Hugh closed the book and stood up. He replaced it on the shelf and turned to look at Adele. The room was dim, the only light coming from the candles they'd each brought with them. Adele set hers on the mantle over the fireplace, as if she knew she was about to need both hands.

Hugh went to her. She was hard to see in the low light, but the way the thin fabric of her nightgown skimmed right over her skin was tantalizing. She wore no corset now, no drawers or petticoats or other undergarments. Hugh himself wore only an old dressing gown. Very little separated them, something that became immediately apparent when he kissed her and she pressed her chest against his.

He wanted her. He wanted to rip off the flimsy nightgown and have her right on this table. The lust he'd been banking since she'd moved into his house was suddenly begging to be let loose.

She pressed her hands to his chest and pushed him away slightly. "Can you wait until our wedding night?"

"No."

He moved to kiss her again, but she stopped him. "I was not jesting. What happens if your mother catches us, well, *in flagrante*."

"We're about to be married, Adele. What does it matter?"

"It matters, Hugh. We are not husband and wife yet."

With a sigh, Hugh stepped back. "Fine, fine. Mother sleeps like the dead, by the way, and her room is at the far end of the hall."

"You have less than two weeks to wait. Is that really so difficult?"

"Yes."

She laughed. "Well, we definitely cannot… take liberties in the library. Someone will hear us."

Hugh sighed. She was, of course, right, but that didn't stop him from putting his hands on her waist and dipping his head to kiss her shoulder. "But on our wedding night, I can take liberties?"

She picked up his face and met his gaze. She actually smirked at him, a seductive look in her eyes. "You can take all the liberties you want then."

He laughed. "I adore you, you know."

"And I you. But we must behave ourselves for, what, nine more days?"

"If I make it that long."

"You have untold stores of strength, Your Grace. I have faith in you."

She patted his shoulder, grabbed a book from the shelf, and went back down the hall. He watched the sway of her hips as she walked and realized that neither had resolved the issue that was keeping them awake.

Well, he'd respect her wishes. But she'd as much as told him that she wanted him as much as he wanted her, and he had some doubts about her ability to hold out until after the wedding. But he was not an animal; he could bide his time. She'd either succumb to her own lust and spend a night with him again, or their wedding night would be all the sweeter.

HUGH WALKED INTO the club with a smile like the cat who got the cream. Lark found it unsettling.

"I cannot stay long," Hugh said as he sat in the chair across from Lark. "I worry about what may happen if Adele and my mother spend too much time together. But I wanted your opinion."

Lark narrowed his eyes. "Why *my* opinion?"

"Well, not yours specifically. You fellows. But Fletcher and Owen are not here. Are they?"

"No. Both had other engagements this evening."

"Are you drinking alone?"

Lark looked at the snifter in his hand. He knew he could trust the old Hugh, but he still wasn't completely sure what Hugh knew and didn't know, and if this new Hugh would accept things or not. Still, he said, "Well, if you must know, I'm meeting

Beresford. Time is a bit of a loose concept for him, however, and he is running quite late."

Hugh stared at him for a long moment. "You and Beresford are lovers, aren't you?"

Lark looked down. "Yes," he said quietly.

"It's all right, you know. I don't have those inclinations myself, but I know sometimes men prefer their own sex."

Hugh sounded sincere, so Lark looked up and said, "I prefer everyone. Although right now, I prefer Beresford."

"How long?"

"Oh, here and there for a few years, more regularly the last two months or so."

Hugh nodded. "I thought you didn't like him."

"Me too. He grew on me." Lark rubbed his head. "What did you want my opinion on?"

"Oh." Hugh reached into his coat pocket and withdrew a large jewelry box. "I bought this for Adele. Do you think it's too much?"

"How should I know?" But Lark waited while Hugh opened the box. "Wow."

Hugh revealed a necklace with a huge emerald surrounded by diamonds. The necklace was gorgeous. Breathtaking. Lark struggled to picture it on the neck of someone as austere as Adele. "It's lovely."

"You think so?"

"A necklace befitting a duchess. Adele will think it too much."

Hugh frowned. "I know. I could not resist it, though. I've never seen anything like it. When I saw it in the case I could picture exactly how it would look at Adele's throat. I thought she could wear it to the wedding."

"I do not know much about women's fashion, but this is a very nice emerald. What if she wears a color not suited to emeralds to the wedding?"

"Then she can wear it to a ball or something. I don't know anything about women's fashion, either. I just thought it would look pretty on Adele. Or, hell, she could wear only the emerald and I would be happy."

Lark laughed. "Well, of course."

Hugh closed the box. "She's going to hate it."

"No, I don't think anyone could hate a necklace like that. But wearing it will make her self-conscious. You've agreed to marry not only a wallflower, but one who blends right in with the wall."

Hugh shook her head. "No, that's ridiculous. She's beautiful."

"I know, but she hides her beauty in order to fade into a crowd. She is not interested in being the sort of woman whose beauty everyone admires. I don't think she will be comfortable with the sort of attention a duchess commands."

"On the other hand, she spent a fair bit of my money at the modiste. Although, based on how Adele described the visit, my guess is that once the modiste discovered she could bill me, she was deceptive about the costs of things with Adele. I can't see her spending that much money knowingly."

"Are you angry about it?"

"Not at all. I gave the modiste permission to bill me for anything Adele wanted. I don't anticipate her causing me any financial hardships. You're right, Adele is not extravagant, and I can afford it anyway."

"Speaking of people with financial hardships, I ran into your cousin the other day."

Hugh frowned at that. "My cousin?"

"Collingswood. He's still in town."

Hugh made the face he made when he couldn't remember something. "And he has financial troubles?"

"His property in Jamaica has experienced some hardships." Lark watched Hugh for any reaction, but Hugh still seemed lost.

"He has not asked me for money," said Hugh.

"No, he is too proud for that." Lark frowned. "The thing is, Collingswood is your closest relative and he stands to inherit your title, which is unlikely to happen now that you've married. I don't know him well enough to say if that matters to him. Maybe it doesn't. In the meantime, I've received word that Collingswood thought he'd be inheriting some tract of land but lost out on it, then he tried to buy a piece of land in Surrey but was outbid for it, so he has thus far been unsuccessful at buying land in England."

"That is curious."

"In what way? Collingswood's desire to own more property is well known."

"I don't know what to make of it, honestly. But I have the sense there's something I don't remember here. A connection I can't make because some things are still lost to me. Do I like Collingswood?"

"You are not close. Your feelings toward him have always seemed… ambivalent."

"Hmm. Are he and I… that is, do we compete? Is there ill will?"

"If there is, you have never spoken to me about it, but it wouldn't hurt to take a look at your land holdings to see which of them Collingswood might have tried to make a play for."

"That is a good idea. I will discuss it with my man of business."

"Please do. I can't say anything for certain, but I have a nagging feeling about him. Still, perhaps it is of no consequence and I am biased because I personally find Collingswood somewhat repellant. Did you invite him to your wedding?"

"Mother took care of the invitations, but I imagine she would have. He is my cousin, after all, and a Baxter, and Mother has been lecturing me about Baxters and Swynfords and reputations all week. I believe her intention of explaining that my ancestor Such-and-So Baxter fought with Henry V at Agincourt is to somehow impress me into seeing that Adele is unworthy. Luckily she does this only when Adele is not around, but I think Mother will not cease with this until the wedding is over and done."

Lark nodded. "She'll come around. She needs to see with her own eyes that nobody cares. If Adele is pretty and charming in public, she'll do just fine."

"Are you sure nobody cares?"

Lark crossed his arms. "I have given this some thought. I think we're in the midst of a quiet social revolution, actually."

"What do you mean?"

"I think it is the fate of daughters and sons to feel dissatisfied with the lives of their parents. What year were yours married?"

"I have no idea."

"Your memory is still faulty, so I will forgive you that. Mine were married in 1778. Think about all that has happened since then. We lost the American colonies. We went to war in Europe. The king went mad. We defeated Napoleon. Not only that, but women want different things now. Did you read Wollstonecraft? Well, if you did, you won't remember, but she argued that women should have equal rights. I think we can see a future where what we do in the privacy of our homes stops mattering."

Hugh sat back in his chair and raised his eyebrows, so Lark decided to plow forward with his speech.

"Can you imagine men and women having the right to choose whom they go to bed with? You could marry whomever you wanted to without fear of being cast out by your family or by society. You could decide not to marry if you don't want to, or decide not to have children."

"You could marry for love."

"Yes. And I appreciate that you are doing just that. I fear I will not have that luxury."

Hugh nodded and was silent for a long moment. "Do you love Beresford?"

Did he? Lark was fond of Anthony and he was surprised by the depths of Beresford's character, but love? "I do not know."

"Beresford himself said you'd have a moment where you'd just know. I haven't had a moment like that with Adele, but I can see where what we have may grow to that. In some ways, I feel like we barely know each other. And yet I cannot imagine marrying anyone else."

"That is a luxury. It's not like I can marry Beresford. And you, by the way, are giving my parents ideas. Isn't it time *I* settled down, my mother keeps asking. In truth, I do not wish to marry at all. I can bequeath the title on my nephew, perhaps."

"It is of no consequence to me, as long as you are happy."

"Yes, and I think that is at the crux of our lives right now. You and I are both wealthy men. We can afford to be happy, or we should be able to. Why shouldn't you marry your Adele? Why does it matter what anyone thinks of it?"

"Is that how you think people will view it? You seemed pretty dead set against our marriage just a couple of weeks ago."

Lark shrugged. "Perhaps I have grown. And anyway, scandal is fleeting. At the end of the day, you're marrying an earl's daughter, and there's not much objectionable about that when you take the public regard of Canbury out of the mix. Maybe a few people will object, but they'll forget in a week when the next scandal occurs."

"So why were you and Owen and Fletcher working so hard to talk me out of it?"

Lark sighed. Why had he? He liked Adele. It was clear Hugh cared for her. "I can't speak for Owen or Fletcher, but the old Hugh had not been ready for marriage, so I merely wanted to make sure you were not rushing into something you would regret later. And I do like Adele. I've never met a woman with a more practical head on her shoulders. The fact that you are buying emeralds for a woman who I am certain would find emeralds too ostentatious is just evidence that you are confident in your decision, and so I will support it."

"Thank you, I think." Hugh tilted his head. "I appreciate your support."

Lark laughed. "Yes, well. You'd better go home to her now before your mother does her in. Here comes Beresford anyway."

Hugh turned around in time to see Anthony heading their way. Today, Beresford looked like Beau Brummel had dressed him in the very height of dandy attire, in an ornate jacket with gold trim, the correct shade of yellow on his waistcoat, and his long hair was tied away from his face in queue at the base of his neck. He grinned when he and Lark made eye contact.

"Hello, Your Grace," Anthony said to Hugh.

"He was just leaving," said Lark.

"What have you got there?" Anthony asked, pointing to the jewelry box in Hugh's hand.

Hugh opened the box and showed it to Anthony. Anthony gasped. "That is gorgeous. I take it you bought it for your future wife and not this oaf." He gestured toward Lark.

"Yes. A wedding gift for Lady Adele."

"Beautiful. The color of that emerald is something else. It will look lovely on her."

"Tell me, Beresford," said Lark. "You have your finger on the pulse of gossip among our peers. Has anyone said anything about Swynford's impending nuptials?"

"No, not really. Well, a lot of surprise, but no one seems especially bothered that Lady Adele is Canbury's daughter, not the extent you all seemed to fear at any rate. Mostly they're not over the shock that Swynford finally picked someone, and basically the last woman they expected. And Eugenia Sackville is spitting mad, but that seems poetic justice."

"Fair enough," said Hugh. He stood. "This will all be fine, right?"

Beresford smiled. "I do believe that everything will work out as it should."

Chapter Twenty-Two

A DELE WAS STILL not in her gown when there was a rap at the door.

"Daisy, will you see to that?" she asked her maid.

Adele was beginning to feel anxious because everything was taking a long time to accomplish, but all she wanted to do was get to the church and Hugh so that they could have this wedding over with. Standing in front of a church with a hundred eyes on her sounded like her idea of hell, and although she very much wanted to be married to Hugh, she now regretted asking for this big wedding.

Not to mention, the mere process of getting into her wedding gown was being done in the slowest, most painstaking way possible.

Daisy opened the door, and when she saw who it was, said, "You may not come in, Your Grace. Lady Adele is dressing for the wedding. It is bad luck to see her now."

So it was Hugh. Adele wanted to see him but looked down at her half-dressed body and thought better of it. She slid a little deeper into the room so that she would not be in Hugh's line of sight through the half-open door.

She heard him sigh. "Very well. This is a gift for her. I leave it up to her if she wants to wear it or not, but please give it to her now."

"Of course, Your Grace. She will see you at the church shortly."

"Yes. Thank you."

She heard his footsteps retreating down the hall and Daisy close the door. Daisy brought Adele a large jewelry box, which Adele opened immediately.

She gasped. Inside was the most beautiful emerald necklace she had ever seen. "This must have cost him a fortune," Adele said. Daisy was the only one in the room, but Adele had said it to herself as much as anyone. "I cannot possibly wear this."

"It will look lovely with the yellow gown, my lady."

"Do you think I should wear it?"

"I think it was a valuable gift from the man about to be your husband. Wearing it would honor him."

"It is so much. I've never worn anything like this."

Daisy took the necklace from Adele, removed it from its box, and then draped it around Adele's neck. "This will look lovely."

"But—"

"You are about to be a duchess, my lady. You should look like a duchess."

"So people keep saying."

Daisy told Adele to sit in front of the vanity and carefully combed her hair. After she pinned Adele's hair up with soft tendrils to frame her face, she picked the necklace back up and fastened it around Adele's neck. Adele gazed at her reflection in the mirror and admired it, thinking she did look quite like a duchess.

There was another knock at the door. "What now?" asked Adele with a sigh.

Daisy went to the door, and this time it was the dowager, whom Daisy let in. Adele and the dowager had made some sort of peace in the last few days, although Adele did not much trust her. Helena seemed more resigned to Adele's presence than accepting.

"I want to give you something," said Helena, holding up a small box. "My, that is a breathtaking emerald."

"A gift from your son," Adele said.

Helena nodded. "Indeed. He has always had good taste. Anyway, I wanted you to have something. This has been passed down through a few generations of Duchesses of Swynford. I last wore it to Princess Charlotte's wedding."

Adele took the box and took a deep breath. Inside was a tiara affixed with diamonds. "This is lovely," Adele said. "But I could not possibly—"

"You shall. It is tradition. Daisy, let us help Lady Adele into her gown so that she might see the complete picture."

And so Adele stood in the center of the room in only her many layers of undergarments as Helena Baxter, the Dowager Duchess of Swynford, and Daisy, the lady's maid Adele had hired two weeks before, lifted the gown Madame Auguste had made for her and slid it over head. Then they both insisted Adele sit carefully back down so as not to wrinkle her dress, because Adele was so tall. They carefully worked together to place the tiara on Adele's head and pin it in place. Daisy handed Adele a pair of white lace gloves, so Adele pulled those on, too.

She almost did not recognize herself in the mirror. In her mind, she was Adele Paulson, a spinster and paid companion, a plain girl with few expectations, but the woman looking back was the future Duchess of Swynford.

Daisy helped Adele stand back up. Helena gave Adele a long appraising look. "Yes. You look lovely, my dear. Appropriate."

"Like a duchess?" Adele asked.

"Yes. I thought your appearance would be vastly improved once we got you out of those dull muslin dresses and gave your hair a less severe style. Daisy shall style your hair every morning from now on. Oh, one more thing." Helena walked over to the table and picked up the diamond earbobs Adele had left there. She helped Adele put those on, too. "Perfect."

Adele sighed. "Your Grace, I do hope we can grow to respect and even be fond of each other. It was never my intention—"

"Yes, I realize." The duchess gave Adele a furtive smile. "You are not one of the money-grubbing society chits who has had her eyes on my son. I have seen your reluctance in these last two weeks. I do believe that you and Hugh are marrying because you are fond of each other. And I know I have not been terribly supportive. I'm sure you understand why."

"Yes," said Adele, because she did.

"I only want what is best for my son. You will understand one day when you have children of your own. But Hugh is determined to see this marriage through, so I will see it through, and I will accept you as a member of our family."

"But?"

Helena sighed. "I would like to get to know you. You seem to be a good woman, and Hugh keeps reminding me that you are not your father, whom I have made no secret of not caring for. This is the way of things, I suppose. My friends keep telling me the youth of today have different notions of propriety than we did in our day."

"If it makes you feel better," said Adele, glancing at her reflection again, "I am dreading the wedding itself. I think I will feel much happier when it is over and I do not have to be paraded in front of society like… like a pet peacock."

Helena laughed. "Well, we still live in England, my dear. There may yet be some parading. That is the nature of marrying into a family like Hugh's. I was not completely comfortable with it at first, either, but I adjusted."

Adele glanced back at the mirror. She felt so unlike herself. Oh, she felt beautiful and she imagined Hugh would agree, but the trappings of being a duchess were not at all familiar to her. She could only hope that she was not making a grave error.

HUGH SUPPOSED EVERY groom knew a moment of doubt as he stood at the front of the church, wondering when, or if, his bride would appear. Even knowing she'd been dressing for this very event when he passed her the emerald had not assuaged the fear that had plagued him the whole carriage ride to the church.

It was his mother's off-hand comment as he'd been leaving. She'd mentioned she'd had a talk with Adele, which had brought a startling cold fear to Hugh. "What did you tell her?"

"I gave her the Waterdown Tiara and told her that since she is about to be duchess she should look the part. She is uneasy with the role, I think."

Hugh had suspected as much. It hadn't seemed to sink in until the last few days that Adele would be not just any wife, but a duchess, one married to a powerful, wealthy man. And although she kept telling him not to spend money on her, he had anyway, and he saw how it made her uncomfortable. He appreciated that. But now he wondered if she might be so uncomfortable that she'd decide they should not be married after all.

But then she appeared at the back of the church like an angelic vision. Her gown was such a pale yellow that it looked almost white underneath the lights of the church. It made her skin look pink and creamy. And there was the emerald at her throat, and it brought out the color of her eyes. And there was his mother's most precious Waterdown Tiara, an object that had belonged to Duchesses of Swynford for more than a hundred years. It all looked like it belonged to Adele, that she would be the most stunning of all the duchesses past and present, and she was about to marry Hugh.

When she arrived at the front of the church, she smiled at him and Hugh's heart stopped.

He hardly heard the words of the priest. He spoke when prompted to do so, but otherwise, he concentrated on his lovely bride. Her eyes were blue like the sea and her hair was bright like sunshine and poets should really be writing sonnets about her attributes because there had never been a more beautiful woman. And she was clever and kind and all that Hugh had wanted.

It was then that he had his moment. It hit him quite suddenly, somewhere in the middle of the recitation of vows, that he loved this woman.

He *loved* her.

He felt giddy with this knowledge, happy beyond anything he could have anticipated, and he could not wait to tell her, although bursting out with it right at this moment seemed inappropriate.

When prompted to do so, Hugh kissed Adele, probably a little more forcefully than was appropriate in church, but he didn't care.

The priest declared them man and wife. Hugh wanted to jump with glee.

He held out his arm to escort Adele back down the aisle. She smiled as she took it. It was only now that Hugh allowed himself to see who had attended. His mother, of course, and Lord Canbury. A few women Hugh did not recognize, likely friends of Adele's. Lark, Owen, and Fletcher sat together. All of the Baxter cousins who lived within half a day's ride of London, including Collingswood.

As he made these observations, Adele seemed to be yanking him down the aisle.

"There is no rush now, my love," he said. "We are married."

"I know, but I wish to leave before—oh."

The church doors opened and a massive crowd had gathered outside. Hugh knew immediately that they were here to see the new Duchess of Swynford, and he also knew that this was the last thing Adele would have wanted. The way between the door and his coach was blocked by a great number of people.

Hugh looked around. Ventnor, Hugh's valet, and a number of footmen in Swynford livery were standing behind him. He leaned over and told Ventnor to ask the footmen to create a path.

Thus it took several minutes to get Adele from the door of the church to the coach. And it was only once they were inside that Adele seemed to breathe.

"We've done it now, Adele. We just promised to love, honor, and obey each other for the rest of our days in front of God and our friends and families."

She laughed softly. "I hope the worst part is over."

"You know, normal brides call this the happiest day of their lives. They love the gowns and the jewels and being the center of attention."

"I am clearly not a normal bride."

"No. You are far better." Hugh leaned over and kissed her.

She smiled at him when he pulled back away.

"Have I told you how beautiful you look today?"

"No, Your Grace, we have hardly spoken today. Thank you for the emerald, by the way."

"Seeing you wear it is all the thanks I need."

"It was far too generous a gift."

"You know, for a moment before you walked down the aisle, I worried you might have been spooked by my mother and would not come today."

"Well, I was a bit spooked, but I wanted to marry you more."

Hugh smiled at that. He opened his mouth to tell her he loved her, but he heard a noise outside. He looked out the window and saw that the street outside was lined with well-wishers. "So many people," he murmured.

"I quite regret rejecting your suggestion that we elope."

Hugh laughed. "You do understand that these well-wishers have good intentions. They want to celebrate the new Duchess of Swynford. Since so few of the king's daughters seem inclined to marry, this is the closest to a royal wedding these people may ever witness. And I am related to the king, you know. My mother has reminded me of this several times this week. So we are practically royalty."

Adele looked a little green.

Hugh took her hand. "It will be all right. We will remain in London only as long as necessary and then leave for Swynford House, hopefully without my mother in tow, and we shall have quiet and privacy there. I think I should greatly enjoy quiet and privacy with you."

Adele sighed. "Yes. I think so, too."

Chapter Twenty-Three

THE WEDDING BREAKFAST and subsequent party had been a lot. Adele had felt obligated to entertain her guests. Then, finally, mercifully, as the sun sank in the sky, Hugh walked over and told her he sensed she was tired, and really the only thing keeping all these people in the house was the happy couple's presence in the Swynford ballroom. He invited her to retire while he kicked everyone out of the house.

Now that she was up in Hugh's bedroom—their bedroom, she reminded herself—and Daisy was taking the pins out of her hair, Adele was nervous. Would Hugh be upset she'd wanted to end the party early? More than that, it was now their wedding night. In a way, she was glad they'd spent a night together already because she knew what to expect. But something about this being their wedding night made it more important.

She'd been given a gift. She didn't care about the title or the relation to the king or the fancy house. What she cared about was that she'd married a good man and soon they might have a child. She'd been telling herself for the last couple of years that a child wasn't something she would ever have, and she'd made her peace with that, but from the moment Hugh had proposed, she'd been thinking about it. Her main duty as a duchess was to give Hugh an heir, and in all honesty, she wanted that more than anything in the world. Hugh had taken her life in an entirely new direction, and though she wasn't too keen on the title and all that, now she could have the family she'd always longed for.

Daisy helped Adele out of her gown and into a loose night-gown and a pale-pink dressing gown that had been a gift from Hugh a few days before. She dismissed Daisy and moved to lie on the bed.

She looked around the room. It was well-kept and masculine. The large canopy bed had a green damask bedspread that matched the fabric hanging from the posts above. In a way, the bed felt a bit like its own little world, like they could undo the ties on the fabric curtains and hide in here, away from everyone else in the house, everyone else in London. After a day of smiling at near strangers, it was something that had a certain appeal.

She closed her eyes, relaxing. Then her stomach growled.

Had she eaten at the party thrown in her favor? There'd certainly been a lot of food there, but Adele couldn't say that much had made it into her body.

Hugh walked in then, and he had a tray in his hand.

"Hello, my love," he said. "Sorry that took so long. A few of our guests were pretty deep in their cups. Also, I don't know how you feel, but I'm famished. I hardly ate a thing. So I've commandeered some of the leftovers from the party."

"Bless you," she said, pushing herself into the sitting position so she could see what he'd brought.

He placed the tray on a table near the bed, then sat beside her. He smiled. "Do you feel completely overwhelmed?"

"Not *completely*."

Hugh chuckled. Then his expression became more serious. He touched the ends of her hair. "I love your hair loose around your shoulders like this. You never wear it this way."

"I always just wanted my hair out of my face. I didn't much care for fashionable styles. My lady's maid has been playing around with doing my hair in different ways, so I will look like some of the other gentlewomen of London. And I suppose if I keep shopping at Madame Auguste's, I shall compete with them."

Hugh smiled. "You are so beautiful, Adele. You could set

your own fashions if you wanted."

Adele felt heat flood her face and looked down. "I am plain."

"No. When I saw you coming down the aisle today, I thought that there has never been a more beautiful woman."

"That is because I had on an expensive gown and the emeralds you gave me and Daisy did my hair."

"No. I thought you were beautiful from the first moment we met. When I woke up in the Sweeneys' house and didn't know who I was, I thought it might be all right because you were taking care of me."

"Beauty and ability to care for someone have no relation to each other. I could have been a monster." Adele smiled.

"You aren't, though." Hugh ran his hands through Adele's hair. "You know what else I realized today?"

"What?"

"That I am completely, irrevocably in love with you. I saw you walking down that aisle and I just knew."

Adele's heart felt like someone had reached into her chest and squeezed. "Oh, Hugh…"

"You don't need to say it back right now. I just wanted you to know that in these last weeks, you've come to mean a lot to me. I truly treasure you. I didn't even know how much until today."

Adele stared at Hugh in disbelief. She'd been so focused all day on just getting through the day that she hadn't stopped to look at him. He was still dressed from the wedding in a black formal coat and breeches, with a crisp white cravat at his neck, a white shirt, and a white waistcoat. He'd combed his brown hair forward, as was fashionable, and his blue eyes sparkled as he gazed at her. He looked exceedingly handsome. Why hadn't she taken the time to notice that today? In his formal clothes, he looked very much like the powerful, wealthy duke he was, but the expression on his face was earnest and… vulnerable.

He did love her. She'd wondered in the last few weeks. His reasons for marrying her had seemed at times like a way to help her out of a bad situation, but he'd repeated over and over that he wanted to marry her, that he couldn't imagine spending his life with anyone else, and Adele had taken that to heart. She'd thought they might grow to love each other in time, as many couples did. She hadn't expected him to make a declaration like that on their wedding night.

Did she love him? Yes, she did. She smiled and touched his hair, running her hand through its short strands. She couldn't seem to make her voice work, though.

Hugh leaned forward and kissed her.

She'd had enough friends who had been married who had feared their wedding nights. Who'd been told by their mothers that "marital relations" were something to be endured, not enjoyed. But Adele had the advantage of knowledge. She'd already spent a blissful night with Hugh, who'd told her even then to never feel shame about herself or her body. So she knew this would be good, and as Hugh licked into her mouth, she felt heat spreading through her body.

She pulled Hugh back so that he was laying on top of her on the bed. She put her arms around him and kissed him.

He loved her. He'd proclaimed it plain as day. A thrill went through her.

Had she ever been this happy? She didn't think so.

She reached for the lapels of Hugh's jacket, and a thought occurred to her. "Will your valet be coming to help you undress?"

"No, I gave him the night off. Told him I could manage to take off my own clothes. I'm sure he will give me an earful tomorrow about proper care of my clothing, but I don't care right now. My hands don't seem to want to leave your body." Indeed, Hugh had one hand on her hip and another near her shoulder.

"They may need to, but just for a brief moment."

Adele pushed his jacket off his shoulders then started undoing the buttons on his shirt. He sat up, straddling her hips, and helped her with the rest. He tossed his cravat aside and she watched it flutter to the floor as she laughed. Ventnor definitely would have something to say about how Hugh dealt with his clothing.

Hugh took off his jacket, waistcoat, and shirt and threw them at a nearby chair. The shirt missed and landed on the floor, but Hugh waved his hand dismissively.

Adele ran her hands up Hugh's chest and met his gaze. "Is this all right?"

"Yes. Please touch me. Touch as much as you want. I am yours to do with as you will."

Adele felt powerful suddenly. She shimmied out from under Hugh and moved to take off her dressing gown. Hugh reached over and helped her.

"This was an excellent purchase," Hugh said. "I love how the silk lays on your body. Doesn't leave much to the imagination. But now I mean to toss it aside."

Adele felt heat come to her face, but she felt gratified, too. Hugh thought she was beautiful, found her attractive, and as was plain from the front of his breeches, he wanted her badly. Adele hadn't known she could have such power. As Hugh slipped her nightgown from her shoulders, she watched his face. The astonishment in his eyes as he revealed her breasts was like that of a child opening a Christmas present. She would have laughed if she hadn't felt so aroused.

She felt brave and bold with him.

"You're so beautiful," Hugh said. "And no one will ever know how beautiful you are because only I get to see you this way."

Adele kissed him and reached for his breeches. She worked at the buttons there but found her fingers suddenly tangled and ineffective. He broke the kiss long enough to help her.

Minutes later, they were both naked and tangled with each other on the bed. "Recall what I told you about no shame, my lady. Be open and expressive. If you want me to do something tell me. If you want me to stop, tell me. But, God, love me. Love me with this beautiful body of yours."

"Yes," said Adele. "Touch me everywhere. I am yours, too."

Hugh lifted his head and grinned at her before he dropped again and took one of her nipples into his mouth.

Adele found it hard to look at him without feeling like she might explode, but she moaned and thrust her fingers into his hair. She was surprised when he tailed kisses down her belly and then settled in between her legs.

She thought at first, *No, he wouldn't... why would he?*

But then he did. He licked her between her legs and moaned like he was eating the most delicious feast. And... it felt amazing. His tongue was rough against her, but he applied a kind of pressure that made her squirm. Then it brushed right over—

"Oh," she said.

He lifted his head. "Oh?"

"I didn't know it would feel that way. But it...it was...do it again."

He chuckled softly and bent to kiss her between her legs again. His tongue pressed against a spot that felt raw and exposed but also like it was the place his tongue belonged. Suddenly her body bowed off the bed and she felt like she was hurtling toward something.

"More..." she said, writhing against his mouth.

He touched her then, sliding fingers inside her, filling her, making her feel everything. She threw her head back and surrendered to it.

She slowly floated back into her body as Hugh crawled back up to lay beside her. He kissed her hard and she could taste herself on him, but was not put off by it at all. She put her arms around his shoulders and realized that he was hard against her leg.

She put her hands on either side of his face and lifted his head so that she could look directly into his eyes. He looked at her with such affection she was nearly undone by it. She could feel him in her chest, in her soul, and she knew that she did indeed love him.

"I love you," she said softly.

He smiled. "I can't tell you how happy that makes me. Tell me again."

"I love you."

"I love you, too."

"Hugh, I must ask something of you."

"Anything, my love. I would give you anything."

"I want you to… spend inside me. I want for us to… that is… I want a baby, Hugh. I've wanted a child for so long. And now that we're married, I can have one. Is that… all right?"

WAS IT ALL right? Of course it was; the sole purpose of today's ceremony was so that any children they had would be legitimate heirs.

But then he understood what she was really asking him. That they would have children was a given, considering that the main purpose of dukes and duchesses was to make more dukes and duchesses.

But she wanted to be a mother. She'd likely been thinking about having children since the opportunity had been denied her when her fiancé had died. She wanted to care for their children, to love them, and she was asking him if he would do the same.

He hadn't given it much thought. He liked children, in theory, although he hadn't spent much time around them.

And what Adele was asking him now was to have a child because they wanted one, not because they felt an obligation.

What would that be like? He could almost picture a baby rocking in a cradle near their bed. He could picture a little boy running around Adele's feet while she laughed at his antics. He could picture her holding their child if he scraped his knees or had a bad dream.

Yes. He wanted that. He wanted all of it. He wouldn't be distant the way his own father had been. He would love his wife, worship her forever, and love their children. It was almost like he could see his whole life before him then, and it was perfect. How had he gotten so fortunate?

He placed a hand on her belly and imagined how her body might change, what she might look like when she was swelling with their child.

He kissed her.

"That is all right," he said softly. "I want that."

She smiled. "Good." She parted her legs.

She was still pliant, still a little boneless from her orgasm, but she put her arms around him and hugged him close. He kissed her, feeling overwhelmed with love all over again. He took her into his arms as the press of her skin against his brought back his arousal. He touched her breasts, her waist, her hips, and kissed her body wherever he could reach her.

"I want you inside me," she whispered in his ear.

He didn't need any more invitation than that. He rested his hips between her legs and kissed her again. Then he guided himself forward and slid inside her slowly. She gasped then clung onto him as if willing him to push forward harder.

She was hot and slick and tight and perfect, and he moved in her as he tried to show her how much he loved her, because his body was too overwhelmed to speak. She gasped and moaned beneath him and kissed his chin, his cheeks, his lips. As a lover, she was still a little unsure and tentative, but she would be a quick study and they'd have the rest of their lives to do this again and learn new things from each other.

It didn't take long for the cliff to rush toward him. He pressed his thumb against the little button between her legs and rubbed in a way he'd already learned would make her fly apart, and she rewarded him by arching her back as her eyes rolled back into her head in ecstasy.

He was not far behind her. He held her close and thrust forward one last time before spilling inside her.

They kissed long and languorously afterward, lazily tasting each other. Adele looked like she might drift off to sleep, but then her stomach grumbled.

"Oh, all that food you brought up must be cold now."

He laughed. "I'm sure it's still good. Shall we eat?"

"Yes, please."

They fed each other bits of the feast on the tray, including a roast goose, some sliced beef, a deliciously tart cheese, boiled potatoes, and a variety of other food that was suddenly the second most delicious thing he'd ever tasted—after Adele. She made a face any time he fed her anything, as if she agreed.

When they'd finished and then done an admirable job of licking any wayward food from each other, Adele lay back on the pillows, still completely naked under the bright light of his bedside lamp, and smiled at him.

"I know you don't love attention," Hugh said, "but I hope today was not too much of an ordeal for you."

"It was worth it."

"Was it?"

"Yes. If all of our nights are like this one, then I think we shall have a very happy life together."

He couldn't help but smile back. "I agree, although I suspect not everything will be smooth sailing." He stood and carried the tray over near the door. Then he lifted the covers on the bed and motioned for Adele to get under them. He slid into the bed beside her. "You seem to be winning my mother over, at least."

"She was very kind to me at the wedding breakfast."

"That's good. I just mean, well, there are financial and legal matters and things that I'm sure will distract me in the coming weeks and I—"

Adele pressed a finger to his lips. "We do not need to discuss them now, do we?"

"No. Although also, one thing in the back of my mind, we still do not know who hit me over the head."

That snagged her attention. Her eyes snapped open. "Do you think he will try again?"

"I have no earthly idea, but it's something I've worried about since coming home. The guard is that fellow in the brown coat usually skulking about in the side yard."

"Oh. Indeed? That is a relief, I must say."

"My point is, I believe we are safe here. It's just a concern I have."

"Well, if we are safe here, then let's forget all about it tonight." Adele yawned. "I am quite tired."

"Sleep, my love. We can talk more tomorrow."

"I don't have to sneak out or anything, do I? I belong in this bed with you now that I am your wife."

He smiled at her. "Yes. And I quite like the sound of that. My wife."

"My husband."

He kissed her and pulled her into his arms. She rested her head on his chest.

"Sleep, my Adele."

Chapter Twenty-Four

THREE DAYS AFTER the wedding, Hugh walked into the mistress's bedroom, where Adele was at work packing her new gowns into trunks for transport to Swynford House.

"You can ask a servant to pack everything for you, you know," said Hugh.

"I know. I prefer to pack everything myself."

"Actually, you might as well *un*pack. I have just found out I may be detained in London longer than expected."

"What?" She turned to face him.

"A legal matter has come up. I must stay in London until it is resolved."

"What legal matter?"

Hugh shook his head as if to say it was nothing Adele needed to worry her pretty little head about, and something about that hit her the wrong way. "Hugh, I need not know the particulars, but you must know by now that I am not the sort of docile wife who just nods and smiles when you speak. I should like to know what detains us in London past our planned departure date." Adele looked at the shawl she held in her hand. She'd been in the process of folding it when Hugh had walked in. She tossed it on the bed in disgust now.

He sighed. "You are right. I apologize. It is the matter of a plot of land in Kent adjacent to my property. A distant cousin of mine bought the land some time ago and never did anything with it. He intended to build a house, I believe, but died before the plans were completed. The plot of land has been tied up in a legal struggle among my extended family. I intend to buy them all out."

"Do you know who the land rightfully belongs to?"

"It belongs to me. My cousin left it to me in his will. It is adjacent to Swynford House land, after all. But one of my cousins has found some arcane legal argument that he is using to contest the will, and now everyone is trying to get their hands on it." He sighed, looking tired. "It is quite a valuable piece of land. If I have to pay all my relatives off to get my hands on it, so be it. To what end, I have not decided, but my solicitor thinks we have a good case for it. So I need to sort out the legal documents related to the sale. I do not think it will take long, maybe a week or two."

"Very well."

"You are disappointed."

Adele could not deny it. She was anxious to get out of London. She'd been feeling a little restless recently, likely due to the lack of real responsibilities in a house that had enough servants to take care of her every whim. At least in the country, there would be some household management tasks for her.

"You may also be pleased to learn that Mother intends to leave at the end of the week."

That certainly caught Adele's interest. "Are you serious?"

"She prefers the house in Surrey and intends to go there now that the weather is warm. She dislikes London in the summer, which I do not blame her for one bit. I think she also is grudgingly accepting that you and I have made a successful match and that the social repercussions are not nearly what she imagined."

"Just as we were coming to an understanding."

"Were you?"

Adele thought so. She and Helena had in fact had a few pleasant conversations since the wedding. Adele sensed Helena was trying to make amends, although she also guessed that Helena still thought Adele was not good enough for her son, and Adele was not ready to forgive her for that sentiment. So tension remained. Adele thought it would ease with time, or she hoped it would, because she could not imagine being at odds with her husband's mother forever.

"She may even like me a little," Adele said.

Hugh walked closer. "I like you a great deal, and that is what matters."

Adele smiled and put her hands on Hugh's shoulders. "You love me."

"I do. And I'm sorry about us staying in London longer than expected. I will try to resolve these issues as swiftly as possible."

Adele hugged him close. He put his arms around her. "Can you do me a favor?"

"Anything, my love."

"Give me something to do," she said. "I have never enjoyed idle time. I need a task."

Hugh raised an eyebrow. "I can think of something you could do right now." He nudged her with his hips, making his intention clear.

She laughed. "I'm serious."

"I know. You should sit down with Mother before she leaves, and she can show you what her daily household tasks are. You may choose to take on as many of those as you like. She likes to meet with the cook in the morning to plan the day's meals and she oversees shopping and the household budget, among other things. Do those seem like suitable tasks?"

"Yes. I shall meet with your mother tomorrow to discuss." She smiled. "I hate feeling… ornamental."

"Ornamental?"

"Like my job here is just to look pretty. I can handle running a household. I did it for the Countess of Sweeney after all."

"I have the utmost faith in you. And please do not hesitate to ask if you need anything. The management of Swynford House will be a much larger undertaking, but I have no doubt you will master it. One of the things I like most about you is how clever you are. I imagine you could run Windsor Castle if you put your mind to it."

Adele grinned. "I appreciate your faith in me."

Hugh kissed her forehead. "I do love you, Adele. I hope I give you no cause to doubt that."

"I do not. I love you, too."

"I would very much like to show you just how right now, but I must get back to my work. Hold that thought until tonight, will you?"

"I will."

"HOW IS MARRIED life treating you?" Fletcher asked.

Hugh grinned as he settled into a chair at the club. "It's very good."

Lark sighed. "That's because the dowager has declared the season over and gone to her country home. I gather from the look on your face that you and your new wife have spent most of your marriage in bed."

Hugh shrugged.

"What brings you here?" asked Owen.

"Adele is having dinner with her father tonight before he, too, leaves for the country, so I found myself at loose ends. I suppose I could have joined them, but it seemed better to give them room to talk. And besides, my wife and I cannot possibly spend every waking moment together."

"Nice of you to remember us, then," said Fletcher.

"I apologize for my absence, but you will understand when you get married."

Fletcher smiled. "I was kidding. I don't blame you at all."

"How is everyone?" Hugh thought to catch up with his friends, since he'd spent the better part of the last two weeks either dealing with the land sale or in bed with Adele. His mother had, he suspected, begun to feel a bit extraneous, and though he did enjoy her company when she was not lecturing him on the history of the family, her departure had been something of a relief.

"Lady Louisa and I went to see that Swedish singer at the opera house again," said Fletcher. "I know none of you cannot abide by opera, but this woman is extremely talented. Voice like a songbird. And if you stop to listen, you may learn that the opera house is good for more than just social intrigue and public assignations."

"And how is Louisa?" asked Lark.

"Great. She told me this hilarious story about Lord Castlereigh, but it loses something in the retelling." Fletcher laughed to himself as if this story were the funniest thing he'd ever heard.

"You aren't married to Lady Louisa because…" said Owen.

Fletcher waved his hand. "She is my friend. Like a sister. We don't like each other romantically."

Hugh opened his mouth to make a half-formed joke about that when his cousin George, Lord Collingswood, appeared.

Hugh could recall enough to know that he and George had grown up together but were not close as adults, and Hugh had the sense that he did not like George much but could not remember why.

"Hello, Your Grace," said George, and he sounded friendly enough.

"Hello, Collingswood. How has your day been?"

"Good, good. I barely got to talk to you or your lovely wife at the wedding, so since you are here, I wanted to convey my sincere congratulations to you."

"Thank you. I will pass that along to the duchess."

"Much obliged. Marriage is suiting you well so far?"

"Idyllically."

"Good."

Hugh glanced at Lark, hoping Lark might be able to step in and help Hugh remember whatever it was that he couldn't, but

Lark shrugged. Whatever reason Hugh had for not trusting George, he had not confided it to Lark before he'd been hit on the head.

"How are things with you?" Hugh asked.

George shrugged. "A little difficult. There was… an incident at my plantation in Jamaica that resulted in some property damage, and the crop yield is little less than what I'd hoped for, but I'm managing. I may need to sell some of my property there to make up for the shortfall."

Hugh wondered if by "property," George meant slaves. Hugh remembered suddenly that George owned a large number of people, which turned his stomach. But he said, "I'm sorry to hear that."

"Cost of doing business. The bizarre weather we're having this year hasn't helped, but that is out of my hands."

"Yes."

"But enough about me. I just wanted to congratulate you again. Have a good evening, gents."

Everyone remained silent until George had disappeared into another room.

"Did you know he was a member here?" asked Owen.

"Yes," said Lark. "He got the membership here because of Hugh, but he's rarely in town, which is why we don't see him."

"I never liked him," said Fletcher. "No offense, Hugh, but he always seems like he has an ulterior motive."

"Agreed," said Lark. "When we were boys, he used to skulk around the Swynford property like he was angry it was made out of bricks."

Hugh remembered George as a boy following him and Lark around and shook his head. "I don't trust him, but I cannot remember why."

"I can't think of anything specific," said Lark, "although I don't trust him, either. He was a bit of a bully when we were boys. I can't see that he's changed much, although I guess he was perfectly polite just now."

"Maybe he's resigned himself to never getting the title now," said Fletcher.

"What do you mean?" Hugh asked.

"As your only first cousin, he was your most logical heir. But now that you are married, your future son, assuming you have one, will be the clear heir to the dukedom."

His future son. Hugh had assumed he and Adele would have a boy, and given how much time they'd spent in bed, they may already have conceived one. Of course, they might have a girl first, one he'd dote on just as much as he would a boy. He hoped if they had a girl, she'd be as pretty as Adele.

He shook it off and focused back on his friends.

"Where did you go just then?" Lark asked softly.

"Apparently I am ready to have children now. Adele and I have discussed it already, in fact."

Owen frowned. "I don't know about this love business. It does strange things to your mind."

Hugh laughed. "No one is more surprised by this turn of events than I am. But back to the topic at hand, you think Collingswood might harbor some resentment toward me now that I have married and all but assured the title will go to another?"

Fletcher shrugged. "Or he wants money but is too proud to ask with so many witnesses. You heard him. He's having financial issues."

Hugh considered the problem. "He has set his solicitor on me to try to get a parcel of land in Kent that was willed to me by one of our distant relations. The lawyer found some loophole in the law that he is trying to exploit to question the will. I would gladly buy Collingswood out if money is what he wants."

Lark pursed his lips and stared at the direction George had gone for a long moment. He turned back toward Hugh. "Is that why he's back in London?"

"I can't say. Does he normally live in Jamaica?" Hugh asked, not able to remember.

"Yes, most of the time."

Hugh shook his head, as if it would rattle the memory loose. He knew something about George, but he didn't *know* it. It was hiding somewhere behind the gray curtain.

"Collingswood is a swine," said Lark, "and a cowardly one, but if you and he had been arguing before your head injury, you did not tell us about it."

"Fair enough."

"Perhaps we should discuss a happier topic," said Owen. "I am postponing my trip back to Wales."

"This is happy news?" asked Fletcher.

"My ancestors are going to strike me down for this, but I prefer London to Caernarfon. What is even there besides a dusty old castle?"

"The beach?" Fletcher suggested. "As I recall, Caernarfon is close to the sea."

"And you refer to the dusty old castle your family owns, no?" said Lark. "The one Edward I built five hundred years ago?"

"Aye, the same," said Owen. "Do you know why Prinny is called the Prince of Wales?"

Hugh laughed. Owen was drunk, his accent becoming more pronounced. Likely Hugh had heard this story before, but he was game to hear it again as if for the first time. "Why?"

"When Edward built that bloody castle, he created the title of the Prince of Wales. The Welsh made him promise that no man who spoke a word of English would ever hold the title of Prince of Wales, and he agreed. So King Edward bestowed the title on his infant son, who did not speak a word at all. Ever since, the firstborn sons of the kings of England have been called the Prince of Wales."

"Thank you for the history lesson," said Fletcher. "You are not allowed to have any more whisky."

"Why are you postponing your trip?" Lark asked.

"I have a new nephew! My sister did not make it out of London before he wanted to join the world."

"Congratulations!" said Hugh.

"Thank you. He bears the unfortunate name of Llewellyn, after the last King of Wales, but he is awfully cute. But anyway, I am staying behind to help out the family before we all adjourn to Wales in a month or so. Hopefully before it gets too hot in London."

"It is already too hot," said Fletcher.

"Are you drinking to celebrate?" asked Lark.

"I will admit to having a tipple before I came out here to meet you gents."

"A tipple or the whole bottle?" asked Fletcher.

Owen just laughed.

Chapter Twenty-Five

ADELE WANTED TO get some kind of a present for Hugh. The legal issues keeping him in town were clearly adding some stress to his life, and the weather in London had been unusual for summer—not too hot, but a great deal of rain—which was probably adding to how tense he felt. But what did one buy for a man who had everything?

Lady Louisa accompanied her to the shops and knew just where to go to find gifts befitting a duke. Adele had been at a bit of a loss; she'd been frugal most of her adult life, and in particular when handling the Countess of Sweeney's money, so she was not sure which shops had finer quality items. They'd had a nice day out, shopping and chatting, and stopping for ices. It had been a long time since Adele had a female friend whose company she enjoyed so much.

But as they approached their last stop, Adele had still not found a gift she thought appropriate for Hugh. They headed to a shop on Savile Road where Louisa had been instructed to pick up an order for her brother. When they arrived, the tailor brought Louisa to a side room to wait while he wrapped up a jacket. Adele examined a display of cufflinks in front of the store while she waited. She spotted a set of emerald cufflinks that were such a smart match for her wedding necklace that she knew at last she'd found a wonderful gift for Hugh. She called a clerk over.

"May I take a closer look at these?" she asked.

The clerk gave her a long look at her. Daisy had done up Adele's hair in a fashionable style that day, and Adele was wearing a fine walking dress from her trousseau, so she was not her normal plain self today. But perhaps she had not quite grown into her status as a duchess.

The clerk said, "Of course, my lady," with reluctance in his voice.

She wondered if she should correct him. What was the social protocol on this?

She leaned over the cufflinks and examined them closely. Conversationally, she said, "I am looking for a gift for my husband, the Duke of Swynford. Do you think these would do?"

The clerk's whole demeanor changed. He stood a little taller and the scowl vanished from his face. "Oh, yes, Your Grace. As you can see, the clarity on these emeralds is quite good. Each emerald is thirty-four carats. An emerald of this size is quite valuable."

Adele knew cufflinks like this would be quite expensive, but she had no idea what a reasonable price would be. She haggled with the clerk a little, knowing better than to accept the first offer. Probably she was still getting swindled, and she felt odd about spending the duke's money on a gift for him, but she arranged for the purchase.

As the clerk wrote up the purchase, a man behind her said, "Hello, Your Grace."

Adele turned. The man standing next to her was familiar but she could not immediately place him. "Hello, my lord."

"Do you recall who I am?"

She squinted at him and tried to remember, but she could not. "I apologize, my lord, but I do not."

"I'm George Baxter. Lord Collingswood. You're husband's cousin. I was at the wedding breakfast."

"Oh, yes, of course. I apologize. I've met so many people in the last month that is nearly impossible to keep them all straight."

"Naturally. I wonder if I might have a word with you."

"Can it wait until I complete the purchase of these cuff links for my husband?"

"No, I'm afraid not. Will you step outside with me please?"

Something in his tone set off all of Adele's alarm bells. She looked for Lady Louisa, who was absorbed in conversation with a tailor in the other room. "What is the urgency?" she asked.

"It is about your husband. Something has happened to him. Will you step outside?"

Adele was reluctant to go with this man, but something very well could have happened to Hugh. Had his assailant returned? Was he injured? Perhaps Collingswood also did not want to call attention, and this was why he was asking her to step outside. He did seem agitated, so this could have been a matter of some urgency. Adele did not think she could ask him to leave or ignore him.

"Is everything all right, Your Grace?" asked the clerk, perhaps sensing that something strange was occurring.

"Yes," she said, not wanting to make a scene. She stepped close to the clerk and said, "I am going to step outside to have a conversation with my husband's cousin for a moment. I shall be back in a few moments."

"Of course, Your Grace."

Adele tried to make meaningful eye contact with the clerk and lowered her voice. "If I do not return promptly, please alert my friend. She is collecting an item in the next room."

"Of course, Your Grace." His tone was cheerful, but she met his gaze and he seemed to understand.

Likely Collingswood merely wanted to give her some inane piece of information he didn't want the clerk overhearing. As far as Adele knew, Hugh was not close to this cousin. If Hugh were in real danger, how would Collingswood know about it? She figured she could listen to whatever he had to say so that he'd go away, then she'd get the cuff links and go home.

"I really must insist you come with me, Your Grace," said Collingswood.

With a last long look at the clerk, Adele followed Collingswood outside.

HUGH WAS NEARLY done. Contracts were signed, money had been
exchanged, and for his trouble, Hugh now owned a patch of land
adjacent to Swynford House that was as yet undeveloped and had
previously belonged to a long-dead relative. Happy to have the
ownership of said land finally decided, Hugh wanted to get out of
London so he could start planning what to do with the land.

He was about to dismiss his secretary when he heard a com-
motion downstairs. He intended to ignore it for a moment, but
curiosity got the better of him. "Let is investigate the noise, shall
we?" he said to his secretary, Killingworth.

When he got to the foot of the stairs, he saw Lady Louisa in a
great state of agitation. Hodges was trying to calm her, but she
was frantic. "He took her! She's gone!" she said when she spotted
Hugh.

He knew instantly something terrible had happened to Adele.
He ran to Louisa.

"What happened?" Hugh asked. "Where is Adele?"

Louisa's face crumpled. Hugh's heart began to pound.

"You'd better start at the beginning," he said.

Louisa nodded and took a deep breath. "We were in Mr.
Pembroke's shop on Savile Road. I left her near the front of the
shop so I could pick something up for my brother. I was gone not
a few moments and Adele was right in my line of sight... until she
wasn't." Louisa started to cry. "Oh, Your Grace, I am so sorry."

"What happened?" Hugh's fear was palpable. "Do you know
where she went?"

"A man came and asked to speak with her outside. Before
they left, she told the clerk to alert me if she did not come back. I
think she knew this man was dangerous, and the clerk said he was

being quite forceful. Once they were outside, the man ran off with her."

"Who was the man?"

"The clerk overheard him tell Adele he was your cousin."

"Collingswood," Hugh said, and then something hit him quite suddenly.

Collingswood was broke. There had been trouble at his Jamaica plantation. He'd been part of the fight for the parcel of land Hugh now owned; it was Collingswood who had been instrumental in sending in his lawyers to quibble about some loophole in the law. Collingswood was in town, which was unusual, and he'd been sniffing around Hugh's social circle. It was perhaps Collingswood, Hugh's heir until he and Adele had a child, who had the most to lose from Hugh's recent marriage.

He had a vision that struck him so hard he had to lean against the wall. As he walked home from the Rutherford ball, someone crept up behind him. He turned just in time to see in his peripheral vision that it was… it was Collingswood who had hit him over the head.

And now he had Adele.

Collingswood likely wanted to get Hugh's attention. To get Hugh's title.

That had been the intention, hadn't it? Collingswood had hit Hugh over the head and left him for dead on a London sidewalk, likely imagining he'd fall victim to a robber or pickpocket or succumb to his injury or the elements, because he was too cowardly to do the deed himself. And now Adele was the only impediment between Collingswood and the Swynford dukedom, or that's how Collingswood must see it. Which meant her life was in grave danger.

Hugh gasped.

He started to head for the door, but Hodges put a hand on his arm. "Before you go storming off into the London night, Your Grace, perhaps you should call for some help."

Hugh saw the wisdom of that. He took a deep breath. Then

he turned to Killingworth. "Go to Lord Waring," said Hugh. "If he is not at his residence, he will be at the club." Hugh thought about that for a moment, trying to think of every possibility. "Or he may be at the Marquess of Beresford's house off Berkley Square. Do you think you can find him?"

"Yes, Your Grace. I shall see to it right away."

No longer able to stand, Hugh sank onto the bottom step of the staircase. He looked up at Lady Louisa, who still looked distraught. She swallowed and said, "We will find her. We will get her back."

"Yes. We will. We must."

Chapter Twenty-Six

L ARK WAS GRATEFUL that he and Anthony were at least mostly dressed when Hugh's secretary came storming into his house.

That had not been true but half an hour before, when Anthony had been under Lark on the settee in Lark's sitting room, calling the names of every god he knew.

Now they were having a post-coital drink and idly discussing going to the club for dinner, but all of that was interrupted when Killingworth rushed in.

"His Grace sent me to fetch you, Lord Waring."

"What could he possibly need with such haste?" Lark asked, although he'd already set his glass aside. The jittery nature of the man's stance told Lark it was urgent.

"The duke's cousin, Collingswood, abducted the duchess while she was out shopping today."

Lark was instantly on his feet. "Return to the front door and tell my butler to ready my coat. I will go with you to the duke's house."

"How can I help?" asked Anthony.

Lark turned and saw the sincerity on his face. He was touched that Anthony would want to help with a matter he had no stake in, aside from knowing the people involved. Lark said, "Go to the club and fetch Caernarfon and Fowler and meet me at Swynford's house. With all possible haste."

"Will you not go to the police?"

"Let me determine what Hugh intends to do first. Likely he plans to storm the gates." Lark paused in the doorway. "I have been guessing for the last few days that it was Collingswood who hit Hugh over the head, but I didn't know how to prove it. I hate that I'm right."

"Are you suggesting he kidnapped the duchess in order to gain Hugh's title?"

"Yes, that is my best guess. He did not succeed in killing Swynford because Swynford is a large man with a thick skull. The same cannot be said for the duchess."

Anthony nodded, likely understanding how high the stakes were. "I always thought he was a snake. I shall go to the club at once."

Lark wanted to kiss him goodbye and wish him luck, but he was conscious of Killingworth standing there, so instead he just murmured, "Godspeed."

After Anthony left, Lark stood in the middle of his sitting room for a long moment, trying to gather his thoughts and his nerve. Then he followed Killingworth to the front of his house, shrugged into his coat, and left for Hugh's house on foot.

Hugh was in a state when Lark arrived.

He paced around the foyer of his house, close to pulling out his hair. He kept saying, "He's got her," over and over.

Lark understood that Hugh had sent for him to be the level head because Hugh was incapable, and this was also the moment Lark understood that Hugh really did love his wife.

"All right," said Lark. "We need to take a few deep breaths and make a plan."

"How can you... how can I... what if he does something to her? If he touches one hair on her head, I will kill—"

"Hugh, go sit." Lark pointed through the open door of the red sitting room. "Your fretting will just make everything worse. If we want to get her back, we must think through this rationally."

Hugh stared at Lark with fury in his eyes for a long moment, then pressed his lips together and nodded. He walked into the sitting room.

Lark needed help, but he sat down to try to figure out what was going on. "Your secretary said Collingswood abducted Adele while she was out shopping. How do you know—"

"Letter for you, sir," said Hodges, walking into the room.

Lark intercepted it before it reached Hugh's hand and ripped the envelope open.

This at least solved part of the mystery.

"What is it?" asked Hugh.

"Have you recently purchased a tract of land adjacent to Swynford House?"

"A distant cousin willed it to me. I've had to sort out a number of issues with various solicitors, which is what has detained me in London past the end of the season. A number of relatives challenged me for the land, but it was clear from my cousin's will that—"

"Is it in your possession now?"

"Yes, as of today."

"Well, Collingswood wants it." Lark turned the letter to show Hugh. "He's essentially holding Adele ransom in exchange for this piece of land."

"A consolation prize, perhaps," said a voice behind Lark.

He turned and saw that Anthony had arrived with Owen and Fletcher in tow. Anthony walked forward. "You said to fetch Caernarfon and Fowler, so here they are. I did some thinking on the way. Collingswood is losing money he doesn't have on his Jamaica estate each day, so what is it he wants more than anything? He wants the dukedom, of course, but he didn't have it in him to actually kill Hugh. What's the next best thing? Land. What Collingswood really wants is money and power, and the best way to achieve that on this godforsaken island is to acquire land."

Lark nodded and looked at the letter. "I thought Collingswood might have taken Adele to prevent Hugh and his wife from producing a new heir to the dukedom, but I believe you are right. He may view the title as out of reach now, so he's resigned to give that up. But he's betting Hugh will give up the tract he just acquired in order to get his wife back. The land in Kent is probably worth more than the Jamaica estate, which he could sell and use the profits to build some grand estate in England."

"That is logical," said Fletcher. "A simple exchange. Adele for the land."

"Let's do it, then," said Hugh. "I am happy to sign that land over to him if that's what it takes. Adele is more important than expanding Swynford House."

Lark patted Hugh's shoulder. "Let's not be hasty."

"Hasty? He has her, Lark. He's got Adele. He could harm her, or—"

"The good news is that she's worth more alive," said Anthony. "He's banking on you making that trade, Hugh. It's all over the gossip rags that you married below your station because the marriage is a love match."

"It is?" Hugh looked almost pleased by that, despite the circumstances.

Anthony smiled. "It is. Collingswood is a spineless coward, which means he doesn't have it in him to harm her. Instead, he'll use her to bargain with you for the land."

"I just said I would agree to his demand," said Hugh.

"What if you could get her back *and* keep the land?" asked Lark.

Hugh frowned. "How do you propose we do that?"

"I have an idea," said Owen, walking into the room.

"Leave it to the Welshman," said Fletcher, a little sarcastically.

Owen didn't look offended. In fact, he grinned. "Several hundred years of the Crown trying to take our land will do that. My father's family may have been loyal to England, but my mother's family is lousy with rebels. I'm named for Owain

Glyndwr, you know."

"You've mentioned," said Fletcher. "Stop trying to give us history lessons."

Owen rolled his eyes. "Listen, here's my plan."

ADELE SAT IN the parlor of a rather shabby house with her hands tied behind her back. The rope was rubbing blisters into her wrists. She'd spent the last few minutes alone in the room, trying to work out how to get out. With her hands bound, she couldn't get the leverage she needed to stand. Even if she could get out of the house, she didn't know where she was; Collingswood had tied a blindfold over her eyes once she was in his carriage.

He'd threatened to harm Hugh again when they'd been standing on the street. He'd grabbed her wrist and ordered her to come with him or he'd shoot Hugh this time instead of just hitting him on the head.

Adele was shocked to recognize the carriage as the one Hugh had been thrown from the night he'd landed on the Sweeneys' doorstep. The truth of what must have happened clicked for her.

She'd gone with Collingswood so that he would not further injure Hugh. Hugh had acted recently like his memory was completely intact, but she knew that he still hadn't recovered everything he once knew and, worse, his short-term recollection was faulty sometimes, too. It hadn't interfered in anything they'd done together, and Hugh's staff had quickly worked out a quick way to help him remember things without making him feel like a fool, but Adele continued to worry about that head injury. Collingswood had clearly been the cause of the injury that still plagued her husband, but as she wished no further harm to come to him, she had gone willingly with Collingswood.

Now she wondered what he intended to do with her.

Worse, she was starting to feel dizzy. She and Louisa had

intended to stop for tea after the visit for the tailors, and Adele had not eaten much that day.

Collingswood stormed into the room. "Where is that idiot husband of yours?"

Adele pulled at her bindings. Her hands were tied quite well; the knot seemed solid. She sighed. "Why do you think he will come here?"

"Because the scandal sheets say he is besotted with you. I sent him a letter saying I'd give you back to him in exchange for a tract of land he recently gained possession of."

So that was his game. "Why do you think he is not fetching the police? You did kidnap me after all." Adele was quite impressed with how reasonable and calm she sounded, despite the churning going on in her belly.

"You came willingly. And I told him not to."

"Oh, well. Unassailable logic."

Before she knew it had happened, she felt the sting of his hand slapping her face. She nearly toppled over onto her side but managed to stay sitting upright.

"He'll come," Collingswood said. "Those imbeciles he spends time with, Waring and his other school chums, will likely come with him."

There was a knock at the door.

"Ah, there they are now."

Adele squirmed against her bindings again. She watched Collingswood leave the room. Did he not have servants? It didn't appear so; she hadn't seen a soul except for Collingswood since they entered this house.

There was a bit of a ruckus outside the door to the parlor, but Adele couldn't see what was happening from where she was sitting. She tried to scoot closer to the door and caught the profile of a willowy man with curly hair—the Marquess of Beresford. Why was he here?

"Now, before you become violent," Beresford said, "I am to tell you that His Grace has sent me as a delegate of sorts. I am to negotiate with you for the release of the duchess."

"Why you?"

Beresford stood tall and proud and said, "I am a neutral party. I could best argue dispassionately for an agreeable solution to this spot of bother."

Collingswood practically growled, "Why didn't that coward Swynford come himself?"

"Couldn't be bothered. Don't believe everything you read in the scandal sheets, Collingswood. There's no love match here. Swynford married her out of pity. He had ruined her, after all. Aristocratic men never know when to keep it in their breeches."

Adele felt crushed, until she realized this might be a ruse. She knew Hugh too well to believe he didn't value her. He'd said he loved her, in fact, and she'd believed him. Beresford acting as though none of that were true must have been the first volley of the war to rescue her.

That also meant Hugh could be walking into certain danger. Collingswood had a gun tucked into his breeches. It was hidden by his coat now, but she'd seen him put it there.

She cursed silently and pulled at her bindings again.

"Let me see the duchess so I can make sure she's all right," said Beresford.

"She's fine. What are you trying to tell me?"

"Swynford is not coming. He values the land in Kent more than he does his wife. Have you any idea what that tract is worth?"

"You're jesting."

"Come now. You know how ruthless the Baxter men can be. You are one yourself, are you not? Trust me, I spend enough time around Swynford to know that all he cares about is money and power. His ruthlessness is how he became so successful. And he doesn't want a slimy eel like yourself to have that land. I believe those were close to his exact words."

While Beresford continued to talk, Adele leaned to the side to try to hear. She nearly toppled over, the bindings keeping her from being able to balance her body well. A noise off to the side distracted her. She turned and saw Owen creeping into the room.

"We have to get out of here," he whispered. "Come on."

Adele turned to show Owen her tied hands. "I haven't been able to stand."

Owen nodded and walked forward on tip toes. The floor creaked, but Beresford's voice had grown quite loud, so hopefully Collingswood didn't hear. Owen helped Adele to her feet but didn't untie her hands. He led her toward the back of the house, but when they were nearly there, Collingswood shouted, "Stop!"

"I didn't think it would be that easy," muttered Owen. "Well, time for Plan B."

Collingswood pulled out his gun and pointed it at Owen. Adele's heart leapt to her throat. She didn't know if Collingswood had the courage to use the gun or not, but she didn't want to take any chances. "Please be calm, my lord," she said, sounding as serene as she could.

"No. Swynford will surrender that land to me, or I will kill you! Then I will go to his house and kill *him*. Then it will *all* be mine, as it always should have been."

While Collingswood's focus was on Owen and Adele, Beresford crept back toward the door. Since there were no servants to stop him, he slipped out the front door of the house. Adele wondered if he was running out on them now.

She and Owen were alone.

Collingswood pointed the gun at Owen and said, "You will go fetch Swynford and bring him to me. If he truly doesn't care about his wife, let him tell me to my face."

Adele felt dizzy, the room swaying and spinning around her. Her hands were still tied, so she couldn't brace herself against the wall, and she worried she might fall over. Beside her, Owen nodded and carefully walked toward the front door. "I will fetch him. I must go to his house, so this may take a little while. Please do not harm Adele."

"Why shouldn't I?"

Owen sighed. "Because Beresford was partially bluffing. Maybe it's not a love match, but I believe Swynford would want to avoid the family scandal should anything happen to his wife. She is therefore more valuable to you if she is alive."

Collingswood pursed his lips but then nodded as if he understood the wisdom of that. But then he reached out and struck Adele across the face again. Adele grunted in pain that time. She lost her balance and her shoulder slammed into the wall. She took a deep breath and managed to use her elbow to push herself back into a standing position, but the dizziness returned, and she was beginning to worry she might pass out before this was all over.

Owen started to march back down the hall. "I swear to all that is holy, Collingswood. If you harm her further in any way, I will see you hanged myself. Forget about Swynford."

"Fine. I won't touch her again. Now go get Swynford. Let's have this done."

Owen opened the front door and now Adele found herself alone in a narrow corridor with Collingswood. She was terrified of the gun in his hand, worried it would go off when he did not intend it to. She tried to back up but tripped over the hem of her gown. The only thing that kept her on her feet is that she hit a wall with her shoulder again and was able to use it to keep herself from falling. She swallowed the cry of pain and leaned against the wall.

"What do you intend to do?" she asked, truly nauseous now. She did not want to be alone with this man. He looked a bit like Hugh, but shorter and less handsome, and he sneered at her in a way that seemed spiteful and dangerous.

His face twisted into a leer. "I can certainly see your appeal. Perhaps my cousin does not love you, but he would be sad to lose such a pretty plaything. If Swynford doesn't want you, maybe I'll keep you for myself." He ran a finger down the side of her face. She pulled at her bindings again, wanting to slap his hand away.

Owen had not gone far, however. Instead the door burst open and a group of men came inside. Beresford and Hugh now stormed through the door, with Lark, Fletcher, and a man Adele did not know on their heels. Collingswood started at the invasion and flailed but did not fire the gun.

Hugh ran down the hall toward her. "Adele. Oh, Adele, are you hurt?"

"I am all right," she said, although Hugh's face was growing fuzzy. "He has a gun."

He took her into his arms and held her closely, maneuvering her so that his body was between her and Collingswood. She was nearly relieved, although her stomach still roiled, and she knew they were not out of danger.

"It's true," said the unknown man. "Collingswood, show your hands."

"He tied Her Grace's hands behind her back," said Owen.

The unknown man said, "You intended to use the duchess to force her husband to give you a tract of land."

"Who are you?" asked Collingswood, still refusing to show his hands.

"Michael Shea. I'm a Bow Street runner. Show your hands."

No one else seemed to be heeding Adele's warning. Lark said, "If you need more, the duke was hit over the head near Grosvenor Square a couple of months ago. That night, his signet ring was stolen. I believe you will now find that ring on the hand of Lord Collingswood."

Adele saw the glint of it—a heavy silver ring with a ruby on it, just as Hugh had described it—as Collingswood waved his hand. Then he brandished the gun.

"Look out!" shouted Adele.

Everyone turned toward Collingswood. He waved the gun around before pointing it up. Who he intended to shoot was not clear.

It did go off then. Everyone ducked. The bullet went up and hit the ceiling; an explosion of plaster caused a white cloud that obscured everyone's appearance.

The Bow Street man, Shea, moved quickly. He grabbed Collingswood's arms and pulled them behind his back, then he took the gun and handed it to Beresford, who placed it on a table.

"Well, this is fun," said Shea. "Crime is down in London. I hardly ever get to arrest anyone anymore."

Beresford chuckled. "Well, show him no hospitality."

Shea looked at Collingswood's hands. He pulled the signet ring off his right hand and examined it. "This certainly does look like the Swynford ring. I believe this belongs to you, Your Grace."

He tossed the ring toward Hugh; Hugh caught it. Without letting go of Adele, he slipped it back on his own hand. Then he put his hand back on Adele's back.

Hugh continued to clutch Adele close as the other men spoke. He ran a hand through her hair. "Your shoulder is red. What did he do to you?"

"Nothing. I tripped and hit the wall."

"After Collingswood slapped her," said Owen.

Hugh let go of Adele then and leapt toward Collingswood. Lark got between them that time. "Calm yourself. Mr. Shea will put Collingswood in jail. The law will sort this out. Adele is safe and you are with her. Let us not make this any worse."

Fletcher produced a pocketknife and walked toward Adele. He went to work undoing the bindings. It took him a long moment to saw through one of the ropes, but when she at last had access to her arms and hands again, she almost wept with relief.

She felt so stupid for going with Collingswood to begin with, but she'd thought it best to avoid any harm coming to Hugh. She hated that Hugh had worried so much. And now he looked like he might murder Collingswood with his bare hands, had Lark not been holding him back.

And now she was even more dizzy. Lights flashed at the edge of her vision. She took a step forward. "Hugh? Help me. I feel…"

Then everything went dark.

Chapter Twenty-Seven

HUGH'S HEART HAD nearly given out when he saw Adele's body go lifeless and crumple toward the floor. Fletcher had been behind her and managed to catch her before she injured herself further, but she had still not regained consciousness by the time they got back to the house.

They'd taken Hugh's carriage to and from the house Collingswood was renting in Cheapside, and Hugh had held Adele in his lap the whole way home, unwilling to let her go. He grew increasingly frantic as they neared his home and she still had not regained consciousness.

"He *hit* her?" Hugh confirmed with Owen.

"Aye, I saw him do it. I doubt it was the first time."

"I swear, I will rip his arms off," Hugh growled.

"You will do no such thing," said Lark. "He is cooling his heels in Newgate Prison by now."

When they arrived home, Hugh carried her upstairs to their bedroom. He was heartened to find her body warm, and she sighed a little as she rested in his arms, but she was clearly quite out of it. He checked her everywhere for injuries, but found none save for a tiny cut on her forehead and a red mark on her cheek.

"Collingswood must have hit her quite hard," Hugh said as Lark hovered behind him in the doorway. "We must get a doctor."

"I'll send Beresford."

Fletcher and Owen kept Hugh company while Lark launched into action and coordinated everything. Beresford returned with the Baxter family's doctor, who immediately went upstairs to see Adele.

The doctor was with Adele for quite some time, though whether it was minutes or hours was hard for Hugh to ascertain. He was terrified she'd suffer the same fate he had and lose her memories. What if she woke up with no idea who he was or what they meant to each other? What if she could not recover her memories? What if the injury was indeed grave? What if she were ill? Fletcher had been standing closest to her when she'd passed out, and all he knew was that she mumbled something about not feeling well right before she fell.

As they all waited, Hodges appeared with a package wrapped in brown paper. "This arrived for Lady Adele."

Hugh took it. He had no earthly idea what it could be, although a card advertising a shop on Savile Road was tucked into the wrapping. Had this been what she was buying when Collingswood abducted her? Hugh held onto it, intending to give it to her when she was awake.

The doctor finally appeared at the door and Hugh held his breath, afraid of the news.

"Her Grace is resting now," said the doctor.

"Did she wake up? Was she hurt badly? Is she quite ill?" asked Hugh, getting to his feet.

"Yes, she did come to. We spoke about how she was feeling and I examined her thoroughly. Her only injuries are the superficial ones you saw for yourself." The doctor smiled, which Hugh was not sure how to interpret. "May I have a word, Your Grace?"

Hugh looked around at his friends. Beresford was there, too, but after everything he'd done that day, Hugh supposed he could be considered a friend, too. Hugh looked back at the doctor and reasoned that whatever his news, it was likely of a delicate nature. Hugh gestured toward the hall.

When they were out of everyone's earshot, the doctor said, "She is not injured or ill. She is with child."

Hugh's heart stopped for a long moment. He was so surprised by this news, he could not move.

"She… what?"

"I knew you would want to know right away."

"Is she… will she be all right?"

"She will be fine. She did not eat enough today, and that combined with the stress of the situation made her pass out. She came around long enough to talk with me and for us to ascertain that she has not had her monthly courses. So I did a more thorough examination."

Hugh was uncomfortable with the doctor taking such liberties and seeing his wife intimately, but he pushed it aside. "You're sure?"

"It is early days yet, but yes, I am sure. She will need lots of rest and hearty meals each day, and she may face some difficulties until the baby comes. But don't smother her, either. She need not be confined to bed." The doctor patted Hugh's arm. "In my experience, women generally know their bodies and what they need, so listen to your wife, and all should be well."

"May I see her now?"

"She may be asleep, but if awake, I think she will be happy to see you."

Hugh instructed Hodges to send up a tray of food and then ran up the stairs. He entered her room and found her asleep in their bed. She looked untroubled.

He sat on the edge of the bed and took her hand.

She stirred and opened her eyes. "Hugh," she said softly.

"How do you feel?"

"Better. Tired still."

"There should be food here in a few minutes. Are you hungry?"

"Starving. I missed tea."

"It's nearly dinner time, but don't feel like you have to get dressed to come down. I'd rather you rested."

"I suppose Doctor Berkley told you the news."

"That you are to have a baby? Yes, he did." Hugh placed a careful hand on her belly.

"Are you happy?"

"Yes. Surprised. I wouldn't have expected it so soon. But very happy. And you?"

"Yes." She smiled. "I've wanted a child for so long, Hugh. I didn't know how much until the doctor told me we would have one."

Hugh leaned down and kissed her gently. "I was so worried about you."

"I imagined you would be. I feel terrible for giving you such a fright."

"No. It's all right. It was my cousin who acted badly. Owen said you were quite brave before I barged into the room."

"Whose idea was it for Beresford to lie about how little I mean to you?"

Hugh smiled and smoothed Adele's hair away from her face. "Owen's. Beresford has a reputation for being a terrible gossip, so we thought he'd be the most likely to be believed if he said I didn't care about you. You know that was a lie, don't you? I love you, Adele. I would have been lost if something happened to you."

"I did know it was a lie."

"The idea was to distract Collingswood so that Owen could sneak in the back door and get you out of there. I would have come in myself, but I was too distraught with worry for you, and Lark told me I'd make a hash of it. If Owen failed, Lark brought a Bow Street runner to arrest Collingswood."

Adele nodded. "I love you, too, Hugh. I'm sorry for making you worry. And it was Collingswood who hit you over the head."

"I know. All is well now, my duchess. We know now who was putting us in danger, and that danger has been removed. So now we will have a beautiful baby, and we will love him or her with all our hearts, and we will live happily ever after."

Adele laughed. "It can't possibly be that easy."

"Probably not. But a man can hope. Cinderella and the Prince lived happily ever after, did they not?"

Adele sat up a little straighter and spotted the paper-wrapped parcel he'd brought up with him. "What have you brought for me?"

"Oh, this." He picked up the parcel. "This came while the doctor was seeing you. I think it was from one of the shops you visited earlier today."

"Oh!" She took the package and peeled off the paper. Inside was a jewelry box. "I bought this for you, actually."

"Oh?"

"I wanted to give you a present. You've been so good to me, Hugh, and you've been stressed out lately, and I wanted to do something nice."

He accepted the box from her and opened it. Inside were two emerald cufflinks.

"They go with my necklace, don't you think?" Adele said.

He was touched that she had thought to find something like this for him. They might yet live happily ever after. He kissed her, hard and fast, and said, "Thank you, my love. These are spectacular. They shall look nice with a few of my shirts. I will think of you every time I wear them."

"You're welcome."

Servants appeared with Adele's dinner then. Hugh sat with her as she ate—he tried to feed her, but she waved him off and told him she could do it herself. As she finished her soup, she said, "I didn't realize you and Lord Beresford were such good friends."

"We aren't, but he's Lark's friend. Apparently he was at Lark's house when I sent my secretary to fetch Lark. I needed someone with a level head, you see."

"Is that how you came to have a whole troop of men come in to rescue me?"

"I was a mess, Adele. I couldn't think straight. Lark thought I would be a liability if I went by myself."

"Thank the Lord for your friends."

"Yes." Hugh was indeed grateful. Lark had been right about Hugh being unable to do anything but make a larger mess. He was glad Lark had taken charge and that Beresford had been so convincing and that Owen had kept Adele safe and that Fletcher had caught her when she'd fainted.

Adele ate some chicken and said, "Are Lark and Beresford lovers?"

Hugh was surprised by that question, but Adele had asked it calmly, without recrimination. "Yes," he said. "I confronted Lark about it about a month ago and he confirmed it. What made you ask?"

"You've suggested a few times that you suspected Lark may have, er, romantic interests in other men. That seems very odd to me, but as long as they're happy and not hurting anyone, I can't find fault with it."

"You are more enlightened than the Crown. They will both be hanged if discovered."

"I promise to keep quiet next time I dine with the Prince Regent." Adele raised an eyebrow. "Although don't you think there is something romantic about that? Two people who love each other enough to stay together even though their lives are in danger?"

"I suppose, although I'd really rather both stayed among the living. And you joke, but we may well have to dine with Prinny one of these days. He is my cousin, after all, if a distant one."

Adele leaned back against her pillows and laughed softly. "This is not the sort of life I ever imagined for myself."

"I hope this is better."

She smiled. "Beyond my wildest dreams."

Epilogue

HUGH NEVER RECOVERED his memories entirely, which taught him to savor each moment as it came because each memory was precious.

He was reminded of this as he and Adele arrived at Swynford House at long last a week after Collingswood abducted her. The expression on her face as the carriage approached the house was priceless.

"I'm reminded again that I am a duchess," she said. "Is this really your home?"

"It is. Mother mentioned at least three times in her last letter that it has been in the family for generations, although according to the records it looks quite different now from its original state as a castle. The records also indicate that I made a number of improvements prior to meeting you, although I cannot recall all of them."

Adele shot him a concerned look that he'd learned meant she was still worried about his head injury, but it passed quickly. She smiled. "Well, show me this giant house of yours."

Adele took to household management like an expert and quickly started asserting herself. She told Hugh in bed one night that she'd never lived in a house she'd had a say in, so he'd given her a few rooms to update and decorate however she liked. When his mother visited, she acted put out that the rooms had been redesigned, but Adele had good taste, and the dowager grudgingly admitted the rooms looked nice.

Hugh suspected Adele and Helena might never be close friends, but every now and then they seemed to enjoy each other's company. Aside from a couple of negative items in the scandal sheets, not much was made of Hugh and Adele's marriage aside from the fact that the most eligible bachelor in England was now off the market. By the time Hugh and Adele returned to London for the next season, the gentry had moved on to the next scandal. This went a long way toward convincing Helena that no shame would come to the family.

But before all that, Lark and Anthony, as Lord Beresford now insisted he be called by his friends, came for a visit mid-summer. Hugh was still adjusting to the idea of them as a couple, but this seemed to be how they were comporting themselves, with Lark requesting that they share a room when they stayed at Swynford House. Hugh had objected at first, but Adele talked him into allowing it. Hugh still worried about the potential consequences—Lark's parents surely expected him to marry, not to mention they could both be hanged—but Adele insisted they honor the relationship if Lark requested it. Lark admitted he was in love with Anthony one night and still wasn't sure what to do about that.

Because of Adele's delicate condition, they opted not to have house parties, but they did entertain close friends. Owen visited for a week, and Fletcher and Lady Louisa came a different week and insisted they were merely friends again. Adele bet Hugh they'd marry soon.

Hugh was so happy throughout the first year of his marriage to Adele that he wanted to commit it all to memory, but he was content to have each moment with her. He was happy for the quiet Christmas they spent together and the snowball fight they got into while on a walk one day and the way Adele liked to walk with him on the Swynford grounds.

Among his greatest memories was the day when his beloved wife presented him with his son.

The doctor and midwife had kept Hugh from entering the room while their son was born, but the moment he was allowed inside, he went to her side and looked at the small, angry baby in her arms. Yet even as the baby wailed, Hugh stared at him in awe, amazed that he and Adele had made this tiny person. They named him Edward, after Hugh's father.

In the years that followed, he kept savoring these beautiful moments. Another was when he met his daughter. And later his youngest son. He taught his children to ride, to play chess, to listen to their mother, and above all, to cherish each moment.

THE END

About the Author

Kate McMurray writes romance novels. She likes creating stories that are brainy, funny, and of course sexy, with regular guy characters and urban sensibilities. She advocates for romance stories by and for everyone. When she's not writing, she edits textbooks, watches baseball, plays violin, crafts things out of yarn, and wears a lot of cute dresses. She lives in Brooklyn, NY, with a bossy cat and too many books.

Instagram/Threads: @katemcmurraygram

www.ingramcontent.com/pod-product-compliance
Lightning Source LLC
Chambersburg PA
CBHW072103300726
48975CB00003B/677